KILLING RAVEN

"Of all the writers of Native-American mysteries compared to Tony Hillerman, Coel is the one who most deserves the accolade."
—*Publishers Weekly* (starred review)

"Readers will be swept up quickly in this novel's rapid stride, its back story, and the tensions evident between Holden and O'Malley."
—*January Magazine*

THE SHADOW DANCER

Winner of the Colorado Book Award for Best Mystery Novel

"Coel not only presents a vivid and authentic picture of the Native American, past and present, but also captures the rugged and majestic atmosphere of Wyoming. . . . The poignant ending will catch even the most astute mystery aficionado by surprise."
—*Publishers Weekly*

THE THUNDER KEEPER

"Coel has obvious respect for the land and people who populate it. . . . She creates dense and compelling characters in complex stories to entertain her loyal fans." —*The Denver Post*

"Coel gets the atmosphere just right. She is on original and interesting ground."
—*Publishers Weekly*

THE SPIRIT WOMAN

"Intriguing Arapaho and Shoshone history and realistic treatment of contemporary Native American issues make this cozy a winner."
—*Library Journal*

"A well-drawn tale. Margaret Coel changes the direction of the series so that there is an added freshness that doesn't lose the essence of the Wind River mysteries."
—*Midwest Book Review*

continued on next page...

THE LOST BIRD

"A truly touching story . . . the whole book is infused with the spirit of Arapaho community."

—Sarah Smith, author of *Knowledge of Water*

"Among the best mysteries of the year. . . . Coel is clearly at the top of her game." —*Booklist* (starred review)

"Engrossing . . . Coel manages to have enjoyable characters and a super mystery—not an easy task." —*Literary Times*

THE STORY TELLER

"Vivid western landscapes, intriguing history, compelling characters, and quick, tight writing that is a joy to read. . . . Holden is a unique mix of the modern and the traditional. One of the best of the year." —*Booklist* (starred review)

"All the strengths of this fine series are present here: Coel's knowledge of and respect for western history, a solid mystery with a credible premise in Indian lore and the struggles of Holden and O'Malley with their powerful, but so far unconsummated, attraction to each other." —*Publishers Weekly*

THE DREAM STALKER

"Seamless storytelling by someone who's obviously been there." —J.A. Jance

"Critics who have called Coel a 'female Hillerman' are right on the mark." —*Daily Camera* (Boulder, CO)

"Murder, romance, a nuclear storage facility and Indian lore blend appealingly in this third mystery. . . . Another coup for Coel." —*Publishers Weekly*

The Ghost Walker

"Margaret Coel guides us mystery lovers on another of her gripping tours of evil among the Wind River Arapahos."

—Tony Hillerman

"Coel is a vivid voice for the West, its struggles to retain its past and at the same time enjoy the fruits of the future."

—*The Dallas Morning News*

"A corking good read. . . . Excellent. . . . An outstanding entry in a superior series." —*Booklist* (starred review)

"A tautly written, compelling mystery, grounded in and sympathetic to the Arapaho culture." —*Milwaukee Journal-Sentinel*

The Eagle Catcher

"Margaret Coel's account of dastardly deeds among the Arapahos on the Wind River Reservation shouldn't be missed by anyone interested in either new trends in mystery writing or contemporary American Indian culture. She's a master at both." —Tony Hillerman

"An uncanny sense of dialogue . . . Coel merges her grasp of history with the mystery genre. The result is so successful, you wonder what took her so long." —*The Denver Post*

"Insightful commentary about Arapaho culture, well-drawn characters and a lively pace." —*Publishers Weekly*

Berkley Prime Crime Mysteries by Margaret Coel

THE EAGLE CATCHER
THE GHOST WALKER
THE DREAM STALKER
THE STORY TELLER
THE LOST BIRD
THE SPIRIT WOMAN
THE THUNDER KEEPER
THE SHADOW DANCER
KILLING RAVEN
WIFE OF MOON

KILLING RAVEN

MARGARET COEL

BERKLEY PRIME CRIME, NEW YORK

KILLING RAVEN
A Berkley Prime Crime book / published by arrangement with the author

PRINTING HISTORY
Berkley Prime Crime hardcover edition / September 2003
Berkley Prime Crime mass-market edition / August 2004

Cover design by Tony Greco and Associates.
Interior text design by Julie Rogers.

For information address: The Berkley Publishing Group, a division of Penguin Group (USA) Inc., 375 Hudson Street, New York, New York 10014.

ISBN: 0-425-19750-6

Berkley Prime Crime books are published by The Berkley Publishing Group, a division of Penguin Group (USA) Inc., 375 Hudson Street, New York, New York 10014.

PRINTED IN THE UNITED STATES OF AMERICA

10 9 8 7 6 5 4 3

ACKNOWLEDGMENTS

MY SINCERE THANKS to those who graciously took time from their busy schedules to answer my many questions and extend their friendship. My life is enriched by having crossed your paths.

In Wyoming: Edward R. McAuslan, Fremont County Coroner; Todd Dawson, special agent, FBI; Paul A. Swenson, special agent, FBI; Mark O. Harris, senator, Wyoming legislature; Virginia Sutter, member of the Arapaho tribe; Rose Stanbury, owner, Books & Briar bookstore, Riverton.

In Colorado: Dr. John Tracy, professor emeritus, University of Colorado; Dr. Peter Steinhauer, Vietnam veteran; Carl Schneider, baseball fan.

In Washington, D.C., John Dix, baseball aficionado.

In Arizona, Mary E. Cook, human resources consultant.

And a special thanks to my friends Karen Gilleland and Beverly Carrigan; my daughter, Kristin Henderson; and my husband, George, for seeing me through the many rough drafts.

To William Patrick Harrison
"Liam"

KILLING RAVEN

Raven: Large, corvine bird having lustrous black plumage and a loud, harsh call.

To Raven: To seek plunder or prey, to eat or feed quickly, to seize as spoil, to devour voraciously.

—UNABRIDGED RANDOM HOUSE
DICTIONARY OF THE ENGLISH LANGUAGE

The raven is a bird of many legends that extend back into time. Always it has been believed to be a bird that feasts on the bodies of the dead and one that hunts with wolves and shares the kill.

The raven is circling above me,
circling above me,
The raven having come for me,
having come for me.

—ARAPAHO SONG

1

THE STARS WERE bouncing across the windshield. Streaks of light that zigzagged through the blackness and plummeted downward before shooting up and out of sight. That was how it seemed, but Lela knew she was the one bouncing in the pickup. Her forehead hit the windshield, her right arm crashed against the door handle. A flash of pain, like a burning coal, gripped her elbow. Someone was screaming—God, she couldn't stop screaming, and her own voice sounded thin and frantic above the pounding beat of Korn and the rushing wind through the opened windows.

Out of the corner of her eye, Lela saw the dark pickup pull alongside them as Tommy stomped on the gas pedal. They roared ahead in a blur of chrome and flickering lights.

"Tommy, look out!" A utility pole rose like a granite tower into the headlights. Lela threw out both hands to brace herself against the dashboard. Tommy was pulling on the steering wheel, throwing his whole body toward the door. They swerved around the pole, which knocked and scraped down Lela's side. There was the screeching sound of metal ripped from metal.

And then they were alone, bouncing through the sagebrush and across the iron-hard ruts, headlights flashing over the empty beer cans and whiskey bottles and the rusted-out parts of old trucks scattered around the bluff. Going slower now, Tommy thumping both fists against the wheel and yelling out his window, roaring to the stars. "We did it! We beat the sonsabitches!"

Lela felt her heart jumping in rhythm with "Clown." She was still holding on to the dashboard, trying to get her breath. The air lodged in her lungs like a cork, the inside of her mouth felt as dry and rough as an old boot. She shifted around until she could see the headlights of the other pickup blinking over the bluff in the distance. Headed toward the river where the party was, and the whiskey and the weed.

She exhaled a long breath, letting out all the air that had been inside her. She felt giddy with relief. She wanted to scream out the window: I'm alive, I'm still alive. She leaned back, letting her eyes take in the man beside her. Sweat glistened on the black tattoo of a raven that seemed to fly over his biceps as he turned the steering wheel. Lines of sweat ran like silver through his black hair, which was smoothed back like a cap over his head and tied into a ponytail. She could sense his excitement, like a fever coming over him. It matched her own. He'd want sex now. That was why he was driving across the bluff, away from the others, to the spot where he'd taken her the first time. She ran her tongue over her lips—cracked and dry and wordless—and laid her head against the backrest. She stared into the night and at the lights glowing among the cottonwoods along the river below.

Tommy leaned toward her and swept one hand under the driver's seat. He lifted a flat, brown bottle, and, balancing it between his thighs, twisted off the top. The smell of whiskey floated toward her, and Lela felt her heart lurch as Tommy took a long drink. The light from the dashboard danced in the brown liquid.

"Lost the mirror," he said, swiping the back of one hand over his mouth. Then he tipped his head back and let the liquid pour into his throat like a fountain before he guided the pickup into the two-track that pitched downward off the bluff and into the grove of cottonwoods. The party was a half mile away, lights flickering like fireflies in the darkness.

"Hot shit." He guided the pickup through the trees, the tires scrunching the underbrush. "It's worth it. Gotta teach those bastards who's boss around here."

Looking straight ahead, Tommy pointed the pickup toward the open area in the cottonwood grove—a campsite close to the river. The headlights streamed over the dirt and clumps of grass, the circle of rocks and charred logs where someone had once built a fire. They lurched to a stop, and Tommy turned off the engine. The stereo went quiet, leaving only the sound of the wind whistling through the trees and the faint echo of the music in the distance. The yellow glow from the headlights hung in the air a moment, before dissolving into the darkness.

"What's that?"

"What?" Tommy handed her the bottle, and she took a drink, wincing at the fire that shot down her throat and into her chest. He had looped an arm around her shoulder and was pulling her so tight that the rough edges of his army camouflage shirt, where he'd cut out the sleeves, scratched against her neck. He smelled of perspiration and whiskey and tobacco all at once in some kind of stew that made her feel slightly sick.

"Over there," she managed, her own voice coming back at her like an echo. She pointed into the darkness toward the campsite where, before the headlights had died, she'd glimpsed something small and unusual in the dirt. Something out of place, left behind and forgotten. Something different. Not one of the crushed beer cans or broken bottles that were strewn around the fire pit.

Lela shrugged herself free of Tommy's arm and leaned forward, squinting through the windshield. The object was hard to make out now, a shadow swallowed by other shadows. It could be a small animal, she thought, a puppy or a kitten. Maybe it was dead, but it might be hurt. Maybe a fox had gotten it. There were fox by the river, and coyote.

"Turn the headlights back on, okay?" she said.

"Jesus, Lela."

She felt Tommy's fingers dig into her shoulder and pull her back. "Forget it. Ain't nothing out there I want. You know what I want." His hand worked its way up under the back of her T-shirt and around, then gripped her breast, squeezing hard.

"Stop it, Tommy," she screamed, twisting herself free and grabbing for the door handle. She pushed the door open and plunged out into the hot darkness, which was tinged with moist, dead-fish smells from the river. Just as she started around the pickup, the headlights flashed on. She stopped. Now she could see the object a few feet away, except it wasn't any kind of animal.

It was a hand—fleshy palm, curled fingers—rising out of the ground, clawing at the dirt.

Her legs felt weak beneath her, as if they'd dissolved into liquid and could no longer support her. She stumbled back a couple steps, both hands pressed over her mouth to hold in the scream erupting in her throat, her gaze frozen on the hand. She tried to turn away, but it was as if the hand itself had fastened onto her and wouldn't let go.

The loud thwack of the pickup door was like a slap in the face, bringing her out of some nightmare. Tommy emerged from the shadows beside her. A wave of gratitude swept over her as his arm went around her shoulders. She felt him pulling her backward.

"Come on, Lela," he said, swinging her around, pushing her toward the pickup. "This ain't your business. You ain't seen nothing."

"What?" Lela tried to turn back, but he pushed her hard and she stumbled against the hood, her legs still jellylike. "We gotta call the police," she managed.

"You crazy?" He gripped both of her shoulders and leaned over her. The smell of whiskey on his breath made her want to retch. "You didn't see nothing, and you ain't calling nobody." His fingers bore into her muscles until she felt the tears pressing against her eyes.

"It's a body, Tommy," she managed. "We got no choice."

He released her, and she wobbled sideways against the pickup, trying to get her balance. In a flash, she saw his hand stretched over her, then felt the hard crash of his palm against her cheek. Her head jerked backward. She crumbled onto the ground, her balance gone now, as if some gyroscope inside her had been turned off. She dug her fingers into the dirt, collapsing into the pain that was spreading through her head.

Tommy was next to her, his black boots a few inches from her face. "Why'd you do that?" she said, feeling like a little girl again, dad standing over her.

"So you get it straight. You keep quiet. It ain't your business."

Lela managed to scrape through the dirt to the hard

ground underneath, then push herself upright along the black boots, the baggy camouflage pants, the shirt with the jagged armholes, the sculptured arms. He was looking beyond her toward the party. She turned her head to follow his gaze. Headlight beams crisscrossed one another in the darkness. There was the pounding sound of the stereos, far away and faint as a memory. She could make out the dark blocks of pickups and the shadows flitting about, dancing maybe, getting laid, getting high, like every other Saturday night this summer. Everybody'd be stoned by the time she and Tommy got back. God, why'd they have to come to Double Dives in the first place?

She looked back at Tommy, his face striped with thin slats of shadow and light, and in his expression she saw a fear as raw as meat.

"You know who it is, don't you?"

"Shut up." He leaned toward her, fists dangling at his sides.

"You had something to do with it." Lela pushed on, her voice thick with tears. "You and the so-called rangers." She thrust her head in the direction of the party. "Like any of you was ever in the army. Whatd'ya do? Whack somebody on Captain Jack's orders? What? One of them guys you been hassling at the casino, just cause they went and got themselves jobs. You ever think maybe you oughta get yourself a real job, 'stead of hanging around doing Captain Jack's dirty work?"

At the edge of her vision, Lela saw the fist come up, but she was already darting alongside the pickup out of range. "Get in." He threw his fist toward her like a club, then started around the hood toward the driver's side. "We're getting outta here," he called over his shoulder.

Lela remained where she was, her head throbbing, Tommy shouting to hurry up. He was already behind the steering wheel, twisting toward the window, his face distorted. He pounded on the horn, sending out impatient blasts of noise that bounced about the cottonwoods and obliterated the sound of his voice. She pivoted around, surprised at the surge of strength within her, and started running, zigzagging and darting through the trees, taking a diagonal path toward the river. She didn't know where she was going, only that she couldn't get into the pickup. She couldn't pretend the hand wasn't there. It was in the dirt, trying to get out.

2

A THICK HEAT had settled over the Wind River Reservation most of the summer. Now it was the third Monday in August, the Moon of Geese Shedding Their Feathers, according to the Arapaho Way of keeping time, and no sign of rain or cooler temperatures. One hot day had stretched into another, and today was no different. The sky was cloudless and was the crystalline blue of a mountain lake, with the sun still high in the east, glinting off the little houses that were set back from either side of Seventeen-Mile Road.

Father John O'Malley, pastor of St. Francis Mission, turned onto Highway 789 and mopped at the sweat that was prickling his forehead. He wished he'd thought to bring along a bottle of water, but he hadn't thought of anything, except that one of his parishioners could be dead.

The phone call had come about ten minutes ago. He'd

just gotten to his office in the administration building. It was Art Banner, chief of the BIA police on the Wind River Reservation. Someone had reported a body at Double Dives. Not a body, exactly. A hand protruding from the ground. They were at the site now recovering the remains—a whole platoon of police officers, sheriff's deputies, investigators from the coroner's office and the Wyoming crime lab, and Ted Gianelli, the local FBI agent. Did Father John want to come over?

He'd felt as if a set of weights had dropped on his chest. Chances were it was a dead Arapaho. One of his parishioners, one of the brown faces that turned up at him during the homilies at Sunday Mass. Or someone else from the reservation, someone he knew. After eight years at St. Francis, Father John knew just about everybody.

And Double Dives was on the reservation, an empty, sagebrush-studded bluff that broke off into an oasis of cottonwood trees along the Wind River, not far from the place where the Arapahos had camped when they'd first come to the reservation more than a hundred years ago. Now the only people who went to Double Dives were the gangs that hung out there, drinking, drugging, racing pickups. Double Dives was wide open. Even the BIA patrol cars stayed away from the place.

"Any idea who it could be?" Father John had asked.

"So far, about all we know . . ." There had been a pause on the other end of the line, the noise of the chief gulping in air. "Poor bastard got shot in the head."

Father John had been barely aware of the clack clack noise of a keyboard, the whir of the printer coming from the office down the hall. His assistant, Father George Reinhold, was probably still working on the mission finances. The man had spent most of the weekend trying to balance the books.

"I'll be right over," Father John had told the police chief. He'd grabbed his cowboy hat from the coat tree inside the door, and, after calling to the other priest that he had an emergency, he'd slammed out the door and headed across the mission grounds. Walks-On, the three-legged golden retriever he'd found in a ditch a couple years ago, had bounded toward him, a red Frisbee clenched between his teeth, a hopeful look in his eyes.

"Sorry, buddy," Father John had said before he slid into the old Toyota pickup parked in front of the residence. He'd had to coax the engine into life—jiggling the key in the ignition, the growing sense of dread gripping him like a sharp pain. He'd had a busy couple of weeks: three funerals for starters, which meant wakes and visits to the families; counseling sessions almost every day; and meetings with the social committee, the youth group, the religious education teachers—endless meetings—plus practice every afternoon with the Eagles, the baseball team he'd started for the kids the first summer he'd been at St. Francis; and, in the evenings, the AA groups and the Gamblers Anonymous group he'd started last month.

Now he eased up on the accelerator and turned right onto Gas Hills Road. He drove several miles east into the bright sunshine. Around a curve, and then a left turn onto an open bluff studded with sagebrush and littered with bottles and cans and the carcass of an old truck. He bounced over the ruts, the windshield fractured by the sun, the line of utility poles running outside the window, and large, black birds circling overhead. Ravens, he thought, with purple-black feathers that shone in the sun and beaks that flashed like lightning against the sky.

At the edge of the bluff, the ruts pitched downward into a grove of cottonwoods along the river. Scattered about were several white BIA police cars that looked gray in the sunlight. Around the police cars were other vehicles—an ambulance, a couple of SUVs, a gray suburban with the blue insignia of the Fremont County Coroner on the sides.

Father John parked behind one of the police cars. Groups of officers, some in uniform, others in slacks and short-sleeve shirts, were milling about. A couple of officers moved through the trees, making a sharp, clicking noise. The instant he shut off the engine, he could hear the sounds of the river through the buzz of voices. He got out into a wedge of shade.

Chief Banner was already making his way over, the light glinting off the silver insignias on his navy blue uniform shirt, his thick head thrust forward like a bull working through the herd. "Coroner's still recovering the body," he said when he was a couple of feet away. "Slow business. Don't want to disturb any evidence. We're searching the area, taking photographs and making diagrams. Grave's real shallow, so whoever did it was most likely in a hurry. Looks like an animal had started working at the dirt and uncovered the hand."

Father John glanced beyond the chief at the circle of investigators about thirty feet away. Five men, down on their knees, hunched over the grave. They might have been praying, he thought, except they were jabbing and brushing at the earth with small tools that flashed in the sun. A couple of photographers stood over them, pointing cameras this way, that way.

"Anybody reported missing?" Father John asked. He was thinking that nobody deserved to be left in this desolate place.

The chief shook his head. "Doesn't mean somebody didn't go missing and nobody thought to make a report. All we got is a body, most likely a homicide victim."

Emerging from the trees was Ted Gianelli, the local fed,

all two hundred and twenty pounds of him in tan slacks, white shirt, and blue blazer, looking as quick on his feet as the linebacker he'd once been for the Patriots. "Girl spotted the hand last night," he said, as if he'd been part of the conversation. "You know her? Lela Running Bull?"

"I know the family," Father John said. "Wayne Running Bull comes to the mission once in a while."

Banner let out a loud guffaw. "Whenever he's sober enough to find the keys to his truck."

Father John didn't say anything. Wayne had been having trouble staying on the wagon ever since his wife died in a traffic accident two years ago. The hardness, the absoluteness of her death, had been following Wayne like a ghost. Nonalcoholics never got it. Just stay off the bottle, they said, but they didn't get the way alcohol sopped up the pain, like a sponge, and made it possible to go on for a while—in the face of the absoluteness. It had been eight years since he'd had a drink, Father John was thinking—not since the year he'd spent at Grace House trying to recover—but there were still times when his defenses were down and the absoluteness came over him. Still times he'd been willing to trade almost anything for a whiskey.

And Wayne—Wayne was struggling to raise a daughter, Lela. The girl couldn't be more than fifteen.

"How'd she take it?"

"Spooked the hell outta her." Gianelli took in a breath and squinted into the sunlight, as if he'd caught a glimpse of one of his own ghosts. "She was out here drinking and raising hell with a bunch of kids. Spotted the hand coming up through the ground and went running to her aunt, Mary Running Bull. Lives over in the trailers on the highway with her two kids. You want to say some prayers?"

This was the reason Banner had called, Father John thought as he followed the chief and Gianelli over to the grave site. A couple of investigators moved aside, and he went down on his knees.

He stared down at the outlines of a figure in the dirt. There had been so many bodies. It never got easier. The sleeves of a plaid shirt had been brushed clear, misshaped hands flopped to the sides, the right hand bent upward toward the sun. The face looked fallen, already decomposing, with smudges of dust on the leathery skin. The right side of the head, above the ear, looked as if it had been bashed in, a mixture of hair and black, congealed blood. The eyes were open, locked in fear. The corpse didn't resemble anyone he knew, white or Indian, but it was difficult to tell. It hardly looked human.

"God forgive you your sins, whatever they may be." Father John spoke out loud, as if the man were alive, sitting across from him in the confessional. "God have mercy on your soul." He was aware of the quiet settling over the area, broken only by the sound of boots scuffing the dirt and the river lapping at the banks.

After a moment, he got to his feet. "Does Lela know who he is?" he asked, looking from Banner to Gianelli.

"Not that she's willing to admit." This from the fed. "Soon as we get an ID, I'll be talking to her again."

"She was pretty upset last night," Banner said.

"Where is she?" The girl was fifteen, Father John was thinking. She'd seen a human hand protruding from the ground. She might need to talk to somebody other than the law.

"A couple of my men took her home," Banner said. "We told her to stay there."

3

FORTY MINUTES AFTER he drove out of Double Dives, Father John turned off Yellow Calf Road and bumped across the dirt yard. He parked in front of a cube-like, bilevel house with pink siding that looked pale and yellowish in the sunlight. *La Traviata* blared from the tape player on the seat beside him. Overhead, rabbit-shaped clouds scudded through the blue sky. The white mountain peaks were hazy in the distance.

Father John pressed the off button on the player. "Ah, *perche venni*" seemed to linger a moment before giving way to the quiet. As he let himself out, the screen door clacked open and a disheveled hulk of a man shambled onto the stoop. Wayne Running Bull looked like he'd just crawled out of bed: faded blue jeans low on wide hips, yellow shirt hanging open over a bulging belly. His black hair sprang like wires out of the braids that hung down his chest.

"How ya doin', Father?" The Indian sank onto the top step, as if he were letting go of a large weight, then clasped his hands between his knees. His hands were shaking.

Father John walked around the pickup. The smell of whiskey hit him like a fastball out of nowhere. "You okay, Wayne?"

"Hey, don't worry none about me. I'm doin' fine." The Indian pulled his elbows in close to his sides and gripped his hands until his knuckles popped out like white marbles. "Hey, Father." He tilted his head back and squinted into the sky. "I got some Jim Beam. How about a drink? What's the harm? Nobody'll know. Let's have a little drink on it." Planting both feet on the concrete step, he started to lift himself upward.

"Drink on what, Wayne?"

The Indian dropped back down. "On how nobody'll ever know." He gave a sharp laugh that rattled in his throat.

Father John folded his arms and leaned back, away from the whiskey wafting toward him like an invisible cloud. He could almost taste the whiskey—it was so familiar—almost feel the heat of it spreading through his chest.

He said, "Missed you at AA last week."

The Indian shrugged, then nodded toward the rear of a brown truck protruding past the far side of the house. "Got me a couple flat tires, Father. Not gettin' around so good these days."

"Look at yourself, Wayne. You're shaking. You need help. Let me take you into detox in Riverton."

"Detox! I need a drink, Father. I don't need no detox." The Indian lifted one hand and began kneading his forehead.

Father John looked away. A light breeze was raking the

patches of grass that sprang up around the yard and pushing little balls of dust down the road. Dear God, he thought. That's how he'd been, nine years ago when his superior had come to his room and said, you need help, John. You're shaking. Look at yourself. He could still see the other priest standing in the doorway, rigid with disgust and contempt. He'd said, what kind of priest are you? And Father John had answered—oh, he remembered it as if it were yesterday—he'd answered the truth: A lousy priest.

He brought his eyes back to the man slumped on the step, still kneading his forehead. Wayne Running Bull had a cache of whiskey. He wasn't ready to quit yet.

He said, "Is Lela here?"

"My kid? Whatd'ya want with her?"

"I want to talk to her about the body she found at Double Dives last night. Where is she?"

"Police come driving up with her last night." The Indian spoke slowly, taking a breath every couple of words. "Said she was some kind of witness and she oughta stay home. I told her to go to her room and get some sleep. She looked like hell. I went back to bed. When I woke up, she was gone. I don't know where she went off to."

"She's fifteen years old, Wayne. You're the only parent she has."

Moisture started pooling in the man's eyes. "Angela left me, Father," he said in a voice hoarse with tears. "Left me with the girl. What do I know about raising the girl? How am I supposed to know what she's up to?"

Father John swallowed hard. Was that how he'd been? Blaming everybody, everything? What had he known about being a priest? How was he supposed to know how hard it would be?

The Indian was shaking his head. "Week ago, Lela packed up her clothes and left with some guy. I don't know who he was. Drove a brown truck. Kept the engine going the whole time she was getting her stuff. Shithead! Exhaust filled up the whole house."

Father John watched the man a moment. Then he said, "Your daughter's had a shock, Wayne. She needs help. If you hear from her, ask her to call me."

At this the man blinked, and for a moment, he almost looked sober. "Lela's got her boyfriend. He's the only one she's gonna trust to help her."

"All the same, ask her to call me." Father John stepped closer to the stoop and leaned over the man. "When you've finished the last of your bottle, Wayne, call me, and I'll take you to detox," he said, then he walked back to the pickup and got in behind the wheel. It was like sliding into a hotbox.

Wayne Running Bull was hunched over in the side mirror as Father John drove out of the yard and onto the road. And then the man and the house and the yard were gone, lost on the other side of a rise, and all that was left in the mirror was a cloud of dust rising behind him.

4

VICKY HOLDEN SMOOTHED the front page of the Wind River Gazette over her desk and glanced at the headlines on the front page. Crews Battle Wildfire. Charter School Approved. Demonstrators Arrested.

The front door cracked shut, sending a tremor through the pine-planked floor of the bungalow that served as her law office. It stood on the corner in a block of bungalows doubling as offices and arts and crafts shops west of Lander's Main Street.

The hushed voices—a protective note sounding in the voice of her secretary, Esther Sundell—filtered through the double glass doors that separated her office from the reception room.

A potential client might have wandered in off the street, but she doubted it. More likely, the visitor was one of Esther's relatives. They were always stopping by, wanting to borrow her car, borrow some money, and Esther was generous. In her fifties now, the woman lived the Arapaho Way, the way of the ancestors, which meant that she probably gave away everything she didn't need. She respected Esther for that.

Vicky went back to the newspaper. Three local men had been arrested at the Great Plains Casino for harassing employees and patrons. Andy Yellowman, Leon Black, Martin Wolf. Arapahos, she knew by the names. According to a spokesperson for the Wind River police, the men taken into custody were employed by Jack Monroe.

Captain Jack Monroe. Vicky turned the page. The captain had made several appearances in the *Gazette* over the last two years, while waging his own war against Indian gaming, preaching about the dangers and evils, trying to drum up enough outrage to stop the casino from being built on the reservation. Despite his efforts, the Arapaho business council had approved the casino. It had been open two months now.

The doors swung inward, and Vicky looked up. Esther had positioned herself in the opening and was leaning on the knobs, her short, stout figure blocking the view of the outer office. "You'll never guess who's here." She kept her face unreadable, but Vicky caught the flash of surprise and disapproval in the woman's brown eyes.

"Why don't you tell me," she said.

"Adam Lone Eagle."

Vicky felt her heart lurch. She hadn't heard from the Lakota lawyer in six weeks, not since they'd had dinner together in Hudson. Two days later, she'd read in the *Gazette* that Lodestar Enterprises had hired him to handle in-house legal work at the casino. She'd told herself she wasn't surprised. It was so predictable. Lodestar had been hired by the business council to manage the casino, and the council had always found outside lawyers to handle the tribal legal work—white men, usually—as if the council couldn't see her, one of their own people. She'd tried to tell herself she no longer cared, but she could still feel the warm flush that had come into her face when she'd read the news.

Adam had never said a word.

Vicky got to her feet and, brushing past Esther who moved back along one of the doors, went into the outer office. Adam stood in front of the desk, as tall and good looking as she remembered: the black hair slicked back around the narrow, sculptured face with the high cheekbones, the long nose with the crook at the top, the dark eyes with the direct, unflinching look, and every part of him imprinted with the confidence and sense of superiority of his Lakota ancestors. He wore a white, short-sleeved dress shirt, opened at the collar, and dark slacks with knife-like creases that folded into the tassels of his polished shoes. Lawyer clothes, she thought, the kind he'd been wearing last spring when she'd needed a lawyer and had gone to Casper to hire him.

"Come in." She waved the man forward.

He led the way into her office, nodding at Esther as she stepped back, then closing the doors. For a half-second, Vicky thought he was about to put his arms around her. She flinched, then walked around her desk and gestured toward one of the barrel-shaped visitor chairs arranged in front. "Have a seat," she said, dropping into her own chair. "What brings you to Lander?"

An amused look came into Adam's face. He took the chair she'd indicated, settled back, and adjusted the creases in his slacks. "How have you been, Vicky?" he said, ignoring her question.

She smiled. So the pleasantries were to be observed. She'd tried to come right to the point, like a white woman, but he wanted to talk like Indians.

She was fine, she told him. *Why hadn't he told her he'd taken the job?* And how was he doing? Also fine, doing great. He brought up the weather, and she joined in. *He could have called.* The long heat spell, the dry, parched earth, when was it going to rain? On and on she went, making small talk, and all the while, folding the newspaper, setting it to one side, rearranging a stack of papers. *She didn't care.* She picked up a pencil and began tapping out a slow rhythm against the edge of the desk.

"Look, Vicky," he said finally, and she knew that they were about to come to the point of his visit, "I've thought about you a lot. I've wanted to call you."

Vicky didn't say anything. She stopped tapping and set the pencil on the desk blotter. *Why did she care so much?* Three evenings together earlier in the summer—they'd gotten on well, she'd thought—and then, nothing.

"Truth is," Adam went on, "after I took the job at the casino, what was I going to say to you? 'Sorry, Vicky. Your tribe just retained a Lakota lawyer instead of you?' "

"You're a good lawyer, Adam." She struggled to keep her voice steady.

"Let's be honest here, Vicky. We both know why the business council didn't suggest you to Lodestar. You're a woman. Why would they suggest a woman when Lodestar could go two hundred miles away to Casper and hire a man, Indian to boot? You've gone up against the traditions. You're not back at the tipi building the fires, cooking the meals, and mending some warrior's buckskin."

Vicky had to smile at that. Most of the women on the rez were like Esther, trying to earn a little extra money for their families. But she wasn't like them. She'd stepped out ahead, like a warrior. She was alone—*Hi sei ci nihi,* Woman Alone.

"Traditions are slow to change, Vicky."

She stayed quiet, unflinching. She would not give Adam Lone Eagle, or anybody else, the satisfaction of admitting the truth of it. If she admitted the truth, even to herself, she would have to close her office and go somewhere else.

Adam had leaned back in his chair. "Fact is, Vicky, Lodestar Enterprises should have retained you, and I told them so." He shrugged and looked past her a moment. "They said they'd made their choice. I could take the retainer or leave it, and frankly, I needed the work. It's not the most exciting legal work I've ever done. Mostly contracts." He smiled and waved a hand toward the desk, as if whatever work she was doing was bound to be more interesting, as if he'd done her a favor by taking the casino job.

"What about restraining orders?"

"You've read the paper." Adam nodded at the newspaper on her desk. "Captain Jack Monroe's a pain in the neck, causing a lot of trouble. We finally got the Wind River police to take notice yesterday. They hauled off three of Monroe's troublemakers. We have to take the legal steps to make certain they don't come back. Which means, yeah, I've got more work than I can handle, so I told Stan Lexson—he's the casino manager—that I'd like some help, and he agreed. I told him I want you. It's a great opportunity, unless you're too busy."

Adam paused, and in that moment, Vicky knew that he knew the truth. Two real estate leases, a couple of divorces, one child custody case—that was the extent of her practice this month, not enough to pay both the rent and Esther's salary and still pay her own expenses, including the payments on the used Jeep Cherokee she'd purchased last summer. She'd been living off her savings for a couple of months now. Everybody on the rez probably knew she was struggling to stay in business. The moccasin telegraph never missed a juicy piece of gossip.

"I'll be up front with you, Vicky," Adam was saying. "Like I said, it's routine, boring work. Mostly contracts with suppliers. Nothing flashy, but it pays well and"—he gestured toward the outer office—"you can keep your own practice. I'm still handling a few clients in Casper. What do you say?"

Vicky pushed herself to her feet. She turned toward the window and, running a finger along the glass, stared outside. The sky was as blue and luminescent as a signal flare. A funnel of shade from the ponderosa spread over the lawn, but the rest of the backyard was bathed in the glaring white sunlight.

"I don't know, Adam." She should jump at the chance, she was thinking. She needed the security of a good retainer. A couple of months ago, she wouldn't have hesitated, but things had changed. She looked back at the man on the other side of the desk. "There's a lot of controversy over the casino."

Adam stood up. He leaned over the desk, gripping the edge and fixing her with the kind of determination that sent a little shiver down her spine. He would be a formidable adversary in the courtroom. "Controversy? There isn't any controversy, despite what that crackpot Monroe says. People know that Great Plains Casino is the best thing that ever happened to the reservation. There's more than a hundred Arapahos working there, and the profits are going to mean better health care, better schools, development of other jobs. The casino's a good thing, Vicky. Monroe's been proved wrong, and he can't stand it. The man's on a mission, thinks he has to save Indians from the evils of gambling. He's tried to stop Indian casinos all over the country. Most of the time he fails, like he did here, but he keeps going. Now he thinks if he harasses people going to the casino he can close the place down. He thinks he can get Arapahos to stop working there and stop gambling there."

Adam stepped back and straightened his shoulders. A thick blue vein pulsed on the side of his neck. "Look, Vicky," he began again, a more patient tone this time. "Come to the casino. Meet Stan Lexson and his people. Look around. Get the lay of the land, and see what you think. What can it hurt?"

Vicky allowed the quiet to close around them a moment, like an invisible cloud moving through the office. From somewhere beyond the cloud came the muffled clacking of computer keys. She couldn't ignore the facts: If she didn't get some business soon, she would have to let Esther go—the first rung down a plunging ladder. Next would be the office; she'd have to work out of her small apartment. And after that, she would have to leave her people again, this time for good.

She heard her own voice cutting through the quiet, agreeing to stop by the casino this afternoon, and then she was walking Adam out, past Esther's desk—the woman curled toward the monitor. After Adam had let himself out the door, Vicky watched the Lakota hurry down the walk, shoulders squared, white shirt clinging to his broad back. He got into a new green SUV parked in the only shade at the curb.

For the briefest moment, Vicky felt as if she were watching a lawyer who'd won a case for his client. The victory had left him even more confident and jubilant, unaware that the client had been diminished somehow and compromised.

"Well, never thought Adam Lone Eagle'd have the nerve

to show his face around here." The secretary's voice came from behind her. The clacking had stopped.

Vicky turned back. "What do you mean?" she asked, although she knew what Esther was talking about.

"Just like one of them Sioux, butting in what's none of their business." Esther raised both eyebrows and stared at the ceiling, the set of her jaw as firm as the gray curls framing the round, brown face. "Just like Lodestar to bring in an outsider to do the law work, when that casino belongs to Arapahos, and you're the one should've been hired. Everybody's saying so."

That was just great, Vicky thought. All the gossip about her career on the moccasin telegraph. "What do you say?"

"I say"—Esther had the same kind of defiant gaze that Adam had leveled on her—"none of our business what lawyer the casino hires. Makes no difference to us."

"Keep saying that." Vicky gave the woman a thumbs-up, then went back into her office. She stood at the window again, looking out at the maze of sun and shadows, trying to sort out the conflicting feelings boiling inside her. What Adam said about the casino was true, and yet there was another side, the shadow side. The divorce case she was handling—Larry and Renee Oldman—was a result of gambling. At the bingo hall, on the Internet, and now at the casino. Larry had lost the house and the truck, and still he couldn't stop.

The truth was, she wouldn't have hesitated to take a retainer when Lodestar had hired Adam. But now—now there were Larry and Renee and Esther's relatives borrowing money to pay gambling debts and . . . she wasn't sure she wanted to be a part of it.

Vicky lifted her black bag out of the desk drawer, then retraced her steps across the office to the front door. Before she made a decision, there was something she had to do.

The secretary blinked up at her, then began rummaging through the papers on her desk. She pulled out a small notepad. "Where can I reach you, in case there's an emergency?"

"You can't." Vicky threw open the door and stepped out into the heat, which was blasting across the front yard like a blowtorch.

5

VICKY DROVE NORTH on Highway 287, which flowed like a river of asphalt through the open stretch of plains, baked in the sun and dotted with clumps of wild grass and sagebrush. Outside her window, rising against the sky in the distance, were the blue-shaded foothills of the Wind River range. A hot wind crashed through the open windows, drowning out Clint Black on the radio and rattling the brown paper bag on the seat beside her. On her way out of Lander, she'd stopped at a convenience store and purchased some gifts: a couple of bags of tobacco, two packages of cigarette papers, four cans of chili.

She hit the power button on the radio. The music dissolved in the wind. She preferred the sound of the wind. It reminded her of summer nights when she was a kid, curled up on the double bed in the back room of grandmother's house, with three or four cousins curled up around her, the room so hot they'd kick the blanket onto the floor and giggle at the way the wind whistled through the windows and made the white muslin curtains dance like puppets on strings.

For the last ten minutes, she realized, she'd been stuck behind a camper with Texas plates. There was a steady stream of pickups and campers crawling along the highway: tourists heading north to Yellowstone Park, she guessed, and most of them stopping off at Great Plains Casino about ten miles ahead. When there was a break in the oncoming traffic, Vicky pushed down on the accelerator and swung out around the camper. Another mile and she turned right onto Plunkett Road, leaving the traffic behind.

She drove east over the ridge, feeling calmer, more at one with herself the farther she went into the reservation, the bluffs and arroyos and prairie rolling away below. Left on Mill Creek Road, right on Trosper. Deep in Arapaho land now. The Shoshones lived to the west and farther north, but the small, rectangular-shaped houses, painted white or blue or yellow, scattered along the road, like blocks dropped onto the dusty earth, belonged to her people. Towels and sheets and shirts flapped on the clothesline poles, and old pickups and sedans stood at odd angles in the bare-dirt yards, some without wheels, propped up on cement blocks. In one yard, a couple of kids were kicking a ball through clouds of dust. A man in blue jeans, shirtless, sat on the front stoop, drawing on a cigarette, keeping watch, his brown shoulders hunched against the sun.

She wondered if the gossip on the moccasin telegraph had reached the houses out here. Of course it had. The whole reservation was probably talking about the fact Lodestar had hired a Lakota lawyer while she was left struggling to keep her office open. She laughed out loud, her voice muffled in the wind. The moccasin telegraph worked on a need-to-know basis. Gossip reached those who needed to know, and she was the last one who needed to know what was being said about her.

Vicky stepped gently on the brake and pulled left, bucking over the logs laid across the ditch. She stopped next to a small, white frame house, lifted the paper bag off the seat, and got out, slamming the door hard. The wind wrapped her skirt against her legs and blew her hair into her eyes. She balanced the paper bag on the hood, combed back her hair with her fingers, and readjusted the beaded barrette at the nape of her neck. The house was quiet. A loose piece of siding snapped in the wind.

Holding the bag in both arms, like an offering, Vicky started down the side of the house. A few feet beyond the back door was the brushshade, small and rectangular-shaped, with willow branches tied to the log frame to form the three walls and the roof. Through the opening, Vicky could barely make out the two old people seated at the metal table in the blue-tinted shade.

She stopped outside and waited until the old man lifted his eyes from the newspaper spread open on the table. "Looks like we got ourselves a visitor," he said, anticipation ringing through his tone. "Come in, come in," he said, motioning her into the shade. "Get yourself outta the heat."

It was at least twenty degrees cooler inside. After a second, her eyes began to adjust to the dimness and the two old people started to emerge out of the shadows. Will Standing Bear was thin as a bunch of willows inside the long-sleeved plaid shirt. A silver belt buckle shaped like a buffalo rose up at his narrow waist, and gray-streaked hair, cut short around the chiseled face, drew attention to his hawk-like nose. And Josephine, plumper, softer, and wearing a blue gingham dress, her hair almost white and pinned into a roll behind her ears, lifted her eyes from the tiny colored beads she was sewing onto the white deerskin moccasin in her lap.

"Sorry to bother you, grandfather, grandmother," Vicky said, using the polite term for elders. She nodded from one to the other, then set the bag of gifts on the dirt floor.

"Bother? You ain't never a bother to us, Vicky." Will was on his feet, opening up an aluminum, webbed chair that had been folded against the wall of willow branches. He shoved the chair toward her. "Only bother is, you don't come around often enough."

"Help yourself to some iced tea." Josephine jabbed a threaded needle into the moccasin and tilted her head toward a small table that held a plastic pitcher and a stack of glasses.

Vicky stepped over and poured herself some tea. The ice cubes clinked against the glass, spattering cold liquid over her hand.

"We got some real hot weather now," Will said as Vicky settled into the chair. Even the aluminum armrests were cool in the shade. She took a long sip of tea and felt herself begin to relax. There would be a good ten minutes of pleasantries.

"We don't mind the weather." Josephine leaned over the table and picked out several tiny beads from an opened cigar box, then slipped the beads onto the needle and down along the thread. She picked at the moccasin again. "We spend the hot days right here where it's nice and cool, like the old ones taught us. They knew what they was doing, the old ones." She slipped another line of beads onto the needle and launched into a story about the way the grandmothers had gathered willows from the rivers and made real nice shades, so the children would stay cool, no matter how hot it was on the plains.

Vicky took another sip of tea and allowed the story to flow over her, the way the old people's stories had flowed over her when she was a child—flowed over her and became her. She thanked the old woman for the story gift, then joined in the pleasantries for another few moments. Yes, everything was fine. Lander was fine, her office was fine. She managed to stay busy, she said, wondering how much of the gossip had reached the old people.

She was aware that Will had been staring at her for several moments. "What's troubling you, granddaughter?" he said finally, leaning toward her.

Now the time was ready. Vicky shifted in the chair. Holding the old man's gaze, she said, "I wanted to talk to you about the casino. I've been asked to handle some of the legal work."

"Heard the Lakota was doing the lawyering."

"I'd be working with Adam Lone Eagle."

"Does that trouble you?"

"Working with Adam?" Vicky gave a little laugh.

"Working for the casino," he said, a solemn note sounding in his voice.

"A white man, Captain Jack Monroe, has people demonstrating at the casino, stopping people from going there."

"Monroe!" Will let out a loud guffaw. "Man don't know his backside from a plow. Comes from somewhere in West Virginia. Appoints hisself the savior of Indian people and goes around the country talking about the evils of gambling. Spent all them months here trying to stop the casino from getting built. Well, he lost that war. Now he's trying to get folks riled up so they'll demand the business council close the place down."

"The demonstrators are Arapahos, grandfather. Arapahos trying to shut down their own casino."

"Hold on, granddaughter." Will thrust his head and shoulders toward her. "Some of the people don't know their own traditions. Three years ago the tribal council come to the elders and says, what d'ya think about building a casino on the rez, like a casino and gambling was some new kind of animal they'd never seen before and wasn't sure if they oughta trap it and bring it home or leave it out there for other people to hunt. We told 'em, you think gambling's something the people never done before? We been gambling longer'n anybody can remember. The old ones, they liked to race ponies and make big bets. Sioux, Cheyenne, all them tribes come around wanting to bet their ponies was faster than ours." The old man shook his head and gave a sharp laugh. "That's how our people got a lot more ponies and blankets and other things, cause we raised the fastest ponies."

Josephine started laughing, as if her husband had conjured out of nothing an old story that she'd forgotten. She had pulled a length of thread off the spool and, still chuckling, was trying to hold the needle steady while she jabbed the thread into the eye.

"You know what we told the council?" Will continued, the story spilling out now, like the thread rolling off the spool. "The people been gambling longer than anybody can remember. Oh, there's some folks that won't know when to stop, but most folks, that ain't the way it'll be. Lots of outsiders are gonna come to the casino, and there's gonna be more money to help the people. We can build us a new hospital and some fancy schools with them computer labs. Some Indians say casinos are the new buffalo. Ain't far from the truth, I'd say. So the Business Council gave the go-ahead. Took three years to get the casino built. Council had to get a pact with the state, and that wasn't easy. Had to go to federal court and get the judge to tell the state they had to make the pact."

Vicky glanced away again. And all that legal maneuvering, she was thinking, had been handled by a firm in Cheyenne. Outsiders. White.

"Trouble was, the casino cost a lotta money to build." Will shook his head and stared at the roof. "That was the toughest part, until Lodestar Enterprises come around. Offered to loan the tribe a hellava lot of money, eighteen million dollars, to get the casino and hotel up and going, and signed on to manage the place, 'cause they know about managing casinos. They done it all over the country, and the Business Council—what do they know about running a casino? They hired Lodestar and appointed three commissioners to make sure everything's running right. They made Matt Kingdom the chairman."

Will sat back, allowing the story to settle into the quiet a moment. "Matt's a good man," he said finally, a strained note in his voice. "One of them guys good with numbers."

Vicky nodded. She knew Matt Kingdom. She'd grown up with his sister.

"Got hisself a new truck he's driving around," the elder continued, "and last month he went off to Hawaii. Moccasin telegraph got real busy. When I see Kingdom over at the casino, I says, what's going on? You the commission chairman, ain't you? Ain't you supposed to keep a watch on how things are going? How come you got yourself a lotta money?"

"Now, Will." Josephine looked up, worry flowing through the lines in her face. "You know it ain't good for your blood pressure to get all upset."

Will waved away the old woman's words, his gaze still on Vicky. "Kingdom says he's got a right to compensation—

that's what he called it—for his work. Maybe so. Maybe so." The old man nodded and looked away. "But compensation ain't all that folks are talking about. You hear about Kingdom's boy? Thirty years old and never had a job, and now he's some kind of supervisor at the casino."

Will let out another guffaw, readjusted his thin frame in the chair, and fastened his gaze on some point across the shade. "Lotta folks are glad to get jobs unloading cartons of hotel stuff off trucks, and Matt's boy gets to be supervisor."

Vicky pushed herself to her feet and, clasping her arms across her chest, stepped to the opening. All around, the land stretched to the sky, like a brown ocean heaving and undulating in the sunlight. She could feel the old couple's eyes on her.

Finally she turned back. "You're asking me to take the job at the casino and keep an eye on what's going on."

Will didn't flinch. He kept his gaze steady on her, his knobby, work-raw hands locked together on the table. "What I'm saying is, you can help your people."

"I'm a lawyer, grandfather." She wondered if she could make him understand. There were different sets of loyalties in the white world, different obligations that took precedence over those in the Arapaho world. "If I took the job, my loyalty would be to my client, Lodestar Enterprises."

Will lifted one hand, as if she hadn't told him anything he didn't know. "Them folks are doing the job they're supposed to do, they'll deserve your loyalty. If not . . ."

Now she understood what the elder was telling her. If she should learn that, in any way, Lodestar Enterprises was not operating the casino within the law, her loyalty to her client would end, and in its place, like an undertow pulling her back, would be her loyalty to her own people.

She swallowed hard at the lump lodged in her throat. Maybe Matt Kingdom had the right to be paid for his time, but who was paying him? The casino? That would be a major conflict of interest. She couldn't imagine that was the case. Lodestar Enterprises operated Indian casinos around the country. The business council had looked into the company's background. And Adam—Adam Lone Eagle working for a company that wasn't honest? She couldn't imagine it.

If she didn't take the job, there were a half dozen other lawyers in the area who wouldn't hesitate. And if it turned out that Will's suspicions were correct—this was what it came down to, she realized—she wanted to be the one to know about it.

"I understand, grandfather," she said. In the old man's eyes, she saw that he had already guessed her decision. She picked up the paper bag and set it on the table. She removed the tobacco and cigarette papers and slid them toward the old man, then she stacked the cans of chili near the cigar box. She smiled at the two old people and promised to come back for a visit soon, then she backed out of the brushshade into the late afternoon sun, which was still beaming overhead like a floodlight.

She drove out of the yard, one hand on the steering wheel, the other pulling the cell phone from her bag. She pressed in the number that Adam had given her.

"Adam Lone Eagle's office." A woman's voice.

Vicky asked to speak to Adam Lone Eagle, and in a moment he was on the line. "Tell me you've decided to join us," he said.

"I've decided to give it a try."

"Great!" A mixture of joy and relief washed through the line. "When can you come over?"

Vicky glanced at her watch. Almost five-thirty, and she should check her messages at the office, make certain nothing important had come up.

"How about first thing tomorrow?" she said.

That would be just fine, he told her, and then he went on about how he was looking forward to working with her, how they'd make a good team when the cell phone went dead in her hand, like a piece of driftwood, leaving only a vacancy and sense of emptiness and the sound of the wind rushing around her.

She drove with the wind a few miles, then turned on the radio, pushing buttons until she had a news station. One could always get news on the moccasin telegraph, but for some time now, she realized, she'd depended on the newspaper and radio for news.

"The body of a Riverton man was recovered from a shallow grave at Double Dives this morning." The announcer's voice blasted through the wind like drumbeats. "The Fremont County Coroner said the man was Rodney Pearson, thirty-four years old, from Two-Valley Road. The cause of death is homicide. Pearson was employed in the oil field at Mexican Flat. Next up in the news . . ."

Vicky pushed the off button. She felt chilled, as if the air had turned cold. Another homicide on the reservation, this one in a dangerous place like Double Dives. Probably a drug deal turned bad. And Father John O'Malley—she always made herself think of him as "Father" now—would have gone to pray over the body. She knew the truth of it as certainly as if she'd been there and seen him. The police had called him, and he'd gone. He would always go.

She guided the Cherokee through the curves on Plunkett Road, aware of her own heart beating. She hadn't seen Father John all summer. There had been times when she'd wanted to call him. She'd even found legitimate reasons—a couple of DUIs, a client arrested on a domestic disturbance—but she hadn't called. They were excuses, that was all. She'd only wanted to hear his voice, and that need in her to be close to him and part of his life, she'd recognized months ago, would never be fulfilled, and so it had to be ignored.

Vicky turned south onto 287 and drove toward Lander, a sense of well-being settling over her, as if she'd given in to the temptation and called him after all and they'd met and talked and caught up with each other, and the meeting had left her resolve shaky and somehow unimportant.

6

VICKY GOT AN early start in the morning, retracing her route on 287, past Plunkett Road, past Fort Washakie, the sun still high in the east, the traffic still light, and the day's heat not yet settled in. From a mile away, she could see the casino and hotel rising out of the plains, giant, dust-colored blocks against the blue sky.

About a half mile from the casino, she slowed behind a couple of RVs. On the billboard looming over the highway, the figure of an Indian warrior in an eagle-feathered headdress blinked in red and blue neon that washed out in the sun. The warrior lifted one hand, as if he were throwing the dice that dropped down the side of the billboard. At the top, in red letters, were the words, *Great Plains Casino.*

She turned into the driveway that curved toward the entrance, which was shaped like a tipi three stories high, trimmed in blue geometric designs. Looming over the tipi structure was the eight-story hotel, with horizontal lines of balconies that jutted from the sliding glass doors off the rooms. On either side of the hotel were parking lots the size of football fields, half full of vehicles, the sun winking off of the windshields.

She followed the driveway past the half-circle of glass doors at the tipi entrance. A group of Indians stood outside—in their mid-twenties, probably—dressed in army camouflage pants and shirts with the sleeves cut out, hoisting signs with black letters: Gambling = Satan. Probably some of the same demonstrators who were arrested two days ago. She could imagine what happened. The tribal judge had fined them for disturbing the peace and set them free. And now they were back. Until Adam got a restraining order, it would no doubt be a familiar pattern.

Vicky drove slowly through the parking lot on the right until she found a vacant spot. The hot asphalt grabbed at her heels as she walked back to the entrance. Ignoring the demonstrators, she darted through the nearest door. A whoosh of refrigerated air hit her and with it, the jumbled sound of mechanical notes racing up and down the scale and coins clinking into metal trays. Underneath the noise was the flat drone of voices. Beyond the entry, the casino floor was a cascade of motion and color, lights flashing, people milling about under the high, conical ceiling. The faintest odor of smoke hung in the air.

Vicky made her way through the crowds and started past the slot machines toward the overhead sign with blue lights that spelled Hotel. Most of the people seated at the slots looked like tourists, but some were Indians, feeding in coins, pushing buttons or pulling metal handles, eyes locked on the red, blue, orange, and yellow figures rolling and jumping on the screens. A siren sounded, and the light on top of a pole started flashing. "All right!" a woman yelled.

Vicky turned into a spacious lobby with a registration desk on one side and a bank of elevators on the other. The casino noise faded into the background. She stopped at the desk and waited until the young woman with dark skin and black hair cut short about her face glanced up from a computer monitor.

"May I help you?"

Vicky said she was here to see Adam Lone Eagle.

"Second floor."

As Vicky started for the bronze doors of the elevators, the woman said, "Wait for security, please."

A gray-uniformed security guard hurried into the lobby, crossed to the elevators, and pushed the button. He glanced around, as if to make certain she was the only one waiting. "Gotta escort visitors to second," he said. "Regulations."

The door opened, and he waved her into the cage. Framed photographs of the reservation hung above the brass railing, and overhead, a chandelier swayed as the elevator started upward. Out of the corner of her eye, she studied the man beside her: bulky shoulders and neck, thin, dark hair, receding from the puffy face, a rim of perspiration at his armpit. He stared straight ahead. The elevator made a ding and rocked to a stop. The doors behind them swung open.

"This way." He pulled his bulky frame around and ushered her into a wide corridor with blue and red carpeting on the floor and framed oil paintings of the plains and the Wind River range on the cream-colored walls. He headed toward the middle door on the right, pushed it open, then stood back. Vicky stepped into an office as large as her bungalow, all buttery colored walls with matching leather chairs, dark blue carpeting, and Remington-like sculptures of warriors and horses on the polished wood tables. Arranged around the walls were large oil paintings of Indian villages and ponies racing across the plains.

Adam was bent over the glass-topped desk on the right, tapping a stack of documents, explaining something in a patient voice to a woman with a hypnotized look in her eyes who was seated behind the desk.

"Vicky!" He sprang upright and came toward her. She had the same feeling she'd had the previous day, that he was about to put his arms around her. She shoved out her hand, which he took, leading her back to the desk.

"Emily," he said to the secretary, who sat back in her chair, "meet Vicky Holden, the attorney I told you about. She'll be joining the team. That's right, isn't it?" He turned to Vicky.

"We'll see." Vicky slipped her hand out of his.

"Emily White Robe keeps me on schedule." Adam nodded at the secretary who was now swiveling toward the computer monitor.

"Glad to meet you," she said over the shoulder of her red silky blouse.

Not true, Vicky thought. The woman wasn't glad to meet any other woman who would be working with Adam. She tried to place the name. White Robe. The White Robe family lived near Ethete. Emily must be one of the daughters, now grown-up, in her twenties and very pretty, and obviously attracted to Adam.

"I alerted Stan Lexson you were on the way," Adam was saying. She felt the slight pressure of his hand on her arm. "He's eager to meet you. Come on, I'll take you over and introduce you. Can't tell you how good it'll be to work with you again," he said, guiding her across the office and into the corridor.

"Last spring, you were working *for* me," she said.

"Then we're even. You'll be working for *me* now. I promise not to be as hard on you as you were on me." He gave a quiet laugh and opened one of the massive double doors at the end of the corridor. Vicky stepped into an office that was almost a duplicate of the one they'd just left, but larger, with creamier walls and plusher carpeting and more of everything—more leather chairs and oil paintings and bronze sculptures, with the detail and patina of true Remington's. The secretary—a white woman about thirty, with sharply cut, shoulder-length blond hair and perfect makeup—smiled at them from behind the desk.

"Mr. Lexson and Mr. Barrenger are waiting for you." The secretary gestured with her chin toward the wooden doors on the right, her eyes lingering on Adam.

Vicky followed Adam into the private office, feeling like a tumbleweed blown farther and farther away from anything familiar. Beyond the overstuffed chairs on the far side of the office, the side tables with more sculptures, and the mahogany desk with nothing on top except an expensive-looking leather blotter, two men stood in front of a panel of windows that probably gave Stan Lexson a view of the casino floor.

It was Lexson coming toward them now, she guessed, a man who looked to be in his forties, about five feet ten, slender, and muscular, like a runner. Despite the way he was dressed—khakis, blue dress shirt opened at the collar, and tasseled loafers—he had the focused, intense look of the bankers she'd worked with on Seventeenth Street in Denver, men accustomed to blue suits, white shirts, and spacious offices in downtown buildings. He had sandy-colored hair, brushed back from his forehead, and light eyes that were boring into her, as if he were sizing up an attorney he might want to hire to handle a major case.

"So you're the Arapaho lawyer Adam's been telling me about." The man held out a manicured hand.

"Vicky, meet Stan Lexson," Adam said.

Vicky moved forward and shook the man's hand. Beneath the softness of his palm, she could sense strength and determination.

"Call me Stan." He had an open, friendly smile, and she found herself smiling back. "Welcome to Great Plains Casino. I like to get to know the people who work for me. Know who they are. What's important to them. We're a close family here."

He motioned toward the man in the beige shirt and pressed blue jeans still stationed at the windows, half-turned toward the room, eyes on the casino below. "Meet Neil Barrenger, head of casino operations."

"Howdy." The man glanced away from the windows. He was probably in his thirties with narrow, slightly stooped shoulders, short-cropped hair going gray and wire-rimmed glasses that gave him the look of someone who spent most days in front of computers.

"A lot of tourists think they're going to get rich down there," Lexson said, motioning them to the window. Vicky followed the man's gaze. Beyond the rows of slot machines was an expanse of felt-covered tables, dealers on one side, players on the other.

"We give them a good chance to win," Lexson said. "Our slots pay ninety-six cents on the dollar. You know anything about the gaming business . . ." he hurried on, not waiting for an answer, "the payoff's excellent. Most casinos take a bigger percentage. We want to keep people happy, so they'll come back. You tried your luck, Vicky?"

"I'm not much of a gambler," Vicky said. She'd driven to the casino soon after it had opened, dropped a few dollars in the slots, and left with less cash than she'd arrived with, plus a feeling of disquiet, as if something had been thrown out of sync. She'd felt the rush every time she'd pushed HIT: This was her lucky hit, this time all the diamonds would line up. It was like alcohol, she'd realized, seductive and warm, a rush of well-being that camouflaged the pain. It could change you, the rush, turn you into someone else.

"We have a rule against employees playing," Lexson said, a new seriousness in his voice. "Technically, you'll be on a retainer, but we have to observe the rules." He nodded at Adam. "You can explain, counselor."

"We have to comply with the pact the tribe made with the state and the Indian Gaming Regulatory Act." Adam gave her a wide grin. "You'll be all too familiar with that in a few days."

"Here they come again." Barrenger moved closer to the window, and Lexson followed.

Vicky looked down on the floor. The demonstrators from out front were marching through the rows of slot machines, jabbing signs into the air. Gambling = Satan. Up and down, up and down. Players swung around on the stools and stared a moment before turning back to the slots. It was like watching a silent movie, Vicky thought. Lights flashing, heads pivoting, mouths opening and shutting.

"We have to get them off the floor," Lexson said.

Barrenger did a half turn and strode across the office. The door clicked shut into the quiet. Adam moved closer to Lexson, who was still looking down on the floor.

"Monroe's people," Adam said.

"See that the district attorney files charges. Trespassing, disorderly, whatever."

"Misdemeanors. Within tribal jurisdiction." Adam held his ground a moment, then walked over to the desk and lifted the phone. "Get the police to the casino," he said into the receiver.

Below, a phalanx of gray-uniformed guards had appeared and surrounded the demonstrators, pushing them into a small circle, which they moved toward the side.

"Where are they taking them?" Vicky asked, watching the circle disappear through a door.

"We have a nice lounge." Lexson let his gaze rest on her a moment. "Maybe we'll give them cookies and coffee and make them comfortable until the police get here."

Vicky waited a couple of beats, then said, "There's something I have to know before I agree to work here. Is Matt Kingdom on the casino's payroll?"

"What are you talking about?" Adam hurried over from the desk.

Lexson laughed. "You were right, Adam. She's tough. A straight-talker, gets right to the point. I like that. Why don't you tell her?"

"Don't know what you've heard," Adam began, "but Kingdom works for the Arapaho Business Council. They hired him; they pay him. Anything else, as you know, would be a conflict of interest."

Vicky pushed on. "What about Kingdom's son? I understand he has a supervisor's job here. How many other employees are connected to Kingdom?"

"Connected?" Lexson jammed his hands in the pockets of his khakis. "You're connected to the tribe. Connected to Adam here. You ask me, everybody on the rez is connected to everybody else. As it happened, Kingdom's son was the best-qualified applicant."

Lexson kept his gaze on her a moment, then turned to Adam. "You see why I wanted an Arapaho attorney on board? What you'll find out, Vicky"—turning back to her—"and what you can tell your tribe, is that we're operating a successful casino, despite what Captain Jack Monroe would like people to believe."

Lexson had wanted her here? Vicky glanced at the Lakota attorney beside her, but his face was unreadable, except, she thought, for the almost imperceptible look of discomfort behind his dark eyes.

"Trouble is," Lexson went on, "some Arapahos think the casino belongs to them. We had a lady come into the restaurant last week, order a big meal, and refuse to pay the bill. Who ever heard of paying in your own restaurant? she said. We have people coming in demanding jobs as dealers. Never dealt a card in their lives. You know how many players come to a new Indian casino hoping to find dealers who don't know an ace from a spade and can't add up to twenty-one? You know how long it would take for such players to wipe out the house? That's why we have to hire the best people, and I don't care who they're connected to. At the end of the day, all that matters is the house profit. If we don't make a profit, neither does the tribe."

Lexson stepped back to the window and tapped his knuckles on the glass pane. "See the blackjack area? We hired an Arapaho as the pit boss. Dennis Light Stone."

Light Stone. Vicky turned the name over in her mind, trying to place the family. "He's not from the reservation," she said.

"From Oklahoma," Lexson said. "Spent six years dealing blackjack in Colorado, and he knows the ins and outs of the game. We want somebody experienced overseeing the other dealers. We want the best, Vicky."

"NEXT STOP, HUMAN resources on the third floor," Adam said. They were walking down the corridor toward the elevator. "After you sign the necessary forms, I'll hand over some contracts for your approval. What d'ya think?" They stopped in front of the closed bronze doors and Adam pushed the up button.

"You're overwhelmed with work," Vicky said, "what with having to deal with Captain Monroe's demonstrators, and you needed help with the contracts."

"Look, Vicky." Adam reached out and took her hand. "I admit that Stan decided it would be a good idea to have an Arapaho on the legal team. It would reassure everybody. I'm the one who recommended . . ."

She cut in. "The only Arapaho attorney around."

"We could have found several in Oklahoma. I wanted to work with you."

Vicky looked straight ahead at the elevator doors. She could see the faint reflections in the bronze: the tall, dark-haired man, the tense, dark-haired woman beside him. "Why didn't you tell me the whole story?"

"Because I knew you wouldn't take the job if you thought you were some kind of token."

"Is that what it is?" How ironic, she was thinking. Will Standing Bear expected her to protect the tribal interests at the casino, while Stan Lexson expected her to assure the tribe that all was well. She felt as if they would pull her apart—her own people, the casino.

"Trust me, Vicky," Adam said. "I need your help." He hesitated. "And maybe you can use the work."

The elevator bell pinged, and they stepped through the sliding doors. Vicky felt the tug of gravity as they moved upward, and then they were crossing another corridor to a door with a dark wood plaque at the side that said Annette Addley, Director, Human Resources. Adam reached past her and opened the door. It was a moment before she summoned the courage to step into the office.

■ ■ ■

THE NOONDAY HEAT rolled through the parking lot in invisible waves by the time Vicky finished filling out the forms the secretary in human resources had pushed toward her. Maybe Adam was right, she thought, passing the parked vehicles that radiated more heat. She could use the retainer fee, that was a fact, and Will Standing Bear and the other elders would be reassured knowing she was working for the casino. A win-win situation. In her bag was a diskette that held several contracts Adam wanted her to review. He'd showed her to a vacant office next to his and said she could take it over, even redecorate if she wanted, but in the end, she'd explained she preferred working in her own office.

She was several cars away when she spotted four men around the Cherokee. Two sitting on the hood, two leaning against the side, arms folded over their chests, egg-size lumps in their jaws. One thrust his head forward and spit out a wad of phlegm.

Vicky stopped and glanced about. Rows and rows of vehicles shimmering in the sun, and no one around. She made herself take in a long breath and continue walking, her gaze on the two men who were now coming toward her, sauntering past the sedan. They were Arapahos with shoulder-length hair slicked back behind their ears, slender builds, and thin, earnest faces. They looked about twenty and were dressed in camouflage clothing. Now the men seated on the hood jumped down. One of them stepped in front of her. The tattoo of a large, black bird wiggled along his ropy biceps.

"Don't mind if we have a little talk, do you?" Tattoo-man said. "You lawyers like to talk, right?"

"What do you want?" Vicky gripped her black bag, getting ready to swing it if she had to.

"You gonna work for the casino?"

"Who sent you here? Monroe?" She shot another glance around the lot. Surely there were security cameras on the lot. Where were the guards? There was no one else in sight. Then she remembered the guards surrounding the demonstrators in the casino and ushering them through the side door. The guards were occupied.

"The Captain's the only guy around here gives a shit about the people. Them bastards there . . ." he tossed his head toward the casino, and a piece of hair fell across his forehead. He let it stay. "All they care about is lining their own pockets. Don't care if people's lives get ruined by gambling."

"It's nothing but Satan's work, Tommy," said one of the others.

"Captain Jack's been telling people the truth." Another joined in. "Don't go to the casino. Don't work in that filthy place. And what do the bastards do? Call the police on the Captain's rangers. Took away three troops yesterday and got some of our people shut up in the casino now. Probably gonna arrest 'em for trespassing or some other shit, like we don't got a right to go in the casino and tell people the truth."

"Don't matter." The man with the tattoo, the man called Tommy, leaned toward her. "Captain Jack'll get 'em out of that stinking jail in no time."

"What do you want from me?" Vicky asked.

"What you do for Kingdom to get a job?"

"What?"

"Don't act all innocent like it's some big secret. It ain't secret no more. The Captain's got it figured out. You want a big-paying job at the casino, you go see Kingdom, the all-mighty chairman."

"That's a serious allegation. What proof do you have?"

"Proof? Look around the casino, woman. How many

Arapahos got good jobs—I ain't talking about sweeping floors. How you think they got them good jobs? 'Cause they're good-looking, like you?" He was in her face now. She could smell the stale tobacco on the man's breath, the musty odor of perspiration. She made herself hold her place. She would not show fear. She would not bear her throat to a raven like a doomed wild animal.

"Use your head, woman. Either you're on the side of the people, or you're on the side of the bastards that're ripping us off. If I was you, I wouldn't be taking no job at the casino."

The man held her gaze a moment, then all four started to move past. Tattoo-man stayed close, not taking his eyes away. And then he swerved into her. She felt the thrust of his elbow into her ribs, felt herself falling sideways. She reached for the hood of the sedan to steady herself, then forced herself to walk on toward the Cherokee. Gripping the door handle to stop from shaking, she looked back at the four men moving through the lot side by side—swaggering—throwing their shoulders around.

"Where can I find Monroe?" she called.

Tattoo-man turned around. She could see the trace of laughter in his expression. "You can't," he called back. "Captain Jack wants to see people, he finds them."

7

"BATTER UP!" FATHER John juggled the ball and waited until Eddie Antelope had raised the bat and adjusted his stance.

"Keep your eye on the ball. Front shoulder in. Stay back. Come through too soon, and you'll be too far in front of the ball."

Eddie wiggled his thin, ten-year-old shoulders, shifted his weight, and locked his eyes above his left shoulder in the direction of the pitcher's mound. Father John pulled back and let go of a slider that ran away from the outside edge of the plate. The loud whack sounded like a gunshot, as Eddie attacked and drove a hard liner in the hole between first and second.

"Good job!" Father John lifted his glove in salute. "Next up. Let's keep moving."

"John!"

His assistant, Father George Reinhold, was hurrying down the third-base line, urgency carved in the forward thrust of his broad shoulders.

"Hold on." Father John motioned toward the kid picking up the bat. Then he walked over to the other priest.

"Somebody waiting to see you." Father George shrugged. "Wouldn't give her name. Insisted she has to talk to Father O'Malley."

"We're about done here." Father John threw a glance toward the kids. Willie Crumble was already dancing into his stance at the plate, hands running up and down the bat. Next Saturday, the Eagles were scheduled to play the Riverton Rams, the toughest team in the league, and they'd been working on making consistent contact. A couple of kids still had another turn at bat.

"I'll be over in a few minutes," he said. "Talk to her until I get there, okay?" He started back to the mound.

"She's in some kind of trouble." The other priest caught up and marched beside him with the persistency and determination of his German ancestors. "It's an emergency, she says, and she had to see you now."

Father John stopped and turned to his assistant. The man was his age, forty-eight, but carried some extra pounds that made him look ten years older. Blotches of sunburn rose on his fleshy face. He was squinting so hard in the sun that his eyes looked like dark slits, and beads of perspiration stood out on his forehead along the edge of his sandy-colored hair.

"Take over here, okay?" Father John pushed the glove and ball into the other priest's hands and headed into the outfield.

"Hey, what do I know about baseball?"

"Just throw the ball," Father John called over his shoulder.

■ ■ ■

HE WALKED DOWN the side of the redbrick residence, then crossed Circle Drive and cut through the field of wind-blown wild grasses in the center of the mission. The buildings huddled among the cottonwoods around the drive, like visitors from the nineteenth century who have stayed on and on. Next to the residence was the two-story gray stone schoolhouse that now housed the Arapaho Museum. Directly across was the white church decorated in the blue, red, and yellow geometric designs of the Arapahos, the steeple lifting through the trees into the blue sky. On the other side of the driveway that ran alongside the church stood the yellow stucco administration building, two stories high with a vaulted, peaked roof and double rows of oblong windows. Behind the administration building, partially visible from the drive, was Eagle Hall, the squat, gray-shingled meeting house and classroom building, and beyond the hall, the two-room guest house.

The noise of a chain saw cut through the sound of the wind in the trees. Leonard Bizzel, who had been the caretaker and all-around handyman when Father John had first come to the mission eight years ago, was standing over some fallen branches in front of the church. A few feet away, Walks-On stretched on his side in the shade. The roar of the saw stopped. The Indian looked up and threw Father John a nod, then went back to sawing one of the branches. Father John veered past the blue truck parked in front of the administration building and took the front steps two at a time.

He found the woman in his office in the front corner, slumped in one of the side chairs, as if she'd just crawled away from an accident. A white woman with light brown hair and pale skin, dressed in blue jeans and a yellow

T-shirt. Still in her twenties, he guessed, with a world-weary look that she wore uneasily, as if it had come without her knowledge or permission.

She raised her head and fixed him with gray, flat eyes. "You Father O'Malley?"

"How can I help you?" he asked, blocking the surprise in his voice. Usually the people who came looking for him were Arapaho.

"I'm Mo Pearson," she said.

He recognized the name. Last night, Ted Gianelli, the FBI agent, had called and said they'd ID'd the homicide victim found at Double Dives: Rodney Pearson, who lived on Two-Valley Road outside Riverton and worked in the Mexican Flat oil fields. Did Father John know him? The answer had been no. And this morning, he'd read the article in the *Gazette.* Rodney Pearson was survived by his wife, Mo.

He pulled over the other side chair and sat down, facing the woman. "I'm very sorry, Mrs. Pearson." His voice was low.

She gave a quick nod of acknowledgment. "Call me Mo."

"How can I help you, Mo?"

"You said some prayers over him out at Double Dives, right?"

That was right, he told her.

She started laughing, a brittle sound edged with hysteria. Then she ran her fingers over her cheeks, wiping away the moisture. "You know how funny that is? Rodney would've had some kind of heart attack if he'd seen you praying over him." She stopped, as if she'd remembered something. "If he hadn't already been dead. He never believed in priests and God and all that stuff."

Father John let a couple seconds pass, then he said, "God believed in him."

"What?" She squinted at him for a long moment, as if she were trying to comprehend. "Whatever," she said finally. "I just wanna get the bastard that killed him."

"Who do you think it was?"

"You saying you don't know?" She jerked her head back and fixed him with a look of disbelief. "Looks like nobody knows. Sure as hell the fed don't know. Spent most of yesterday asking me stupid questions. Who's your husband hang with? Who's he work with? Who's he sleep with besides you? I said, nobody, so shut up." She set an elbow on the armrest and propped her chin in the palm of her hand. A thread of tears ran down her cheek and through her fingers. "Why'd he have to ask stupid questions like that? I told him who killed Rodney. Some Indian, that's who did it."

"What makes you think so?" Father John could almost smell the stench of anger and hatred clinging to the woman like bad perfume.

"Who'd Rodney work with at the oil field? Indians. Who'd he hang with, go drinking with? And all the time telling me, Mo, honey, you and me gonna hit the big time. How the hell was we gonna hit the big time with him hanging around with a bunch of Indians?"

"Look, Mo," Father John began. "Agent Gianelli's a good man. He'll check out everybody your husband knew, and if an Indian's guilty, he'll have him charged with homicide. You'll see justice done."

She lifted her head and gave a shriek of laughter. "Damn right, I'll see justice done. All you gotta do, Father O'Malley, is tell me who did it."

Father John leaned forward and clasped his hands between his knees. "Listen to me, Mo. I have no idea who killed your husband. I'm very sorry it happened. It was terrible. It shouldn't have happened. I'll do anything I can to help you."

"They talk, those Indians." She was shaking her head up

and down. "Oh, I know how they gossip. They brag about everything." She shifted sideways and shot him a defiant look. "All you gotta do is listen, and sooner or later, one of 'em is gonna blurt out that he shot Rodney like he was a deer he scared up out of the brush. Maybe come in your confessional, begging for forgiveness like, and then all you gotta do is tell me who it is."

Father John leaned into the back of the chair, not taking his eyes from the woman. Was she asking for his help so that she could kill the person who had killed her husband?

He said, "What do you plan to do?"

She kept her eyes locked on his. Her face dissolved into what passed for a smile, as if they were conspirators. "Like you said, it shouldn't never have happened, and justice is gotta be done."

"If I hear any gossip," Father John leaned toward the woman, "I'm going to call Gianelli. The fed will track down the killer."

She shook her head so hard that her whole body picked up the rhythm. "The fed's never gonna find Rodney's killer, 'cause you and me both know the Indians aren't gonna talk to him. They're gonna clam up when he comes around, like they don't know nothing. But they'll talk to you, right? I mean, you being the Indian priest and all. They think you're one of 'em."

"You've had a terrible shock, Mo. You're still in shock, and you're angry. That's normal, but what you're thinking about is wrong. Give yourself some time. You'll start thinking differently. Is there someplace you could go for a while? Somebody you could stay with?"

"Relax, Father O'Malley." She waved a thin hand between them. The smile sat frozen on her face, and mockery flashed in the gray eyes. "All I'm asking is that you find out from them Indians who the bastard was that killed Rodney.

I know you'll go to the fed, but you can tell me, too, can't you? That way I can make sure the fed does his job. You'll be doing the Indian a big favor, 'cause if the fed don't find him real soon, Rodney's got friends that're gonna take care of it. You know what I mean?" She swooped up the small brown purse next to her feet and dug out a pen and notepad. After scribbling something on the top page, she ripped it out and handed it to him, then jumped to her feet.

"Killer's gonna get what's coming to him," she said, backing to the door. "One way or the other. Like you said, justice is gonna be done."

And then she was gone. The sound of the front door slamming shook the plastered walls of the old building.

Father John walked over to the window. The kids were circling around Father George as they came across the field, lugging the canvas bags filled with bats, balls, gloves, and helmets. Six or seven pickups were parked around Circle Drive waiting to take the kids home. And Mo Pearson was climbing in behind the steering wheel of the blue truck. The muffled noise of the chain saw drifted over the voices of the kids, squealing and shouting, and the sound of an engine kicking to life.

After a moment, gray exhaust burst from the tailpipe and the truck sputtered onto Circle Drive. Father George reached out and pulled back one of the kids as the truck accelerated past. He stared after it a moment, shaking his head, then ushered the kids toward the waiting pickups.

Father John turned away and sank into the chair behind his desk. He glanced at the paper in his hand. An address on Two-Valley Road, phone number, name: Mo. Why had she come? To pressure him to find her husband's killer by threatening some kind of vigilante action?

The woman was right about one thing. Arapahos had a way of shutting down when the fed came around. But Gianelli was a dogged investigator; he never gave up. He'd keep coming around until somebody let something slip, and then he'd have the murderer . . .

It could take time, that was the problem. And Rodney Pearson's friends would be out in the oil field looking for his killer. They could decide one of the man's coworkers was guilty, and then what? Pay him back in kind? Shoot him in the head? Bury him at Double Dives? Good Lord. There would be a war between the locals and the Arapahos.

He tried to push away the thought, debating whether to call Gianelli. What would he say? Mo Pearson believed that her husband's friends would go after his killer? The woman was obviously in shock. She could be in shock for days, weeks, and the problem was, she might convince Rodney's friends that the only way he could have justice would be if they saw to it.

Mo Pearson was right about something else. There was someone on the reservation who might know about her husband's murder. He rolled a pen across the top of the desk. He should have seen it before. Lela Running Bull had left her dad's house as soon as she could get away. Why? So she wouldn't have to talk to Gianelli again? What was she hiding? The girl was scared. He could feel the truth of it, like a fly ball floating into his glove. She hadn't called the mission today. She didn't want to talk to anyone.

But he had an idea of someone who might know how to get ahold of the girl.

He got to his feet, grabbed his cowboy hat from the coat tree in the corner, and walked to the front door. Father George was just coming inside.

"Before you go anywhere," the other priest said, "there's something you ought to know."

Father John turned and followed the other priest down the corridor, past the sepia-toned photographs of the early

Jesuits at St. Francis Mission, faces wavy behind the old glass, eyes pale, and distant, peering out from behind rimless spectacles. He turned into the office at the far end.

The other priest was already behind the desk, thumbing through a stack of bank statements. The man had been handling the mission finances since he'd arrived three months ago, a job Father John had been glad to relinquish. Always more bills than funds in the mission account, always juggling payments. Which bills to pay this month? Which to set aside and hope the phone company, the utilities company, or some other company would give the mission some slack, that was George Reinhold's job now.

The man actually liked it. He had a complete trust in numbers. "They are what they say they are," he'd said. Definite. Pure. Precise. Not unlike his own philosophy, which was as solid and unmovable as granite. The man even resembled granite, with thick chest and arms, a large head that set directly on his shoulders. No matter what happened, you could always lean upon granite, which Father John realized, probably accounted for the way the Arapahos had taken to the man. There was comfort in the strength of certitude.

"The bank called this afternoon," the other priest said. "It appears we're overdrawn."

Father John nodded. It wasn't the first time.

"By more than a thousand dollars. They covered two checks, but they want the money."

"Thousand dollars?" Father John pushed away from the doorjamb. "How's that possible?"

The other priest tapped the bank statements. "Obviously the bank's made a mistake. I've gone over the deposits and debits. Everything balances. Don't worry. I'll drive over to Riverton tomorrow and get it straightened out. Meanwhile," he picked up a stack of envelopes. "What do you suggest we do about these bills?"

"Hold on to them," Father John said.

The other priest took it in with a grunt. "We can't keep operating in the red . . ."

Father John interrupted. "We've been in the red before. Money has a way of finding us when we need it." Dear Lord, he thought, he was beginning to sound like the elders. "You have to believe in miracles, George."

The priest shot him a pained look. "I'll call the telephone company and tell them we have a little miracle coming. Should arrive any day now."

Father John left the man still peering at the pile of envelopes, and retraced his steps down the corridor to the front door. Then he jogged across the grounds to the pickup. In ten minutes, he was heading east toward the trailer park were Mary Running Bull lived.

8

THERE WERE A half dozen trailers with gray aluminum siding that slid to purple in the shade of the cottonwoods. Trucks and cars stood outside the trailers, and clotheslines, some sinking with towels and sheets, hung between the trees. He started to pull over at the side of the road. He had no idea where Mary Running Bull lived. He'd have to work his way from trailer to trailer, starting with the closest.

And then he saw her, the heavyset woman with long black hair, standing in the doorway of the white trailer, a toddler slung on one hip. She stared in his direction a moment before stepping back out of sight. The door slammed shut.

Father John drove ahead and stopped, then made his way across the churned dirt and dried brush and knocked on the door. No answer. He knocked again. "Father O'Malley, Mary," he called. "I'd like to talk to you. It's important."

Several seconds passed before the door creaked open. Mary Running Bull stood back in the shadows. From somewhere inside came the subdued noise of a television. The woman might have been a high-school girl, he thought, dressed in short, cutoff jeans and a pink blouse tied at her waist, with a tiny silver earring in one nostril. She leaned sideways and adjusted the round-faced little girl on her hip. The child was eating a peanut butter and jelly sandwich, and specks of red jelly dotted her face like measles.

"Come on in, Father," Mary Running Bull said, a sharpness in her tone that failed to mask the notes of defeat and weariness.

He stepped into the stuffy space with a closet-sized kitchen at one end and, pushed against opposite walls, a sofa with an Indian blanket thrown over the cushions and a small table with a half loaf of bread, jars of peanut butter and jelly, and paper plates on top. In the corner, another child—a small boy—sat cross-legged on the uneven vinyl floor in front of a television that had cartoon characters jumping across the screen, falsetto voices that punctuated the metallic music. The boy gripped a sandwich in his pudgy hands.

"Just getting the kids some supper," the woman said in what might have been an attempt at polite small talk, except Father John had the feeling she was stalling.

"Lela's not here," she said after a moment. "That's why you came, isn't it."

"I want to talk to her."

"Well, you're gonna have to get in line. Police, FBI. They all been around wanting to talk to Lela. I told them the same thing I'm telling you. She's not here."

The woman crossed in front of him, set the little girl down next to the boy, then stepped into the tiny kitchen and folded her arms, leaning back against the counter. Behind her, shoved against the wall, were cereal boxes and a couple of soup cans. "I been telling Lela Tommy's no good," she blurted, as if unpinning an idea that had been wound in her mind. "Get you pregnant, I said. That's all he's good for, so he can brag to his buddies. No way is he gonna stick by you, I told her."

She threw a glance over at the two children and exhaled a long breath. "Lela's like me. Can't tell her anything. Gonna have to learn the hard way."

She was silent a moment, and Father John waited. The crackle of metallic music floated between them. Finally, she said, "I was going to college." She nodded, as if she wanted to convince herself of some half-forgotten reality. "Wyoming Central. I really liked college. It was like, you know, the world started getting bigger."

"What happened?" he asked.

"Found out I was pregnant." She started laughing, and, for a moment, he thought she might burst into tears. "Some no-good I'd gotten mixed up with that summer. So I had to quit school and get a full-time job. Got on at the supermarket over in Riverton. I was lucky. Then Jeb was born, and everything was going real good, until my no-good boyfriend starts coming around, being real sweet and saying we were gonna get married, and then I was pregnant with Amanda, and Mr. sweet-talking, no-good sonabitch was gone."

She pushed away from the counter. "Don't know why I'm going on like this. Besides, don't get me wrong, Father. I love my babies, and my auntie, she takes care of them while I'm at the store, so things are okay. I'm making it okay."

He started to say he was glad to hear it, but she'd only stopped for a breath and was already hurrying on. "Sometimes I think about what I was learning. Programming and business management, and I try to hold on to it, you know. I try to remember. I don't want it to go away, 'cause I think someday . . ."

She spun around to the sink, turned on the faucet, and, leaning over, started splashing water in her face. Her shoulders were shaking. She reached out like a blind woman and patted the counter until her fingers curled around a towel. Then she turned back, mopping at the mixture of water and tears that ran down her face and matted the sides of her hair. "God, I don't know why I'm going on like this. You must think I'm some kinda nutcase."

Father John put up his hand, palm forward in the Plains Indian sign of peace. "It's okay, Mary," he said. "I understand. You're worried that Lela will do the same thing."

"Lela's real stupid for a smart girl." She tossed the towel back onto the counter. "She oughta graduate from high school, go to college, get herself a good job."

"What's she frightened of?"

The woman stood very still, her face taut.

Father John pushed on. "That's why she's hiding. She's frightened of something."

Mary moved to the table and—hands shaking—busied herself smearing peanut butter and jelly on a slice of bread. She slapped another slice on top, cut diagonal pieces and, leaning over, handed one to each child. Then she went back to the kitchen, glancing at him out of the corner of one eye as if to confirm that he was still there.

He waited.

"Lela came running in here a couple nights ago, white as those plates." Mary settled back against the counter and gestured with her chin toward the paper plates on the table.

"Looked like she didn't have any blood in her, 'cept for the welt on her cheek. Said she seen a hand coming up from the earth in Double Dives. I said, we gotta call the police, and Lela started crying and said he'd kill her, too."

"Who, Mary?"

The woman gave another shrug. "Tommy Willard, I guess. The sonabitch likes to knock her around. Why's he gonna kill you? I said, unless he doesn't want you talking to the police. Maybe he had something to do with the dead body, I'm thinking. So we had a big fight. Lela was crying and screaming. But somebody was dead out there, and Tommy didn't want her saying anything. And now I knew about it, and if we didn't call the police, all of a sudden I'm some kind of accomplice. I don't know what her and Tommy been up to, and I got my kids to think about. So I called nine-one-one. Lela was crying hard and saying how she hated me and how we were both going to pay. Cops were here in five minutes. Said she had to take them out to the Dives and show them where she'd seen the hand. She was shaking so hard, she could hardly walk. She said nobody could see her driving around in some cop car. I had to get my neighbor to watch the kids so I could ride with her over to the Dives."

"Where can I find Tommy Willard?"

Mary shook her head. "All I know is, Lela said he lives with a bunch of rangers."

"Rangers!"

"That's what they call themselves. They roam around the reservation like some kind of army. Leader's an old guy, Jack Monroe. Vietnam vet. They call him the Captain."

Father John had followed the stories about the man in the *Gazette*. After the man had failed to stop the casino, he'd stayed on the rez, telling the *Gazette* the fight had only begun.

"Listen, Mary, I want you to give Lela a message." He hurried on before the woman could voice the protest forming on her lips. "Tell her she can't hide forever. Sooner or later, Tommy or Jack Monroe or whoever she's afraid of is going to find her. Tell her to call me." He plucked the small notepad and pencil out of his shirt pocket and wrote down the number at the mission. Then he tore off the sheet and set it on the table. "I'll try to help her," he said.

The young woman stared at the paper, but made no effort to reach for it. She was still leaning against the counter when he left, some kind of argument playing out in her expression.

Father John drove back down the dirt road and made a left onto Highway 789, then a right into the reservation. The sun was almost lost behind the mountains ahead, and tiers of reds, magenta, and orange rose through the sky like flames. There was no traffic, only the asphalt unfurling ahead and a flock of black birds, ravens, most likely—a conspiracy of ravens, he thought, circling over some carrion on the plains, their harsh cries bursting through the quiet.

He kept his speed at a steady forty, judging by the flash of the telephone poles outside his window—his speedometer hadn't worked in years—and tried to arrange the scraps of information he'd picked up so far into a cohesive, logical story. A fifteen-year-old girl had discovered the body of Rodney Pearson and had run away. Most likely she was running away from Tommy Willard, which meant that Mary might be right. Willard could be involved in Pearson's murder, and Lela knew more than was good for her.

He felt chilled. Logic demanded its own truth. Lela Running Bull was in danger. Mary and her two kids could also be in danger.

Dear Lord, he thought. Let Lela call.

9

IT WAS HIS favorite time of the day, that moment during early Mass with the pale sunlight flaring through the red, yellow, and blue stained-glass windows, when time seemed to stand still, and all that had happened yesterday and the day before, all the yesterdays and all the tomorrows, collapsed into the sacred silence.

Father John finished the last prayers of the Mass—"*Oh, give thanks to the Lord, for He is good, for his great love is without end.*" A chorus of amens, hushed and reverent, like a quiet rush of air, came from the elders and those parishioners who had taken to stopping for early Mass on their way to work.

He walked down the aisle and stood at the door in the vestibule shaking the gnarled, work-roughened hands as people filed out into the morning. Last month, he'd spent a week on retreat in the mountain wilderness of Colorado, a quiet time of prayer and reflection that had brought him back to himself, renewed his spirit, his vocation. Everything had seemed different and new when he'd returned: the church with the steeple lifted into the sky, the cottonwoods rustling around the old buildings. He remembered driving around Circle Drive and thinking he'd come home. The mission was all he had ever wanted in a home.

After the Mass, Father John hung his surplice and chasuble in the sacristy closet and helped Leonard Bizzel straighten the cabinets and store the Mass books. As long as Father John had been at St. Francis, the caretaker had assisted at daily Mass. No matter the weather, no matter the icy roads in the winter, at five forty-five in the morning, Leonard's old truck rattled around Circle Drive. He was as dependable as the sun, as the wind blowing across the plains.

The church was quiet as Father John made his way across the altar and genuflected before the small, tipi-shaped tabernacle that the grandmothers had made from tanned deerskin. The faintest odors of aftershave lingered in the air. He let himself out the front door into the orange-tinged daylight and headed across the grounds to the residence.

"Pancakes? Waffles? Scrambled eggs? Name your poison, Father." Catherine Bizzel stood in front of the stove waving a spatula toward him like a maestro conducting the brindisi in *La Traviata*.

"Pancakes," Father John said. The moment he'd come through the front door, the aroma of pancakes and hot oil had rushed over him. He sat down across the table from Father George, who had already sliced away at the half-mountain of pancakes on his plate.

"Your wish is my command." Catherine gave a final swirl of the spatula and turned back to the stove. She scooped some batter out of a bowl and poured it onto the frying pan. Scoop. Pour. Tiny specks of oil popped and jumped around her hands. She worked quickly, going through motions she'd practiced a thousand times.

One of the little miracles, Father John thought, this fifty-some-year-old woman, short and squarely built, with thick brown arms and quick, capable hands. She wore blue jeans and a pinkish blouse that draped around her hips. Her hair was black, streaked with silver and curled about her flat face. There was a perpetual look of surprise in her dark, round eyes.

Two months ago, Elena, who had been the housekeeper longer than even she could remember, had taken a week off to help her granddaughter look after a new baby in Nebraska. The week lengthened into ten days, two weeks, a month. He and Father George had stumbled past each other, burning the eggs, frying granite-hard hamburgers, brewing coffee that looked like ink and tasted like paint thinner, producing laundry with multihued, tie-dyed underwear.

Finally Elena had called Father John to say he might want to get somebody to help out, but it was her job—he shouldn't forget—her house to look after, her mission. He promised he wouldn't forget and wondered who might want a job that belonged to Elena.

The next morning, Leonard Bizzel had planted himself in the kitchen doorway and announced that his wife, Catherine, would like the job.

Father John'd had to restrain himself from jumping up and hugging the man. It wasn't until a week later, after Catherine had returned the residence to running order, that she'd confided how she and Leonard needed the extra money. It had surprised him. Leonard never missed a day at the mission. He fixed the plumbing, touched up the paint, pruned the cottonwoods, cleared the wind-blown debris from the grounds, and generally kept St. Francis Mission presentable. He and Catherine ran a small ranch—ten head of cattle, a couple acres of hay. Father John had assumed that, between the ranch and what Leonard took home from the mission, they were making ends meet. And Leonard was a private man. He hadn't said anything.

Father John pushed a forkful of pancakes into the syrup and took another bite. After a moment, he lifted his eyes to the woman. "Tell me something, Catherine. You think Arapaho women served pancakes on the plains?"

The woman set another stack on the table. "Thought you got done with all that history research when you come to the mission."

Father George let out a guffaw, then helped himself to the new stack.

"Catherine. Catherine. Research is never done." Father John took the remaining pancakes, spread on a slab of butter, and drizzled on some syrup, allowing the memory to linger: he, the graduate student and then the American history teacher at the Jesuit prep school in Boston, lost in the library stacks, searching for one more document, one more piece of evidence to explain the past and restore something of all that had been lost.

"It's the joy of research," he said. "It has no ending."

"Ah, just like heaven." Father George pointed his fork across the kitchen, as if he were pointing to some demonstrable proof that had just materialized in the doorway.

"Just like the work around here." Catherine dropped into a vacant chair, clasped her hands over the table, and stared at the ceiling a moment. "The grandmothers got flour and sugar and cornmeal from the whites," she began. "They already had buffalo tallow. Wouldn't surprise me none if the warriors got pancakes." She paused and wrinkled her nose. "I'm not sure how they tasted."

Father John took another bite, while Catherine went on about how the grandmothers had picked wild asparagus and turnips and beat the bushes with sticks until the ripe berries covered the blankets they'd spread underneath, then pounded the berries into strips of buffalo and dried the strips to make pemmican for the winter. "Oh, they knew what they were doin', all right," she said.

His own thoughts had already returned to Lela Running Bull, fifteen years old, half-child, half-woman, caught up in something too big to grasp, and too frightened to pick up a telephone.

He'd offered the Mass for her this morning. Dear Lord, he'd prayed. Let her call, and let me find a way to help her.

"BY THE WAY," Father George said. They were walking through the field surrounded by Circle Drive, the wild grasses crinkling under their boots and the morning sun already hot on Father John's shoulders. The breeze made a whistling noise in the cottonwoods. "I went to the bank in Riverton yesterday and talked to the manager. There's a discrepancy between the bank records and ours."

"What's the discrepancy?" Father John said, following the other priest up the concrete steps in front of the administration building.

"Deposits for the last three weeks seem to be missing." The other priest stopped on the landing and turned to face him. "Not likely they were all lost somewhere."

Father John leaned against the metal railing and watched a tumbleweed scuttle across Circle Drive and lodge behind the rear wheel of the Toyota pickup in front of the residence. He was trying to remember if he'd been the one to drop the deposits at the bank. Usually Father George handled the deposits—the Sunday collections, the donations—but a couple of times, his assistant had given him the envelope. *You going into town? Take the bank deposit.* Once he'd found the thick deposit envelope under the front seat of the pickup two days later, and when the bank statement arrived, Father George had stomped into his office and demanded to know why the deposit had been late. But three deposits missing?

He looked up at the other priest who was at the door, rattling his key in the lock. "What did the manager say?"

"He agreed to reexamine the bank records for incoming deposits." The other priest gave the door a hard shove and stepped inside, a mixture of worry and frustration outlined in the slope of his shoulders.

Father John followed. The warm, musty odor of past decades and old problems clung to the plastered walls. He turned right and went into his office.

"You can imagine what the bank manager was thinking." George had propped himself against the door frame. "Maybe you priests forgot to bring in the checks and cash? Maybe there weren't any checks and cash?"

"How much are we missing?" Father John sat down at his desk, his eyes on the bills stacked in the small wooden box, waiting to be opened and handed over to his assistant.

"Three thousand, nine hundred and seventy-eight dollars and twenty cents. All in checks, except for a couple hundred from the collection baskets. We're overdrawn by more than a thousand."

Father John groaned. A fortune. The checks had come in from around the country—the little miracles that had kept St. Francis afloat for more than a century, mailed in from people who had never seen the mission, never met an Arapaho. *Use this to help somebody.* He hadn't even finished thanking the donors. Now he'd have to explain that the donations were lost and ask for new checks. It could be weeks before they arrived.

"There's something else, John." The other priest stepped into the office and perched on one of the side chairs, hands clasped between his knees. "I didn't want to bring it up until the bank looks into the matter. Always the chance," he shrugged, as if he didn't believe what he was about to say, "that the bank donated our deposits to some other account."

"What are you getting at?"

"Last four weeks, Leonard's volunteered to run the deposit envelopes over to the bank."

Father John kept his eyes on the other man. It wasn't unusual for Leonard to take the deposits. Over the years, the caretaker had often stuck his head in the door. "Anything for Riverton, Father?" he'd say. "Gotta go to the hardware store," and Father John himself had handed the man the envelopes. He would trust the man with his life.

And yet . . .

"We can use the extra money," Catherine had said.

Father John got up and walked over to the window. Leonard's green truck was parked at an angle in front of the church. Ah, yes. Leonard had mentioned this morning that he intended to fix the two broken pews.

"He turned back to the other priest. "The bank screwed up somehow."

"I don't have to tell you, this has me worried." Father George got to his feet and headed for the door.

The man was right about that. He *didn't* have to tell him. "They'll find the deposits," Father John said, but he was talking to himself. His assistant had already left, and only the clack of the man's footsteps in the corridor indicated he was still close enough to have heard what Father John said. And probably wasn't any more reassured than he himself felt.

Father John sat back down at the desk and looked at the phone, debating whether to pick it up. This was the kind of problem he would have liked to talk over with Vicky, hold it up to the light of her sharp, legal mind. Friend, confidante, partner in how many cases? Divorces, adoptions, DUIs. Always the first person he'd called when somebody else had a problem. So what would be wrong with calling her now?

Who was he kidding? It was only an excuse to hear the sound of her voice. There had been times when he'd used any excuse to call her, but there hadn't been an excuse all summer. He hadn't looked for one. And during his retreat, he'd come to understand that he could love her, that love was God's most precious gift. He could love her and let her go.

He had no idea how she was doing. Fine, he supposed, because, otherwise, someone might tell him. He wondered about that. None of the gossip on the moccasin telegraph about Vicky ever seemed to reach him, although he suspected there was always gossip. But lately, it was as if an invisible bubble had descended over the mission, intercepted everything about Vicky and sent it bouncing back, so as not to disturb the pastor or upset the resolution he'd made during his retreat. It was as if the people wanted to protect him from his own weakness.

He jumped to his feet and strode out of the office, grabbing his cowboy hat from the rack as he went. He'd promised to have coffee with the elders over at the senior center this morning. He was about to let himself out the front door when the phone rang.

He walked back into his office and lunged for the receiver among the piles of papers on his desk. "Father O'Malley," he said into the mouthpiece.

There was no response, only a dead quiet, but Lela Running Bull was at the other end. He could sense the fear pulsing down the line. "Talk to me," he said.

"This is Lela." Her voice was small and hesitant. "Mary said you been looking for me."

"Don't be afraid, Lela." He kept his own voice steady. "I want to help you."

"I ain't afraid of nothing."

"Where are you?"

Silence, except for several quick intakes of air.

"Tell me where you are," he said. "I'll come there."

"You can't come here!" The words burst down the line like the scattering of buckshot. "Tommy'll . . ."

"Tommy! You're with Tommy?"

"It's okay, Father. That's what I called to tell you. Everything's okay, so you don't need to be worrying about me."

"You're afraid of him, Lela."

She didn't say anything, and he knew he'd guessed right. "It's true, isn't it?" He was talking fast against the possibility that she might hang up. He could picture her moving the receiver away from her ear, hesitating, trying to decide what to do. "Listen, Lela, if you know anything about the man who was murdered at Double Dives, you could be in danger. Let me come and get you."

He realized that she'd started crying, and now she was gasping and sniffling. Finally she said, "You'd run to the fed, and Tommy'd kill me for saying anything."

"Why, Lela? What is Tommy afraid of?"

"The guy they dug up was a white guy." The words came like a gasp, as if they had a will of their own. "Tommy didn't have nothing to do with any white guy."

"Rodney Pearson?" And then he understood. Lela Running Bull had expected the body to be somebody else, which explained why she was afraid. She thought Tommy had been involved in another murder at Double Dives. It also explained why Tommy had taken Lela from her father's house. He wanted to make sure she didn't talk to Gianelli. Which only confirmed his own fear that Lela was in serious danger.

"You can stay at the mission," Father John said, hearing the urgency in his voice. "You'll be safe here until all of this is straightened out."

"I'm telling you, I'm okay." She was shouting. "Tommy didn't have nothing to do with the white guy that got shot. Pearson, whatever his name was."

"What about the other guy, Lela? Who did you expect to be in that grave at Double Dives?"

She was quiet for so long that, for a second, he thought she'd hung up. Finally, she said, "I thought maybe it was gonna be some guy named Dennis, okay? But I got things mixed up, so I was wrong. There's nothing to it. Forget it, okay?"

"Dennis who?"

"Jesus, Father. Whyd'ya keep . . ."

"What's the last name?" He was beginning to lose patience.

"Light, or something." She paused. "Light Stone. Some Oklahoma Rap that deals at the casino."

Deals at the casino. Pieces of a picture were beginning to come together in his mind. The girl's aunt had said that Tommy worked for Captain Monroe—one of Monroe's so-called rangers—and yesterday, in the *Gazette,* there was the article about the three Arapahos arrested for trespassing and disturbing the peace at the casino. The Arapahos worked for Monroe.

He said, "What's going on, Lela? What happened to make you think Tommy killed Dennis Light Stone?"

"He didn't kill him!" Father John heard the defiance shooting through her voice—something new, a rocket fueled by fear. "Nothing went down. Just leave me and Tommy alone." The connection cut off, leaving a buzzing noise that bore into his ear.

He hung up the receiver, walked around, and dropped into his chair, a new scenario playing out in his mind. Light Stone was Arapaho—Rap, Lela called him. A dealer at the casino. He represented everything Monroe had been railing against for months: an Indian ripping off other Indians. Suppose Monroe sent Tommy and the other rangers to harass the man, force him to leave his job, and Light Stone had refused. Then what happened? Had Monroe ordered Tommy to kill the man as an example to other Arapahos working at the casino?

Suppose further—a new idea taking shape now, making his blood run cold—suppose that Tommy had shot the wrong man.

Which meant Dennis Light Stone, if he was still alive, was also in serious danger.

Father John picked up the receiver and dialed the number for the FBI office in Lander. An answering machine picked up, and he left a message for Ted Gianelli to call him, then hung up. He stared at the phone a moment. He had no idea who Dennis Light Stone was, except that he was Arapaho and he worked at the casino.

He picked up the phone and dialed the senior center. This time, someone answered, probably the woman who was setting up the coffee. He left a message for the elders that he'd stop by tomorrow. An emergency, he said. Then he headed back out the door.

He had a new destination now. He had to find Dennis Light Stone and warn the man.

10

FATHER JOHN WAS in a line of RVs inching along 287 toward Great Plains Casino, the afternoon heat lifting off the asphalt and engulfing the pickup in smells of hot oil and tar. On the billboard ahead, the figure of an Indian warrior in an eagle-feathered headdress flashed in red and blue neon lights. White dice with black numbers rolled down one side.

The RV ahead took the turnoff into the casino driveway. It was then he saw the demonstrators lining the highway: a half dozen men dressed in camouflage, with thick, black belts and laced-up boots. They looked about eighteen, anger cut into their stances. They might have walked away from boot camp, he thought, except for the signs they thrust toward the passing vehicles: Gambling Kills People. Say No to Casino. Stay Away.

So these were the demonstrators he'd read about in the *Gazette,* led by a white man who called himself "Captain" Jack Monroe and preached against the evils of gambling: addictions, broken families, corruption, crime.

Father John followed the RV past the demonstrators and down the driveway lined with rope-tied stick trees, the skeletal branches waving in the breeze. The RV turned left, and he turned right and drove through the parking lot until he spotted an empty space. He walked back to the entrance, past the small cubicle with "Valet Parking" above the opened door and two Arapaho men slumped in the shade inside.

"Hey, Father," one shouted. "What're you doin' here?"

"Came to see a friend." He waved at the cubicle.

"Sure, Father." The voice trailed after him. "Good luck."

The automated glass doors parted, and he crossed the carpeted lobby that curved away toward the hotel. A wall of noise rose in front of him: coins clanking and ringing. He was facing a field of slot machines with people hunched on stools, pushing buttons and pulling levers. A couple of amber lights blinked from the top of metal poles. He recognized three parishioners down one row: Abby Huntinggirl, Bob Shoemaker, Jolene Thunder—eyes glued to the screens, fingers jabbing the buttons, as if the machines were extensions of their arms.

He looked down the next row and the next—four, five, six other parishioners. A couple had been at the Gamblers Anonymous meeting last week.

He pushed through the group of tourists flowing around him and made for the side wall, not wanting to see any more parishioners plugging hard-earned dollars into machines. Another amber light started flashing; the wail of a siren burned through the noise.

"Can I help you?"

A dark-haired woman, with bright red lipstick and thick

black eyelashes, pushed a change cart in front of him. She was dressed in black shorts and a black blouse, buttoned low enough that he could see the cleft of her breasts.

"Need some change?" She gave him a hopeful smile, and for a half-second, he had the feeling she might welcome any advances he wanted to make.

"I'm looking for somebody," he said.

"Oh?" She tilted her chin and stared up at him out of suddenly wide eyes.

"Dennis Light Stone."

"Blackjack tables, but haven't seen him for a while." She tossed her head toward the rear.

He thanked her and made his way around the cart and down the rows of slot machines. He spotted the blackjack tables: small and curved, with seven seats on one side, the dealers on the other. He headed over. At the nearest table, a woman with hair wound into a white-blonde braid that curled at the nape of her neck and long, red fingernails was dealing the cards to two players. He was struck by the almost religious ritual of the motions in the way that she laid the cards and stacked the chips.

After a moment, the players slid off the stools and, shaking their heads, started toward the craps tables. The woman began shuffling again, the red nails snapping the cards. "Care to try your luck?" She gave him a sideways glance.

"Don't have any." He stepped closer to the table.

"Everybody has luck." She stared frankly at him. "I know you. You're the good-looking mission priest."

He said she'd gotten part of it right. He was the mission priest. "You must be from around here."

"Riverton. A gambling priest." She smiled, as if that was an original idea.

"We're all too human."

She was still smiling. "What other vices do you have?"

"You think gambling's a vice?"

She laughed out loud and glanced beyond him. He followed her gaze. An archway opened along the side wall below a red-neon arrow and the word *Poker.* But it was the slim, youngish man with gray hair and wire-rimmed glasses standing next to the archway who'd caught her attention.

Father John turned back. "Where can I find Dennis Light Stone?"

"Look, Father." She seemed nervous now, shuffling the cards faster. "We're not supposed to fraternize. Maybe you ought to play a hand just to keep me out of trouble. I'd like to keep my job." She gave a little laugh and threw another glance toward the archway. "Casino's the best thing ever happened to these parts. I'm making a decent living for me and my kids."

He moved to the wide curve of the table and perched on the stool in the center. He hadn't played blackjack since the casino nights at the prep school where he'd taught American history. It had taken a year of casino nights—third Saturday of the month—to raise enough money for the new gym.

"What do I need?" He pulled a five-dollar bill out of the pocket of his blue jeans.

"I can see you're a high roller." She took the bill and set a red chip in front of him, then dealt them each two cards. Both of his cards were faceup: sixteen points. Only one of her cards was up: a jack.

He brushed his cards in his direction to indicate that he wanted another card.

She held his eyes a moment. "You sure you want a hit?"

He nodded. She dealt him a five of clubs. Twenty-one.

She turned over her other card. Two of spades. She dealt herself a ten of hearts, then swept the played cards into the discard pile. "Not bad for an unlucky man," she said, setting a red chip next to the one he'd bet. "Wanna go again?"

"Why not?" he said. "Tell me where Dennis is."

She dealt another round. "Hasn't been in for a while."

"What do you mean?" He had nine points. The dealer had a seven of clubs showing. He brushed the cards.

"Just hasn't been around." She dealt him a three of hearts. "You know Indians. Maybe they show up sometimes, maybe they don't."

"Has Dennis ever not shown up before?" Another brush.

"Not that I know of." Shc dealt him another card. Twenty points now. He moved the two red chips to the edge of the cards, and she dealt herself a nine of hearts, then a six of spades, for a total of twenty-two.

"I'd say you're very lucky, Father O'Malley." She swept the cards into the discard pile and set two more red chips in front of him. Then, tilting her head toward the archway, she said, "You might want to check with the boss over there."

Father John picked up the chips. He'd started with five dollars, now he had twenty, and with the weight of the chips in his hand came a familiar surge of expectation. He was winning! He could win more, all he had to do was set down the chips and say, "Why not another game?" and the world would shift in his direction. *All he had to do was pour another three fingers of whiskey and he would be in control, and the loneliness would disappear.*

Dear Lord. He felt as if the wind was bearing down on him, pushing him onward. He backed away from the table.

"Come back sometime." The dealer flashed him a smile and started reshuffling the cards. A couple of white women in pink slacks and flowered shirts were sliding onto the stools.

Father John worked his way around the tables to the archway and stopped in front of the man planted against the wall. "Neil Barrenger," the man said. "How can I help you?"

The firmness of his handshake surprised Father John. The man was medium height with a slight frame and stooped shoulders. He wore wire-rimmed glasses that made his gray eyes seem oversized, like the eyes of a small fish in a tank. There was a little strip of white skin where his hair had pulled back from his forehead.

Father John gave his name and said he was from St. Francis Mission. He was looking for Dennis Light Stone.

The man's thin eyebrows cocked into pyramids. "Dennis? He's been out sick last four days. Must've picked up the flu."

"Where can I find him?"

"Sorry, Father." The man pulled in his bottom lip, as if he meant it. "Can't give out information on our employees to anyone, not even to a priest."

"Can you give him a message? Ask him to call me at the mission."

The man seemed to consider this a moment. "What's this about?"

"Dennis Light Stone could be in danger."

"Danger! You mean from the demonstrators?"

Father John nodded.

"Don't worry, Father." Barrenger took hold of his arm. His grip was like a vise, as if all the man's strength were concentrated in his fingers. "We have the matter under control. Monroe and his demonstrators aren't going to bother folks around here much longer."

Father John thanked the man and headed back across the casino, wishing he felt more assured. He was in the lobby when he felt another hand on his arm—a light touch, tentative. He turned around. A dark-haired woman with black, slanted eyes and little hollow spaces below her cheeks stood in front of him. She was Indian, but not Arapaho. Lakota, maybe, or Crow. She tossed her head toward the rear of the casino, "Sheila said you're looking for Dennis, and I seen you talking to Barrenger."

He said that was right. Did she know where he could find Dennis?

She shook her head so hard that her shoulders were trembling. "He hasn't been comin' to work. I've been . . ." She hesitated. "I mean his friends have been worried."

"Did you call him at home?"

A startled look came into her eyes. "It's not my place. I mean, what would she think . . ."

"He's married?"

"Yeah, Her name's Theresa. Dennis said don't ever call him at home. Maybe you could go to his house and check . . ." Another pause. "Those bastards out there," she raised one hand toward the highway, "they been bothering Dennis, stopping him in the parking lot, threatening him."

"Did he report it to the police?"

She looked at him with wide-eyed incredulity. "You don't know Dennis. He told 'em to go to hell, they weren't gonna run him out of the casino. But . . ." She looked back at the demonstrators. "The casino got a restraining order or something to keep 'em out of the parking lot. I'm still worried, with Dennis not showing up for work. What did Barrenger say?"

"Dennis called in sick."

The woman stared at him in disbelief. "That's a lie." It came like a scream for help. "Dennis told me he's never been sick a day in his life."

"Any idea where he lives?"

"Lander, someplace. Theresa works over at the Rendezvous Motel. Maybe you can look for her there. You could ask her where Dennis is, and she wouldn't get suspicious. Please, Father, if you find out anything, please tell me."

He left the woman standing in the lobby, a forlorn look about her, as if Dennis Light Stone had evaporated into the atmosphere and she had no expectations of ever seeing him again.

Father John pulled his hat down against the sun that was blazing over the mountains and headed back to the parking lot. The sky was on fire, with red, orange, and violet flames streaking overhead. The discomfort curled into a knot in his stomach. Dennis hadn't been at work in four days, and the man's boss had no idea where he was. Why else had Barrenger lied?

Four days. Three days ago, Lela Running Bull had stumbled upon Rodney Pearson's body at Double Dives and had thought it was Dennis Light Stone.

The pickup was like a firebox. He got behind the steering wheel and cranked open the windows before backing out of the space. Then he drove back through the lot, his thoughts still on Dennis. The man could be hiding from Monroe's gang. But if he was in hiding, then he already knew that someone wanted him dead. Maybe he'd been warned, or maybe he'd just figured it out, or maybe . . .

Father John tried to shove the thought away. Maybe Dennis Light Stone was already dead.

11

THE BLACK-AND-white images flickered into the darkened room. Vicky watched herself on the screen coming out of the casino and walking along the sidewalk. Waiting for a sedan to pass now, crossing the driveway, heading into the southern parking lot.

Now she had a bird's-eye view of the expanse of the lot from a camera atop a pole somewhere, and she was the small figure hurrying down the rows of parked cars. At the far end of the lot, two other figures got into an SUV, which backed out of the parking slot and lurched off the screen.

"Here we go," Neil Barrenger said into the silence.

Vicky shifted forward in the leather chair, her eyes fastened to the screen. The faraway image telescoped into a closer frame of four Indians around her Cherokee: two seated on the hood, two lounging against the door, all looking in the same direction.

Watching her! She saw herself walk into the frame and stop abruptly, her senses snapping into alert. Then she started out again, shoulders back, steps deliberate.

"Notice the tactics," Barrenger said. His voice was calm and matter-of-fact, as if he were analyzing an annual report.

Vicky struggled against the impulse to jump up and walk out of the stuffy room. She had no desire to relive the encounter about to take place on the screen.

Barrenger said, "Look at the way a couple of them get right in your face then circle in back in case you try to get away. That's how they've been intimidating our people. Accosting them in the lot. Warning them to stop working at the casino. Check out how the other two step in front of you."

The man's arm thrust past her and clicked the remote in his hand. The image froze on the screen. He clicked again and brought in a close-up of the man on her right.

"Do you know him?"

"I didn't recognize any of them," Vicky said. Then she explained that she'd spent a lot of years in Denver. She didn't know all the kids who'd grown up while she was away.

"You were scared out there. You can see it in your expression." Barrenger clicked again until her face filled up the screen. Underneath the impassive mask that she remembered plastering on was the animal look of fear, the kind that could draw wolves and ravens.

"People get scared and everything starts to blur." The man sounded as if he were speaking from experience, and she wondered whether he had ever been frightened. "When it's all over, if they're still alive, they start remembering.

That's why police bring victims in to look at photos and lineups. Jogs their memory. They say, oh, yeah, that was the guy, but you ask beforehand what the guy looked like, they couldn't tell you. It's afterwards people start putting it together."

The image on the screen shifted back to the young man on her right. "Take your time. Sure you don't recognize him?"

"I'm afraid this is a waste of time." Vicky started to get to her feet. She felt the operation chief's fingers tapping lightly on her shoulder, nudging her back into the chair.

"Hold on. Here's the main troublemaker." The image focused on the man leaning toward her, shoulders forward, brown, sinewy arms dangling out of the jagged armholes of his camouflage shirt. The tattoo of a black bird crawled up his right biceps.

Vicky was quiet a moment. "They called him Tommy."

"Now we're getting somewhere. So that's Tommy Willard. First lieutenant in the army of Captain Jack Monroe." Barrenger clicked the remote until the man's face ballooned across the screen, smashed and distorted looking, dark eyes lit with an anger that funneled into the room.

"So far," the man went on, "our videos show Willard and the others stopping people in the parking lots, as if they only want to talk. But we have them now. No more restraining orders, no more arrests for trespassing and disorderly conduct. They're going to do jail time for assault."

"Assault!"

The images began flashing. Tommy pushing her, knocking her sideways. She, scrambling for her balance and darting for the Cherokee. The video stopped, then went through a fast rewind before coming again into focus. The image froze on Tommy throwing his weight against her. She saw the flash of surprise and fear on her face.

"You agree that's assault, don't you?" There was a note of satisfaction in the man's voice. "We're going to play hardball with these guys."

"There might be another way."

"We've tried being reasonable, Vicky. We've had them arrested for trespassing. They keep coming back. Even if the tribal court gives us a restraining order, I doubt it will stop them."

"What other way?" Stan Lexson's voice emerged from the dimness behind her. Vicky glanced around. She could barely pick the man out of the shadows. She wondered how long he'd been there.

"Could we have the light," she said, getting to her feet.

Light burst over the room. Lexson was coming toward her, arm extended. He took her hand and held it in both of his, his pale eyes narrowed in concern. "Let me say how sorry I am that this happened to you, Vicky. I hope you're all right."

"I'm okay." Vicky slipped her hand free.

"We've learned from this unfortunate incident. We've increased the number of security vans in the parking lots. Response time will be much faster. Unfortunately, you were already inside your vehicle before the van approached. The BIA police were twenty minutes away, so we decided to let the men leave the casino premises. We have the evidence we need to pursue an assault charge."

"Tommy Willard made a disturbing allegation," Vicky said.

"Oh? And what was that?"

"He said that anyone who wanted a good job at the casino had to see Matt Kingdom. Is that true?"

Lexson drew in a breath between clenched teeth. "As I've explained to you, Vicky, we're trying to operate a successful business. We hire the best people we can find. What

Willard and the rest of Monroe's gang think is of no concern to us. I believe that after the BIA police study this video, they'll agree assault charges are in order."

Vicky looked back at the screen and the images of herself and Tommy Willard reduced to black-and-white tracings under the fluorescent ceiling lights. If what Tommy Willard said was true, then the commission chairman was working hand-in-glove with the casino he was supposed to oversee. A serious allegation, but where was the proof? The fact that Kingdom's son had been hired as supervisor of maintenance? Suppose he was the best-qualified applicant, as Lexson said? In any case, if Monroe had any proof, he would have gone to the tribal council, the newspaper, the FBI. He would shout it from the rooftops.

Instead, he sent out the rangers to harangue the casino employees and patrons about the evils of gambling. Why? What did he hope to gain? Did he really expect to close down the casino? Or was Captain Monroe playing a waiting game, keeping up the campaign, keeping the casino in the newspapers until . . .

Until he found the proof that the commission chairman was really working for Lodestar Enterprises?

Vicky turned back to the manager. "If there's any truth to Willard's allegation, Lodestar Enterprises could face disciplinary action from the Indian Gaming Regulatory Commission, as well as civil lawsuits from people locked out of jobs."

"Yes, yes." Lexson put up both hands. "Trust me, Vicky. We understand our business," he said, a new sharpness in his tone. "We need you to take care of the vendor contracts and not worry about the business end of things. I'd like to see them by the end of the week."

"As a lawyer, I have the duty to advise you . . ."

"This is a business decision, Vicky, not a legal matter.

We'll handle Monroe and the rangers in our own way." Lexson nodded at the operations chief, who stepped over, opened the door, and nodded her out.

Vicky walked past: Lexson on the left, Barrenger on the right. The instant she stepped into the outer office, the door slammed behind her. She kept going—across the plush carpet, past the blond-haired receptionist, with the phone pressed against her ear, through the door, down the corridor.

What had she signed on with? A company more concerned about third-rate troublemakers than with the possible corruption of the tribal gaming chairman? Who were Lexson and Barrenger? For that matter, who was Lodestar Enterprises? And what kind of pact had they made with Matt Kingdom?

It was none of her concern, she told herself. She'd been hired to handle the contracts with vendors and equipment suppliers, not to ensure the legality of casino operations.

Or had she? Had Lexson wanted an Arapaho lawyer so that the business council and everybody else on the rez would discount Monroe's accusations, lulled into the belief that everything at the casino was as it should be, since one of their own was on the legal team?

She was at the door to the legal offices when she turned around and headed back toward the elevator. She could walk away, she was thinking. Ride the elevator to the first floor, walk across the hotel lobby and out the door. And not look back.

Except for Will Standing Bear's voice pounding in her head like the incessant beat of the drums. *You are Arapaho, granddaughter. Arapaho. Arapaho.*

She pressed the up button. The elevator doors slid open, and she stepped inside, pushed the button for the third floor, and made herself take several slow breaths—in and out, in and out—until her heart stopped racing. If Matt Kingdom controlled the best jobs at the casino, she was going to find the evidence.

She felt herself being lifted upward in a silent vacuum toward—she didn't know what—knowing only that she could not turn back.

12

ANNETTE ADDLEY. DIRECTOR. *Human Resources.*

Vicky studied the name on the plaque next to the door. She'd noticed the name yesterday when Adam had brought her to the office to fill out the employment forms, but it hadn't meant anything. An Addley family lived in Fort Washakie, but she didn't remember anyone in the family named Annette.

She opened the door and stepped into the narrow waiting room, with padded chairs arranged around the walls and a desk across from the door. Behind the desk was the same secretary—white, fiftyish, with dark roots visible in her light-colored hair—who had pushed a clipboard and some papers toward her. After Vicky filled in the forms and handed them back, the woman had slipped them inside a folder and smiled across the counter: "Welcome to Great Plains Casino," she'd said.

Now the woman gave her a startled look, as if she hadn't expected her to return. "Yes, Ms. Holden? Your papers were processed yesterday. Any questions?"

"No. No." Vicky waved away the offer. "I'm here about another matter. Could you pull up some records for me? I'd like to become familiar with the department heads I'll be working with."

The woman brought her penciled eyebrows together and glanced down at the computer as if she expected the monitor to flash the answer. Then she backed to a door, reaching behind her for the knob.

"One moment." She opened the door and slid inside.

Vicky waited. Two or three minutes passed before the secretary reappeared, another woman behind her. Tall, striking-looking with black shoulder-length hair, smartly cut, and prominent cheekbones that emphasized the hollowed space in her cheeks. Annette Kingdom—whatever her last name was now—didn't look much different from the way she had looked in high school. Still the flawless complexion, like polished bronze, and the wide dark eyes that always seemed to know more than they saw.

"Vicky! Ho'heisi!"

Matt Kingdom's younger sister threw both arms around her and hugged her tight. Then she stepped back and, grabbing Vicky's hand, pulled her forward into a spacious office, with two sofas on either side of a glass table and an L-shaped desk against the far wall below a painting of the Wind River range.

Annette dropped onto one of the sofas, guiding Vicky down next to her. "Ho'heisi!" she said again, giggling now. "You remember, don't you? We were the mad women. I was so excited to see that the casino had hired you," she hurried on. "I can't believe we're going to be working together. I mean, once I heard you went to law school, I thought, man, she'll be so high-and-mighty. Never speak to me again. But here we are. We'll have to go to lunch. It'll be like old times."

Vicky forced a smile. The last thing she wanted was to relive the old times when they were seventeen, giggling together in the lunchroom, calling themselves by a secret name: Ho'heisi. She'd met Ben, her ex-husband, by then, five years older and fresh out of the army, and so handsome her heart had constricted every time she saw him. She'd been pulled into Ben Holden's orbit, like a planet with no gravity of its own. All of which she'd poured out to Annette Kingdom over bologna sandwiches and Coke. It made her cringe to realize the woman had known her when she was the most helpless, when she was mad—mad for Ben.

She said, "I didn't realize you'd gone—" She stopped herself from saying, to college. "—into human resources."

Annette blinked. "You never did think I was very smart, Vicky. Well, I'm smart enough." She flicked red-tipped fingers at the office. A diamond ring glistened on one finger.

"I didn't mean . . ." Vicky heard herself stumbling.

"I have lots of experience. Six years, head cashier over at the Thrifty. Believe me," Annette drew in a long breath, "I know how to deal with people."

"What about human resources?"

"Listen, Vicky," the other woman leaned closer, her expression suddenly familiar—the expression she'd always used when she had a secret to confide. "The great thing about Lodestar Enterprises is, they believe in people. There aren't a lot of people on the rez with business experience. They're willing to give Arapahos a chance. I can pick up the phone, call the human resources department in Chicago, and they walk me through the job. Besides, I got a secretary knows what to do."

Vicky was quiet a moment. Maybe that's how the management jobs were handled: pick up a phone, call the main office, and they walk you through the steps. People could learn the job and get experience at the same time. Still, how many people in management owed their jobs to Kingdom?

"What I came by for, Annette," she said finally, "is to see the list of managers. Can you pull it up for me?"

The woman's expression froze. "Oh, I'd certainly do that for you, Vicky. I mean, it's no problem. I could have my secretary—" She leaned over and thumped Vicky's hand. "What a hoot! Me with a secretary. I'd have her pull the list in a minute, but . . ."

Vicky sat very still, waiting for the blow.

"The boss's orders," Annette hurried on. "Lexson called about five minutes ago and said nobody in the company can see the personnel records until further notice. I don't know what's going on." She shrugged. "Soon's he changes his mind . . ."

"I'll be back." Vicky finished the woman's thought and got to her feet.

A DIFFERENT CLERK in a tailored blue suit was behind the hotel desk peering at the computer monitor. Behind her, on the cream-stuccoed wall, the six Arapaho business councilmen seemed to be looking out across the lobby to the casino from their bronze-framed portraits. Farther down the wall, past the door that, Vicky guessed, led to the hotel offices, were portraits of the gaming commissioners: Jules Ledger, Robert Oldman, and, in the center, Matt Kingdom, in a white shirt and dark, western-style jacket, cowboy hat tipped forward, smiling into the camera.

"Excuse me," Vicky said.

The woman looked up. "Oh, sorry. What can I do for you?"

She was Arapaho: Sharp cheekbones and narrow black eyes, black hair shiny under the fluorescent lights, an open, friendly face. The white tag pinned to the woman's lapel read, Nancy Walking Horse. One of the Walking Horse girls who'd been in elementary school fifteen years ago when Vicky had left the reservation for college, law school, a new life in Denver. Nancy had metamorphosed from a gawky ten-year-old into a beautiful young woman.

Vicky introduced herself, and the woman smiled. "Oh, yes. I'm sure you don't remember me."

"I do remember."

The woman blushed, then drew in a long breath, as if to summon courage. "I've followed your career, Vicky. Law school and all, and now you've come back to Lander to help our people. I always wanted to be like you." She blushed again and looked down, fingers rolling the edge of a sheet of paper.

Vicky was quiet. A failed marriage, two kids left on the reservation with her mother. It wasn't as if she had set out to become a lawyer with a burning desire to help her people. It had happened, that was all, after everything else had collapsed, with Ben's drinking and Ben's fists and her own life had gone out of control. *Don't be like me.*

A second passed before she said, "I'm doing some legal work for the casino. I'd like to meet the hotel manager."

"Len Herfly. You know him, don't you?"

Oh, yes. Vicky could still see the skinny, awkward kid with the slumped shoulders, black ponytail and ragged blue jeans. He'd been a couple of years ahead in school. In the same class with Matt Kingdom.

"He should be in pretty soon." The woman threw a glance

toward the glass entrance. You can talk to the assistant manager, Marcia Kammer. She's in a meeting with some vendors right now. Just between us," the young woman looked around, then leaned forward, "Marcia's the one that runs the hotel. She's real sharp. Worked for an Indian casino in Mississippi before she came here. You want to wait?"

"No, thanks," Vicky heard herself saying. "You've been very helpful." She gave the young woman a smile, then started across the lobby, feeling as if she were trying to walk across the bottom of a lake. The human resources director, Kingdom's sister; the hotel manager, Kingdom's former classmate. But an assistant manager ran the hotel and the secretary ran the human resources office—and no doubt both had worked for other Indian casinos run by Lodestar Enterprises. How many other people connected to Kingdom had a manager's title while someone else handled the work?

A wall of noise rose in front of her as she entered the casino. She stepped aside for an attractive woman in black shorts and a thin white blouse that showed her bra, who was pushing a change cart. Dodging through the knots of people, Vicky made her way past the entrance to the buffet toward the neon-red sign high on the back wall: Raven's Nest.

The restaurant hostess—another young Arapaho woman—was at the desk inside the door. Behind the desk was a spacious dining room, with rows of tables covered in white cloths that draped over the floor and, on top, white napkins folded in peaks. A wall of murals lit from behind curved around the room, giving the illusion of rivers and mountains and lush valleys outside.

"Early dinner?" the hostess suggested.

"Another time, perhaps." Vicky introduced herself and said she'd like to see the manager.

The hostess allowed her dark eyes to trail downward, then upward, and Vicky had the uncomfortable sense that she was on display: Vicky Holden, Arapaho lawyer, mid-forties, blue linen dress, silver chain at her neck, black hair, cut to her shoulders. Lipstick probably faded. She looked half-dead without lipstick.

She said, "Is the manager in?"

"This way." The woman led the way through the tables. An elderly white couple, tourists by the look of them—dressed in khaki shorts and short-sleeved shirts—sat munching on club sandwiches in the corner.

The woman headed down a hallway and rapped on a door. It swung inward, and in the opening, was a stocky, square-shouldered woman who appeared to be about forty years old. A breed, Vicky thought, with the sharp cheekbones and narrow black eyes of an Indian and the pinkish complexion and the light brown hair of a white.

"What is it?" There was a jolt of impatience in the woman's tone.

"This here's Vicky Holden from the legal department. Wants to see you."

"It'll only take a minute," Vicky said.

"Good. That's all the time I have." The manager motioned her inside.

Vicky stepped into the small office, which had a desk against the side wall and two upholstered chairs. "I'm on retainer with the casino," she said.

"I heard. What's Stan want to know? I told him he'd have the quotes tomorrow. Jesus, the man's impatient."

"You've managed restaurants before?"

"What is this? A little background check?" She threw her head back and laughed. "That's good. That's really good. I've been managing restaurants for Stan for five years now, and he still doesn't trust me. Doesn't trust anybody."

She shouldered past Vicky, flung open the door and gestured toward the hallway. "Go back upstairs and tell Stan everything's working just fine in the Raven's Nest. Tell him to send his watchdogs someplace else."

Vicky started into the hallway, then turned back. "I didn't get your name."

"Betty Monarch." The woman paused. "Comanche, case you want to know." The door was shutting, and Vicky had to step out of the way.

She stood in the hallway a half minute. The muffled rattle of pots and pans and dishes sounded through the wall behind her. *Comanche.* A former employee of Stan Lexson's. Vicky felt her theory starting to evaporate like a cloud of smoke. Here was one management position Matt Kingdom didn't control.

There could be others. The blackjack pit boss. An Arapaho from Oklahoma. What had Lexson said his name was? Dennis . . .

Dennis Light Stone.

Vicky walked back through the dining room—another table occupied by two more tourists, a long-legged waitress in a short, black uniform scribbling in a notepad. Into the casino, past the rows of slots toward the gaming tables. The noise faded behind her. She stopped at a craps table. Four players sat across from a man in a white shirt and black vest, watching the dice roll over the green felt. "Twelve," the dealer called, sweeping in the chips of those players who had bet wrong.

Vicky wandered to the next table, where another craps game was in progress. Six players, one grinning and raising his fist in salute to whatever gods of luck had just paid a visit. She headed into the blackjack area. It was quieter here, players seated on stools, hunched over the half-moon-shaped tables, cards spread in front, and dealers slapping down other cards, pulling in chips, shuffling, dealing again, the action fast and concentrated.

Vicky waited until two players at a table got up and wandered off. She stepped closer.

The dealer, a middle-aged white man with a black toupee and a southern drawl, nodded toward a vacant seat.

"I work in the legal department."

"Ah." The man nodded. "That Arapaho lawyer they brought on."

"Who's the pit boss on this shift?"

"You don't know?" The man was shuffling a deck, then snapping down cards, as if to keep his fingers and wrists flexible. "Thought all you Arapahos got together at pow-wows or something. Usually, it's Dennis Light Stone. Good man, Dennis. Been in the business a long time. Come here from Colorado. Me, I'm from Mississippi. Worked in a Choctaw casino, then started knocking around, going from casino to casino." He shrugged. "Way to see the country."

"Where can I find Light Stone."

The man stopped laying out the cards and stared across the room. "Popular guy, Dennis. You're the second person today to come around asking for him. Some priest playing at Sheila's table wanted to find him."

"Some priest? You mean Father O'Malley from the mission?"

"Yeah, that's the one."

"Did he say why he was looking for Dennis?"

The man shrugged. "Wanted to talk to him, I guess. Same as you."

Vicky glanced around, half-expecting John O'Malley to emerge from the tables. Now that she knew he'd been here, the place seemed filled with him—the look of him, the way he walked, the way he smiled at her. She wondered why he'd been looking for Dennis Light Stone.

"Haven't seen Dennis around last few days," the dealer was saying. "Must've taken some time off. See that guy delivering the fill to Sheila?" He shifted his gaze toward the bulky man with the close-cropped blond hair, who was handing a box to the dealer at the adjacent table—a woman with a blond braid wrapped into a ball at the back of her head.

"The what?"

"Fill. Table needed more chips, so the dealer signaled Felix—he's the pit boss with Dennis gone. Felix went to the cage and got the extra chips."

"Who is he?"

"Felix Slodin. Been knocking around casinos like me. We worked together down in Mississippi."

Vicky thanked the man and started back through the casino. So Dennis was just another Arapaho, with a good job and somebody to back him up, somebody who'd worked for Lodestar Enterprises in the past. As she started down the rows of slots, she sensed something change in the atmosphere. Her skin felt warm and clammy, as though a spotlight had turned on her. Someone was watching her.

She glanced around. Tourists hunched over the slots, or milling about, looking for the next payoff. Then, as if her eyes were drawn upward on their own toward the white glow of the ceiling lights, she saw the blank, cream-colored wall high over the casino. But it wasn't a wall, she knew. It was the one-way window in Lexson's office. She could imagine the manager standing there, hands in the pockets of his slacks, looking down on the floor.

Watching her.

Vicky fought the temptation to wave, to let him know that she knew.

She hurried back through the hotel lobby and stepped into the elevator.

■ ■ ■

THE DOOR TO Adam's office was open, and Vicky caught a glimpse of him as she walked through the waiting room. He was leaning back in his chair, tasseled black loafers crossed on the corner of the desk, head bent toward the legal-sized document folded over his hand.

As he glanced up, his feet thudded against the floor. "Vicky! Wait up."

She was already through the door to the other office and reaching for her black bag in the desk drawer.

"How'd it go?" Adam stepped inside and shut the door. "You see the video?"

Vicky fixed the strap of the bag over her shoulder and turned to face him. "What's going on here, Adam?"

"What're you talking about?"

"Assault! Lexson and Barrenger think they can discredit Jack Monroe's accusations by having his men charged with assault."

"It was assault. You know that."

"Tommy Willard said that Matt Kingdom controls the good jobs at the casino."

"There's no truth to that accusation. I told you, Monroe wants to close down the casino. His men will say anything if they think it'll stick."

Adam stepped toward her. "I've been going over the employment contracts, Vicky. If there were anything wrong with the way we hire people, don't you think I'd have detected it by now?"

"What about Lexson and Barrenger? Who are they, Adam?"

He moved toward her. She could smell the scent of him, a mixture of soap and aftershave and the faintest hint of perspiration. "They're men who know how to run casinos. They've run casinos for other tribes. The company they work for loaned the tribal council eighteen million to build this place and sent Lexson here to manage operations. They have the management contract for seven years. Do you think Lexson would do anything to jeopardize the company's eighteen million?"

Vicky crossed the office to the windows outside. The sky was as placid and blue as a stilled sea. A small plane curved close to the foothills, disappeared, then reappeared—like a blackbird circling its prey.

What Adam said made sense. Tommy Willard worked for Captain Jack Monroe, whoever he was. A man who'd tried to stop Indian casinos and, when he failed, launched his own personal vendetta. Suppose that was all it was? A vendetta.

She turned back to the Lakota who stood with his hands at his sides waiting, the quiet, patient look of her own people on his face, as if he would wait forever, if it were necessary. "Where does Monroe get the money to pay the rangers?" she said.

Adam shrugged. "He's a nutcase, Vicky. Who knows where he gets the money. Maybe he's wealthy. What does it matter? We can't allow him to destroy the casino. Look," he took a step toward her. "Lexson knows how to take care of Monroe. We have our own work to do." He hesitated. "You're not going to quit, are you?"

"No, I'm not going to quit," she said, brushing past him and opening the door. Not until she found out who else had sham management jobs and whether they were also connected to Matt Kingdom. "I'll have the first batch of contracts ready in the next couple days," she said over her shoulder.

"Have dinner with me tonight," Adam said.

Vicky turned back.

"We can talk about this." He hurried on. "You'll see there's nothing to worry about."

"You're suggesting a business dinner?"

"Business and—" he gave her a wide smile. "Pleasure."

"Hasn't anyone ever told you that mixing business and pleasure is a bad idea?"

"I never believe half of what people tell me. How about that place in the foothills? Say about seven o'clock?"

Vicky left her eyes on his a moment. Finally, she said, "Why not."

13

"YOU HAVE A hotel reservation?" A woman with black hair, worn long and swept back like a veil, came along the other side of the registration desk toward him. She was strikingly pretty, Father John thought, probably in her thirties and dressed modestly, almost like a nun, in a navy blue skirt and blouse, with a silver bar pinned on the collar. *Theresa* was etched in black letters across the bar.

"Are you Theresa Light Stone?" Father John asked.

The woman halted in mid-step next to the computer that emitted a low buzzing sound, like the buzz of a fluorescent light. She gave him a wary look.

"I'm Father O'Malley from St. Francis Mission," he added hurriedly. "I'd like to talk to you." He watched the wariness in her expression dissolve into fear, and then her face froze, as though she was preparing herself for a blow.

A priest. Priests delivered bad news. She glanced about, as if she wanted to summon help: the upholstered chairs across the lobby, the newspaper opened on a side table.

The look of fear dug in deeper. "Nothing's happened, has it, Father? Everything's okay, isn't it?"

He put up the palm of one hand in an attempt to reassure her, although he wasn't sure himself that everything was okay. "I've been trying to reach your husband," he said. "Can you tell me where I can find him?"

She looked stunned, as if he'd slapped her, and the slap had come out of the blue. She flicked her eyes toward the whoosh of the double doors sliding open at the entrance. A man with a garment bag hanging over one shoulder and a bulky briefcase in his free hand was coming across the lobby. Bringing her gaze back, she nodded toward the door at the end of the counter. "Wait in the office while I take care of this guy," she said.

Father John walked over and let himself through the door into a short hallway. Another door led to a small room crowded with a couple of chairs, a wall of filing cabinets, and a desk. The computer on the desk was wedged between stacks of papers and folders that spilled over the surface onto the chairs.

It was several minutes before he heard the door in the hallway open and shut. Theresa stepped into the office and, gathering up the papers from one of the chairs, motioned for him to sit down. She walked around, gathered another stack, and dropped into the chair behind the desk, clutching the papers against her chest.

"Dennis came to see you, is that it?" She was nodding, as if she'd answered her own question.

"What are you talking about?"

This made her hesitate. She leaned forward and dropped the papers next to the keyboard. "I figured he's . . ." she took in a long breath, then plunged on. "Pretty upset about us splitting up, so he went to talk to a priest."

Father John was quiet a moment, trying to bring a new picture into view. Dennis was having marital problems. A man with marital problems might decide to get away for a few days to think things over. That could be all there was to it. He could be mistaken thinking that Dennis was hiding out someplace, or worse. Thinking that Dennis was dead.

He said, "I'm sorry you're having problems."

"Oh, the problems are gonna be gone, Father." She gave a halfhearted shrug. "Soon's the marriage is gone. It's really quite simple, at least for me, but Dennis, well . . ." She shrugged again and pressed backward into the chair. "He kept saying how he didn't want things to be over between us, how we'd come a long way and been through a lot. God, he had that right, or partly right. I'd been through a lot with that man. He said he was gonna change, but he was always telling me he was gonna change and quit screwing every bimbo that came within screwing distance."

She gave the chair a quarter turn and stared at the window. Beyond, a line of cars and trucks blurred along Main Street. "Last year, down in Colorado," she began, as if she were pulling the memory from the outdoors, "Dennis got involved with that nineteen-year-old stripper. Exotic dancer, she called herself. What a joke. I told him that was the end, but he said, no, Theresa, honey, we'll go to the Wind River reservation and be with our own people and follow the Indian road. He said he had a job offer to be the pit boss at the new casino, and everything was gonna be just fine. Guess I don't have to tell you what happened. First thing, he got himself a girlfriend."

Theresa swung the chair back and stared at him. "You're a priest," she said. "You've never been married."

He didn't say anything.

"Let me tell you something, Father. You know when your partner is having an affair. And with Dennis, I've had lots of experience. I told him to get out and stay out. That was four days ago. I'm not surprised he went running to a priest. Problem is, Dennis doesn't see why other women ought to come between us. 'You're the one I love, Theresa.'" The words came from deep in her throat. "I can imagine the story he told you to get you to come here."

"That's not why I'm here," Father John said. "Your husband never came to see me."

A shadow of disappointment passed across the woman's eyes. "Then what's this all about?"

"Dennis could be in trouble," Father John began, selecting his words. He didn't want to alarm her, and yet . . . he wanted to find Dennis, talk to him, assure himself that the man was okay. "He hasn't been at work the last four days, and Jack Monroe's gang has been harassing . . ."

Theresa cut in. "They didn't bother Dennis. Call themselves the rangers, but they're nothing but park rangers, drunken Indians that hang at the parks. Get their kicks causing trouble. Dennis figured soon's the casino was up and running good, they'd slink back into the muck they crawled out of. Think about it, Father." She was shaking her head. "Thugs like Monroe, they're not gonna close down the casino. Too many people need the jobs. Too many people making money. Besides . . ." she paused, some interior argument playing out behind her dark eyes.

"Besides what?" he prodded.

She dropped her eyes and let out a long breath. "I shouldn't tell you this. Dennis made me promise not to tell, but what the hell? He broke all his promises to me. Every single one," she said, raising her gaze to his again. "Dennis carried a gun. If Monroe and his gang get too close, he knows how to take care of himself."

Father John sucked in a column of air. This was bad. He'd wanted to warn Dennis that he might be in danger, but the man already knew he was in danger. He was carrying a gun!

"Where's he staying?"

She was shaking her head. "Try his girlfriend's."

"You know who she is?"

"You want the truth, Father?" The woman gave him a too-frank stare. He forced himself not to look away.

"Truth is," she went on, "if I knew who she was, I'd kill the bitch."

He knew who she was, Father John was thinking. The girl back at the casino, worried about Dennis, asking him to let her know the minute he heard anything. And the truth was, Dennis's girlfriend didn't know where he was.

"When you find him," Theresa remained seated behind the desk as he got to his feet, "give him a message from me. Tell him not to bother coming home."

FATHER JOHN STARTED to tap out the telephone number at the FBI office on his cell as he pulled out of the parking lot, then gave it up, tossed the phone onto the seat, and turned left onto Main Street. With a little luck, he might catch Gianelli in his office. He parked in front of the flat-faced brick building with the gift shops on the ground floor and took the black-vinyl-covered stairs two at a time to the lobby on the second floor. He pushed the button on the intercom next to the wood-paneled door on the left. Cool air wafted from the vents overhead.

"Help you?" Gianelli's voice boomed over the sounds of *La Boheme*. The agent was the only man in the area who loved opera as much as he did—and knew more about it, a fact Father John didn't like to admit.

"John O'Malley," he said into the speaker.

It was a moment before the door opened. "So you got my message," Gianelli said over his shoulder as he led the way into an office with long, old-fashioned windows that overlooked Main Street. He dropped into the swivel chair behind the desk and motioned Father John to a side chair.

"What message?"

Cupping one hand around his ear, Gianelli swiveled toward the bookcase and turned a knob on the CD player. "Che gelida manina" faded into the background, a soft undercurrent of sound.

"Stopped by the mission," Gianelli said. "Father George said you'd call as soon as you got in. Give me the whole story, John. No holding back. Everything you know about the Pearson homicide. Mo Pearson says some Indian on the reservation shot her husband, and you know who it is."

Father John hung his cowboy hat on one knee. "She's mistaken," he said. And then he told the agent what Lela Running Bull had said, how she'd expected the body at Double Dives to be Dennis Light Stone, a pit boss at the casino who happened to be Arapaho, how Tommy Willard and the rest of Monroe's gang had been harassing the man, and how nobody had seen him in the last four days.

"You telling me that Monroe's gang went after Light Stone and shot a white man by mistake?" Disbelief was plastered on the agent's face. "Come on, John. This isn't a story from an opera. This is real life, man."

"I just talked to Dennis's wife . . ."

"Wife?"

"Theresa. Works over at the Rendezvous Motel. They've been having some problems, and she asked him to leave."

"Aha!" Gianelli brought a thick fist down on the desktop. A pile of papers skittered sideways. "She threw him out, and he's gone on a drunk somewhere."

"Dennis has a girlfriend, and she hasn't seen him either. She works at the casino."

Gianelli tilted his chair back and studied the ceiling a moment, considering. "Captain Jack Monroe," he said under his breath, "has turned into a royal pain in the ass. Looks like I'm gonna have to lean on the captain a little and find out what he knows about Pearson's death and the whereabouts of Light Stone."

The front legs of the chair dropped onto the floor with a thud, and Gianelli jumped to his feet. "Look, John," he said, leaning over the desk. "Mo Pearson's right about one thing. Those Indians talk to you. If you learn anything, I expect . . ."

"Don't worry." Father John got to his feet and started for the door. "You'll be the first to know," he said as he let himself out the door.

14

THEY ATE DINNER at the Timberline Lodge, the kind of restaurant with white tablecloths and heavy napkins curled into the wineglasses. Conversations from nearby tables buzzed around them, like the flow of an electric current. The waiter hovered at their shoulders, sweeping the plates away, a magician making rabbits disappear. Adam kept up a stream of small talk during most of the meal, the polite dance of her people, and Vicky felt a warm flush of gratitude toward the man for observing the traditions. She tried to hold up her end, nodding, smiling, aware of the attractive blond woman with the diamond ring flashing on her finger who kept looking over and smiling at Adam. They'd caused quite a stir when they'd come in, Vicky had noticed. Adam, with the bearing of a chief, in a white dress shirt, a tan leather vest, and pressed blue jeans. The heads of other women had swiveled around as they'd walked past.

She took a sip of coffee, aware that his eyes were on her, following each small movement. She felt a little thrill of excitement. He'd called about five to remind her about dinner. She'd just finished several contracts. Standard boilerplate, nothing out of the ordinary. She'd gone through them quickly, making a few changes here and there to the benefit of Great Plains Casino, changes she expected the vendors' lawyers to line out, as she would in their place. All afternoon, she'd been stalked by the feeling that Matt Kingdom had sold out the people. But there was no proof. No records, no physical evidence, nothing that she could take to the Business Council and say, look, the chairman who's supposed to oversee the casino is handing out management jobs. So what if the man's sister and onetime classmate had management positions? Lexson would probably argue that they were the best-qualified applicants.

She'd agreed to meet Adam at the restaurant in the foothills outside town. Lights from the dining room blinked through the trees as she'd pulled into the parking lot. He was waiting for her at the entrance.

Now he leaned toward her. "I took the video to the BIA police at Fort Washakie this afternoon," he said. "Tommy Willard and the other three men will be arrested and charged with assault. A couple of hours in jail, and they'll start spilling their guts to make a deal. Jack Monroe will be charged with conspiracy to commit assault. That should be the end of it, Vicky."

The waiter appeared and began clearing their plates, then he refilled the coffee cups and slipped a leather case on the table. "Have a good night, now," he said, a strained note of cheeriness in his tone.

"What about Dennis Light Stone?" Vicky asked after the waiter had turned away.

Adam shook his head. "Good worker. Best blackjack pit boss in the house, but he's stopped coming to work. Probably got tired of running a gauntlet of Monroe's goons every day. We could lose other good employees—like you, for instance. We could lose you if the police don't get Monroe out of the way."

Vicky was quiet a moment. "I don't think people just walk away, Adam."

"What's bothering you?" Adam's eyes were almost black, half-closed, as if he were trying to bring her into sharper focus.

Vicky set the coffee cup in the saucer, wondering whether to confide in the man across from her: A Lakota. The Lakotas were not exactly the enemy in the Old Time. They were too numerous, too powerful. Arapahos couldn't afford to have them as an enemy. No, there had been an uneasy alliance between her people and the Lakotas, but you could never trust them, grandfather said. The ancestors had never trusted the Lakotas.

"Stan Lexson and Lodestar Enterprise," Adam said, as if he'd lifted part of her thoughts out of her head. "For some reason you don't trust them. Listen, Vicky . . ." He pushed his cup and saucer away and sat back, not taking his eyes from her. "If I thought Lexson wasn't on the level, I wouldn't have gone to work for the casino. I certainly wouldn't have dragged you into the job. You're making good money reviewing contracts. Standard contracts that you'd find at any hotel or restaurant or casino. What is it that worries you?"

Vicky held the Lakota's gaze a moment, debating whether to confide in him, finding herself wishing it were

John O'Malley across from her. She pushed the thought away, as she'd trained herself to do. Whenever it came, always at unexpected moments—when she was sitting across the table from a man that every other woman in the restaurant had been watching—she could push the thought away. What she hadn't yet mastered was the ability to keep it from returning.

She realized that Adam hadn't taken his eyes from her. She drew in a long breath and said, "I found a couple of people in management jobs with ties to Matt Kingdom."

"A couple?" A look of relief came into the man's eyes. "Kingdom probably knows everybody on the rez. A couple out of several dozen or more on different shifts?"

Vicky folded the napkin on the table, conscious of the tension locking onto her shoulders. For a half-instant, she wondered if Stan Lexson had sent Adam to have dinner with her. Have a little talk with her. Calm her fears. Put blinders on her so she wouldn't look around at whatever may be happening.

"How do you know Lodestar Enterprises is a legitimate company?" she asked.

"You kidding? The Business Council researched the company. Lexson has been with Lodestar Enterprises for years. He's spent ten years running Indian casinos and making a lot of money for other tribes. He knows what he's doing. Kingdom flew to Mississippi and Michigan and interviewed the tribal councils that Lexson had worked for. They gave the man glowing recommendations."

"Matt Kingdom handled the investigation?" The idea was so ludicrous, Vicky had to stifle a laugh.

"Kingdom helped put the deal together between the Business Council and Lodestar Enterprises. The company agreed to put up the eighteen million for the casino, when no bank was willing to loan that kind of money. Not enough people in the area to support a casino, the banks said. Well, Lodestar knew that busloads of people would come from Nebraska and Montana and Utah. They took a long, hard look at the odds and were willing to take the chance. The irony is, they're not gamblers. They only place their money on sure bets." He gave her a wink and, shifting sideways, pulled his wallet out of his back pocket.

Vicky started fumbling in her bag for her own wallet, her thoughts still on Matt Kingdom. The man had made a deal with Lodestar Enterprises, she was sure of it now. He'd researched the company and found something that let him cut a deal.

Adam waved away the credit card she tried to hand him and slipped his own card into the leather case. Almost instantaneously, the waiter materialized and whisked the case away.

"Relax, Vicky," Adam said. "A lot of lawyers drew up the contracts between the tribe and Lodestar. The Business Council's firm in Cheyenne, Lodestar's lawyers in Chicago. Everything's legitimate. All we have to do is handle the routine legal matters. You can finish reviewing the vendor contracts, collect your fee, and take a vacation. Ever been to Hawaii?"

Vicky watched the Lakota sign the charge slip, fold the small piece of paper, and tuck it inside his wallet. A careful, meticulous man, she was thinking. The kind of man who would be the first to spot something wrong in the casino operations unless . . .

She looked away, trying to outdistance the half-formed idea gaining on her. Unless Adam Lone Eagle was more than a part-time legal adviser. Unless he was being paid not to see any problems.

■ ■ ■

ADAM'S HAND WAS warm against her arm as he guided her through the restaurant and down the graveled walk toward the parking lot. "Listen," he said, pulling her closer to him. "The river."

They stood very still, and through the sound of the wind in the pines, Vicky could hear the Popo Agie River gurgling and sighing.

"Come on," Adam gripped her hand and pulled her into the trees. The faintest trace of light, soft and creamy, shone through the branches. She followed him down the slope, his hand still holding hers as they ducked around the branches.

And then she saw the river running like molten silver, rushing over the rocks, lapping at the banks. She could feel the sprays of moisture on her face and arms. A large black bird, a raven, she thought, was flapping overhead. Suddenly, the bird dove toward the bank, then swooped upward, the small creature clutched in its beak emitting a tiny, shrill scream that remained in the air even after the raven had streaked into the darkness.

"Did you see that?"

"Don't let it bother you, Vicky." Adam pulled her over to a concrete bench on a little plateau above the river, then sat down beside her. "Nature can be cruel."

"So can humans."

"We're part of nature. You have to look away."

"But then you become part of the cruelty."

"Look at this now." He waved toward the river and the pines on the other side, swaying in the breeze, black against the graying sky. "What a beautiful evening. Nothing can ruin it." He took her hand again.

Vicky was quiet a moment, feeling herself relax into the wind and the cool, damp air washing over her. Finally, she said, "Tell me about yourself, Adam."

He squeezed her hand and laughed. "Now that could ruin the evening."

"Have you ever been married?"

Several seconds passed, until she thought he'd already given her the only answer he intended. Then he said, "Once. Her name was Julie. She put up with me for about ten years, then, one day, she put my shoes outside the door, and I knew that was the end. I never blamed her."

"What happened?" Vicky felt the muscles in her chest begin to tighten. Another recovering alcoholic, she was thinking. She was sitting on a concrete bench watching the river and the man beside her was another recovering alcoholic. Just like her ex-husband. Just like John O'Malley. But she'd trusted John O'Malley to be strong, and she'd never trusted Ben. She wondered which kind of man Adam Lone Eagle might be.

He was quiet for so long that Vicky was sure she'd overstepped an invisible boundary and the conversation was over. "I'm sorry," she said, starting to get to her feet. "It's none of my business."

She felt his hand tighten around hers, pulling her back, closer to him. "Let's just say," he began, "that I lived like a chief in the Old Time. I thought I needed more than one woman."

Vicky turned to him. "You cheated on your wife."

"I'm not proud of it, Vicky. The day our divorce was final was the blackest day of my life. If I'd been a drinker, I'm not sure I would have ever gotten sober." He shook his head. "I'd tried to convince Julie that I could change, but she didn't believe me. She couldn't forgive me, and I don't blame her. I threw myself into work. Worked nights, daytime. Whatever job I could get. UCLA law school took a chance on me, so did Howard and Fergus in Denver. Your old firm, I believe. Too bad we weren't there at the same time."

"Any kids?" Vicky said after a moment.

"A boy, Mark. About to finish law school at the University of Denver. I pray all the time that he doesn't follow in the footsteps of his old man."

"What was Julie like?" Vicky stared at the river. She could feel his eyes searching her face.

"Nothing like you. She was traditional."

"I'm traditional."

"That's what you tell yourself," he said. "But the fact is, you're caught up in a world where men are supposed to live. It's a tough place, Vicky, and dangerous. Yet, there you are. Maybe that's why I'm attracted to you. I'm trying to understand you."

Vicky felt an odd pang of disappointment. John O'Malley had understood her, reading her mind and heart, and he'd done so without trying. She tried to push the thought away. Freeing her hand, she got to her feet. "We'd better go," she said, starting up the slope toward the lights from the restaurant blinking through the trees.

When they'd reached the Cherokee, Vicky found the key in her bag and jabbed at the lock.

"Allow me." Adam took the key and opened the door. Then, slipping the key into her palm, he took her hand in both of his. "How about I follow you home?"

"It isn't necessary, Adam. Thank you for dinner and a lovely evening." She started to slip past him.

"I'd really like to, Vicky." Now his hands were on her shoulders, and he was leaning toward her. In an instant his mouth was on hers, his lips warm and sweet tasting, and she gripped the edge of the door to keep herself from moving closer.

Finally she backed away, conscious that the hardest part

had been the decision. "This isn't a good idea, Adam. We have to work together."

"We're two attorneys. Independent contractors. That means we can call our own shots."

Vicky shook her head and started to get inside, but he held her in place.

"I thought you liked me," he said. "I thought you and I were hitting it off, that there might be something starting between us. What is it? Somebody else? Your ex-husband wasn't right, was he?" He gave a forced laugh. "It's not that priest?"

"Oh, Adam, please." She slipped out of his grasp, got in behind the steering wheel, and started the engine.

"Couple years ago . . ." Adam paused.

Vicky flipped on the headlights, then looked up at the man holding the door open, leaning toward her.

"I sued the archdiocese on behalf of a client," he went on. "She'd gone to a priest for counseling and he took advantage of her. Inappropriate sexual contact, is how we put it in the lawsuit. Fact is, she was in love with the man. He made her a lot of promises, and she believed him. Made plans, gave up her own career, but her own life on hold. When she realized he had no intention of leaving the priesthood, she was devastated. Priests don't leave, Vicky. Sure, some of them do, the ones you hear about. But you don't hear about all those who stay. They're the ones who believe they have a calling from God, and no woman has the power to make them give that up."

"There's no point to this, Adam." Vicky grabbed hold of the handle and started pulling the door closed.

"I'm glad to know your ex-husband was wrong. Maybe that means I have a chance."

"See you at the office tomorrow," Vicky said before she slammed the door.

15

THE TWO-LANE road carved out of the foothills and dropped into the valley where the lights of Lander blurred in a yellow phosphorescent glow. Vicky tightened her grip on the steering wheel and stared at the column of asphalt in the headlights ahead, swallowing back tears that kept coming despite her wishes, as if they had an existence of their own. Damn! She did not need more complications in her life. She did not need a Lakota, another man she couldn't trust. She could still see the women's eyes trailing the man through the restaurant. She did not need Adam Lone Eagle.

She guided the Cherokee through a curve and out onto a straightaway. The northern reaches of Lander lay ahead, the lights from the streetlamps and gas stations and houses as sharp now as Christmas lights on a tree. Everything seemed clearer. She would tell Adam that she was not ready for a relationship, or whatever he might have in mind. She didn't have to explain; what would she explain? That her ex-husband had been dead three months now, yet she still looked up and saw him coming down the street, rounding the corner, walking into the office? Always someone who looked like Ben, the same slope to the shoulders, the same black hair flecked with gray at the temples, the same dark, confident eyes. She had stopped loving Ben years ago, and yet . . .

She'd never loved anyone else until . . . five years ago she'd walked into the administration building at St. Francis Mission and locked eyes with the red-headed man behind the desk. "You must be Vicky Holden," he'd said. She could still hear his voice. "I've heard a lot about you."

She wiped at the moisture on her cheeks with the palm of one hand. She'd always known that John O'Malley was who he was. He could no more give up the priesthood than he could change the color of his skin or the tenor of his voice or the way his eyes went from blue to gray when he laughed.

What does that have to do with us? Adam's voice in her head now, as strong as if he were seated beside her. Vicky turned into the traffic on Main Street and tried to compose an answer. Nothing, she supposed. She'd already resolved to move on, find closure and create her own space. She laughed out loud at the psychobabble clichés, all of which seemed to apply to her. She wondered at the note of hysteria that lingered in the air after the sound of her own laughter had faded.

She passed the turn to her apartment and, two blocks farther, took a right at the intersection. The dashboard clock glowed red: 10:15. *He sei ci nihi,* Woman Alone. The grandmothers had given her the name not to define her, but to make her strong. Strong enough to be as she was. Still, she was not ready yet to face her apartment alone.

She parked in the shadows in front of the bungalow. The black letters on the sign in front, Vicky Holden, Attorney at Law, looked smeared in the darkness. She still had a couple of contracts to finish.

The instant she turned off the headlights, the night seemed to close in, as still and warm as if a blanket had dropped over her. She walked up the sidewalk to the porch and, fumbling with her key in the darkness, managed to unlock the door. She stepped inside, conscious of the desk on the right, the chairs on the left. A faucet was dripping in the kitchen at the back of the house.

She switched on the ceiling light and walked through her office to the kitchen, dropping her bag on the desk as she went. She opened the cabinet over the stove and rummaged behind the stack of books, diskettes, and packages of printer paper until she found a glass. Then she opened the refrigerator and started to reach for the pitcher of iced tea.

Something shifted in the atmosphere, as if the air currents had changed direction. She stood very still, her hand suspended over the plastic container. *Be aware in all things.* She could hear grandfather's voice. *You will sense when the enemy is near. You must be ready.*

The refrigerator hummed in the silence. She closed the door—slowly, slowly—and held her breath. There was no sound now, not even that of her own breathing. Nothing but the silence and the sense that something was wrong dropping down on her like an invisible weight.

A second passed. Another. She was barely breathing. From outside came a small noise, no more than a scuff of leaves on the sidewalk. An animal, she told herself, the neighbor's dog or a stray cat skulking past, but she knew it wasn't true. Someone was coming up the front sidewalk.

Explanations streamed into her mind like a fountain. Esther had come back to catch up on some work. A neighbor had seen the light and wanted to make certain there was no intruder. Adam was here.

She shoved away the explanations. They defied the truth that she could sense in every part of her being. Someone who meant her harm was outside. *Be aware, be aware. You will sense the enemy approaching.* Her skin was prickling, her heart knocking. She had the sense of being completely alone. *Then let me be strong.* She waited, muscles tensed, for the enemy to show himself.

The crash came like a shotgun blast, an explosion of glass followed by a loud thud. Vicky felt the shiver run through the floorboards and, for a moment, she thought a truck had crashed into the front of the house. Over the noise of her heart pounding in her ears, she could hear the glass pane clinking like giant icicles, then dropping onto the floor.

She moved along the counter and opened a drawer, her eyes combing the small space for a weapon. White plastic spoons and knives, bottle caps, a bottle opener and, wedged near the back, a screwdriver. She picked up the screwdriver and, walking silently on the balls of her feet, made her way along the counter and around the corner into her office. She stopped at the opened doors and peered around the jamb into the front office. A hole the size of a hubcap gaped in the plate glass window next to the door. Glass hung like stalactites from the top of the window frame, and tiny shards of glass winked on the polished top of Esther's desk and littered the floor like ice crystals. Lying in the center of the floor, as inert as a dead animal, was a baseball-sized rock looped in brown twine. A piece of paper was folded into the twine.

Outside, an engine roared into life, gears straining, tires squealing. Vicky walked over to the broken window. Through the shimmering strands of glass, she saw the dark pickup careen around the corner, up and over the curbing, crushing a small bush, almost hitting the lamp pole, then humping back onto the asphalt. In a second, the pickup was lost behind the bungalows that jutted forward, blocking the view of the side street. A plume of black exhaust floated into the yellow circle of light.

The enemy was gone. Vicky felt her heartbeat start to slow. She drew in a long breath and turned back to the rock, her gaze fixed on the brown twine looped over the surface. The ends of the twine flared out, like the shredded ends of a wire, and little brown slivers poked from the loops. Even more than the rock that had crashed through the window and the folded white paper, the twine seemed to embody the evil. She could not touch it.

Leaning over, she tugged the paper free, unfolded it, and read the black, block-like words: *Get out of the casino.*

She was still staring at the message when she heard the sound of footsteps coming up the sidewalk. The door! God, she'd forgotten to lock the door.

The footsteps were crossing the porch now. She lunged for the door and threw herself against the wooden panels, groping for the lock, but the door was already opening, pushing against her, and she realized a boot was wedged into the opening.

"Police officer." A man's voice.

Vicky moved along the door until she could see through the peephole. On the other side was a bear-like man with a round, reddish face, in a dark shirt with the silver insignia of the Lander police department winking in the dim light.

She stepped back, and the door flung open.

"Everything okay here?" The officer's gaze went from the glass littering the floor to the broken plate glass window. "Somebody practicing for the Rockies?"

Vicky handed the officer the note. "Ever hear of Captain Jack Monroe?" she said.

16

FATHER JOHN HAD almost finished saying Mass when he saw her: the small, dark figure next to the wall in the vestibule, backlit by the early morning light. He felt his heart take an extra beat. He'd known her for how long now? Five, six years? Ever since the morning he'd looked up from his desk and seen her standing in the doorway. He'd recognized her instantly—The *ho:xu'wu:ne'n* the grandmothers gossiped about: Married a fine man, Ben Holden. Oh, he might've had a little drinking problem, and maybe he hit her a few times. No cause to divorce him. Now she'd come home after living in Denver for ten years, as the grandmothers had always known she would, because she was Arapaho and couldn't stay away from all that was sacred—the earth and sky, the way of the ancestors.

During all the time he'd known Vicky Holden, she had never come to the mission unless there was trouble.

"Go in Peace, the Mass is ended," he said. *Ita Missa Est,* he was thinking, the old Latin words the priest used to say when he was an altar boy in Boston. The sounds of kneelers knocking into pews and footsteps scuffing the floor floated behind him as he walked down the aisle. He shook hands with the parishioners who were filing out and looked for her. She was nowhere.

"LOOKS LIKE VICKY'S got something on her mind." Leonard set the missal inside the cabinet in the sacristy. "You hear she's working for the casino now?"

No, Father John hadn't heard. News about her on the moccasin telegraph had been bleeped out before reaching the mission. He hung up his chasuble and waited for the caretaker to continue.

Leonard let a couple seconds pass, as if he were weighing how much to pass on. "Working at the casino some of the time," he said. "Still got that new office over in Lander. Her secretary says things are slow. She's hoping Vicky won't have to lay her off." The Indian nodded toward the door. "Vicky's probably waiting to talk to you, Father. I'll finish up here."

Father John crossed the altar, genuflected in front of the tabernacle, and hurried toward the front door. He found her by the old cottonwood tree at the side of the church. Dressed for the office in a dark skirt and a blouse the color of blue iris that made her hair look like black velvet. She wore a trace of lipstick, but her eyes looked dark and shadowed with worry.

"Do you have a minute?" she said. "I'd like to talk to you."

"Would you like some breakfast?"

She shook her head. "I'd like to talk to you in private."

"As a priest?"

This made her pause. "As my friend," she said, finally.

"Come on." He took her arm and guided her across Circle Drive and through the field to the residence. He could feel the faintest tremor beneath the sleeve of her blouse, as if some invisible turbulence was erupting inside her.

"I'll get us some coffee." He ushered her into the study, then went to the kitchen. Father George was at the table, working on a bowl of oatmeal, Catherine was at the stove, ladling out another bowl.

"Sit down and eat," she said.

"Give me a few minutes." He poured coffee into two mugs, ignoring the other priest's raised eyebrows, and went back to the study.

Vicky was seated in the old leather chair behind his desk, staring at the books in the bookcase against the wall. "You don't mind, do you?" She swiveled toward him.

"Be my guest." He set a mug in front of her, then dropped into the visitor's chair on the other side of the desk.

"I always feel a sense of peace when I come here," she said.

He gulped down some coffee to keep himself from saying, It's been a long time. "Is everything okay?" he managed.

She gave a little laugh that sounded almost like a cry. "If that were the case, John, you know I wouldn't be here. I didn't know where else to go. I'm not sure who else I can trust." She paused. "I'm doing contract work for the casino."

"So I've heard."

"Last night I had a visitor." She kneaded at the black bag in her lap. "Left me a message tied to a rock pitched through the front window of my office. It said, Get out of the casino."

"Captain Jack Monroe," Father John said, almost under his breath. He felt the anger surge through him like a shot of adrenaline. The man who'd harassed Dennis Light Stone and other Arapahos was now harassing Vicky. He studied her face a long moment, trying to detect any sign of fear. There was none, which made him afraid for her. She was good at masks. She would never let anyone see her fear, but he'd felt the trembling inside her. He had to look away a moment to keep from bolting around the desk and taking her into his arms to shield her from whatever madness might be coming her way.

"Tell me what's going on," he said, trying for the impersonal tone of the counselor, the priest in the confessional.

"The man's a lunatic." Vicky tilted her head and began rubbing the back of her neck, as if she could work out whatever tension she was harboring. "He thinks he can force Arapahos out of our own casino."

Father John worked at his coffee a couple seconds. A pattern was emerging in his mind, so clear he wondered why he hadn't seen it before. Monroe had targeted Arapahos in the best-paying, most visible jobs—Dennis Light Stone, a pit boss, Vicky, a lawyer. If the man could scare away people like that, then no Arapaho would take a job there. Arapahos might even stop gambling there. A bold strategy, the strategy of a commander ordering his troops to snipe at the leaders until, finally, the people deserted the village.

"Did you call the police?" Father John set the smudged piece of paper on the desk.

Waving one hand in the air, Vicky said, "An officer showed up minutes later. He was patrolling the neighborhood and heard the window break. He was very nice, very professional. Took down the information, said he'd make out a report. Even helped me nail cardboard over the broken window. You know what he was thinking. An Indian problem that spilled over into town. Whoever threw the rock was back on the reservation in ten minutes. What are the Lander police supposed to do? They can't follow him to the rez. Besides . . ." She drew in a long breath and exhaled. "An assault charge has been filed by the BIA police against three of Monroe's men for stopping me in the parking lot a couple days ago."

"Assault? They assaulted you?" Father John could barely suppress the alarm in his voice.

"A man named Tommy Willard pushed me. But he also said something that I haven't been able to shake. He said anyone wanting a good job at the casino has to see Matt Kingdom."

Father John drained the last of his coffee, then got up and went to the window. Leonard was crossing Circle Drive carrying a bundle of dead branches, and Walks-On trotted along, balancing a long stick in his jaws. The scare tactics were escalating, he was thinking. First, harassment, then assault. Followed by a rock through the window. Is that how it went for Dennis Light Stone? Harassment? Assault? A bullet in the head?

He turned back and told her about Lela Running Bull and the body at Double Dives; how Tommy Willard was the girl's boyfriend; and how, yesterday, the girl had admitted that she'd expected the body to be Dennis Light Stone's.

"So you went looking for Light Stone at the casino yesterday," she said, swiveling around and staring across the study. "To warn him that he could be next."

Vicky kept her eyes straight ahead, and he studied her face a long moment. The muffled clank of a pan in the kitchen broke through the quiet that settled over the study. How well they knew each other, he was thinking. "I hope we can be friends," she'd said when she'd first walked across his office, holding out her hand. He remembered the pinpricks of light in her dark eyes. And in the time since, he'd learned to anticipate her moods. He could read her mind, but she could also read his, as if their thoughts were scrolling in each other's head.

"You think Monroe could be on to something, don't you?"

She swiveled a quarter circle and faced him. "I don't like the man's tactics," she began, "but from the beginning he'd said that the casino would corrupt the people. Kingdom's the chairman of the gaming commission. He's supposed to make sure everything is honest and legal. What if he's been corrupted?"

"They brought you in, Vicky," Father John said. He was trying to work it out. Why would the casino hire an Arapaho lawyer—a woman so tenacious and independent?—if there was anything to conceal?

"My job"—she shook her head and gave him a mirthless smile—"is limited to checking the boilerplate in the contracts with vendors, equipment manufacturers, and soft-goods suppliers."

"You're saying they want you in the legal department because it looks good? It'll reassure people?"

She shrugged. "When I tried to find out if Monroe's claim had any merit, Stan Lexson made certain I couldn't see the personnel records. What difference would it make if I looked at the records? Unless Kingdom is controlling the high-paying jobs. His son is the supervisor of maintenance, his sister is the human resources director. How many other managers are connected to Kingdom?"

So many connections on the reservation, Father John was thinking. Connections through marriage—somebody's cousin married to somebody else's cousin. History—somebody's ancestor rode with Chief Sharp Nose or Chief

Black Coal, who was somebody else's ancestor. Ceremony—the old men who'd sponsored younger men in the Sun Dance and become their spiritual grandfathers. He could never keep track of the Arapaho connections, but Vicky—it was as if she'd inherited some genetic code that sorted them all out.

"There could be something else, John." Vicky flattened both hands on the desktop, pushed to her feet, and walked over beside him. He followed her gaze out the window. Leonard and the dog had disappeared, leaving only the breeze ruffling the grasses and moving the branches. "If Kingdom placed too many relatives in top jobs, the people would be up in arms. They'd demand his resignation. He's too smart for that. What if he reserved only a couple jobs for his closest relatives? What if he's reserved the other jobs . . ."

"You think he's been selling the other jobs?"

"Suppose it's true. Who would know? The people with the jobs aren't going to tell anyone. Even if they're giving Kingdom a cut of their salaries, they're still making good money. And providing Kingdom a nice, steady income."

"What about the other commissioners?"

Vicky shrugged. "Either they don't know what's going on, or Kingdom's bought them off."

Father John didn't say anything for a moment. The picture seemed clearer now, like a section of film freeze-framed and brought up close. "Maybe Dennis Light Stone paid for his job," he said. "His wife said Dennis made a trip to the reservation before he took the job as pit boss in the casino. Monroe could suspect . . ."

"Exactly." Vicky put up the palm of one hand. "He *suspects*. If he had any proof, he'd go to the Business Council. He'd go to Gianelli. He wouldn't stop until he'd closed the casino. He's been trying to intimidate people, hoping someone might break under the pressure and blurt out the truth. The man's like a raven, John. Pecking at the prey until it's helpless. Then he'll swoop down."

"You think he could commit murder?"

"What?"

"Look, Vicky," he said, "Light Stone hasn't been at the casino in four days. Nobody's seen him, not even his wife."

"He could be hiding from Monroe."

He could be dead, Father John was thinking.

"Or . . ." Vicky hesitated, then plunged on, "Lexson could have arranged a leave of absence. Maybe sent him away from the rez." She was warming to the idea now. "Dennis is a lightning rod for Monroe. An Arapaho in a top job on the casino floor. Lexson and Kingdom might have wanted him out of Monroe's sight for a while."

She clasped her hands and started pacing—the desk, the window, the framed print of an Arapaho village on the opposite wall. "This is perfect," she said. Lexson and Kingdom were waiting for Monroe to step over the line, and Tommy Willard did just that. The rangers could be charged with assault and conspiracy to commit assault, and I suspect the tribal court will issue a restraining order that forbids them to come within a hundred yards of the casino. Monroe will be discredited. There won't be anybody asking embarrassing questions about Matt Kingdom and the casino jobs . . ."

"Except you," Father John said.

"You're damned right." A faint blush came into her cheeks. Her eyes sparkled in the light streaming through the window. "If Kingdom's been bought off, I want to know it. I think I'll drop by his office and have a talk with him."

"No, Vicky." Father John took her hand, wanting to lead her away from the chasm he could feel opening in front of her. "If you're right, you'll only warn him. It could be dangerous. Go to the Business Council, tell them what you suspect. Go to Chief Banner or Gianelli . . ."

"And tell them what?" she asked, and he knew that he could not keep her from danger, that she would plunge on until she found the truth. "That I suspect the gaming chairman of colluding with the people operating the casino? I'm no different from Monroe, John. All I have are suspicions. I can't prove anything. I haven't seen the personnel records. I don't know yet who's on the payroll."

"How can I help you?" he asked.

She pulled her hand free, picked up her bag, and started for the door. "I'll call you after I've talked to Kingdom." Then she gave him a wave that had more bravado, he knew, than she felt.

17

IT WAS MID-morning before Father John headed west on Seventeen-Mile Road, *Tosca,* Act III, rising from the tape player on the seat beside him, the road stretching ahead, the plains shining in the sun. His mind kept replaying the conversation with Vicky. She had a theory—no evidence, she'd said—just a theory that something was wrong at the casino. She wouldn't let go.

That worried him. Dear Lord, the worry sat like an ingot in his stomach. If her theory was right, then the man running the casino, Stan Lexson, had something to hide. Something important enough to pay off the tribal gaming chairman with choice jobs.

Father John thumped the steering wheel with one fist and tried to recall what he'd read about Indian casinos.

How tribes hired management companies. How some of the companies had turned out to be fronts for organized crime, and how the companies had skimmed profits from the casinos and stolen from the tribes. The managers had gone to prison.

That was the point, he told himself. Indian casinos were old business now, more than three hundred operating around the country. Surely the Indian Gaming Commission had safeguards in place to prevent criminals from taking over. Surely the Arapaho Business Council had investigated Lodestar Enterprises and Stan Lexson before they entered into an agreement. It was logical.

He felt reassured; logic was reassuring. Vicky had said herself that she didn't have any evidence. Only a theory, and the fact that Lexson wouldn't let her see the personnel records. And yet . . . Monroe had the same theory, and the man had tried to close down other Indian casinos. Is that why he was suspicious? Because he'd seen the way management companies could operate?

Father John was only half aware of the curve ahead and the sky, clear blue and shot through with clouds, dipping toward the road. There was no telling what Vicky might do to prove the theory. He felt helpless with the realization that he couldn't protect her, he couldn't keep her from danger.

He took the curve, pulled into the parking lot in front of the senior center, and slid to a stop, gravel spitting from beneath the tires. He turned everything off—engine, tape player—threaded his way past the pickups and old sedans that were parked around the lot in no particular order and let himself into the center. Coffee and tobacco odors wafted toward him. Seated around the metal tables were groups of elders, cowboy hats pushed back on their heads, bolo ties dangling around the opened collars of their plaid shirts.

"Hey, Father!" somebody called through the hum of conversations.

Father John made his way around the tables, shaking hands, exchanging pleasantries, patting shoulders knobby from arthritis and decades of lassoing horses and digging fence post holes. Finally, he helped himself to a mug of coffee at the counter, then walked over to the table near the window that framed a view of the foothills. He sat down across from Will Standing Bear whose rail-thin body was folded onto a metal chair. The old man gripped the armrest with one hand and moved his coffee mug up and down the table with the other. James Yellow Horse sat at one end, an ancient-looking man with thin gray hair and a beaked nose. At the other end was Dan Utica, the youngest of the three, black hair hanging in thick braids down the front of his shirt, wide forehead wrinkled in a permanent frown.

"How's it going, Father?" Will said.

"Okay." Father John took a pull of coffee, unable to shake the hard worry inside himself. He waited while the other elders joined in about the hot weather, the stunted hay in the fields, the new foreman at the Arapaho Ranch. It was still too early to get down to business.

Finally Will said, "You hear how Vicky's doin' with her new casino job?"

Father John set his mug on the table. "She's worried," he began. "She heard a rumor that Matt Kingdom could be helping people get jobs."

Utica let out a guffaw. "Got that no good son of his an important job."

"Good thing, ain't it?" Will said. "Who else is gonna hire that boy? Hasn't had a job in ten years."

"I hear Matt's sister's working there," James put in.

"Listen, Father." Will unfolded his legs and leaned

toward the table. "If that's all that's goin' on, Vicky ain't got nothing to worry about."

Father John looked from one elder to the other. "What do you think is going on?"

Will sucked in his lower lip a moment before he said, "Ain't gonna be nothing, long as Vicky's looking after things."

Father John pushed back against the rungs of his chair. Vicky was right, he thought. As long as she worked at the casino, the elders and everybody else on the reservation would think everything was fine.

He said, "Captain Jack Monroe's trying to stop people from going to the casino."

Will let out a loud snort. "That white man's been going around saying gambling's the devil's work for a long time. Well, gambling ain't good or bad. Just something the people always liked to do. Sometimes they lose, but it's like giving to charity, you know. Share what you got with somebody might need it more." The old man lifted his mug and set it down hard on the table to punctuate the point. "My grandfather used to talk about the games the people played."

"Yeah, mine, too." James shook his head at the memories. "Men used to carve dice out of bones and plum stones. Not like white men's dice, but different shapes. Circles, rectangles, ovals."

"They painted on the symbols," Will said. "Tipis and moccasins and the four hills of life. Sometimes they'd paint *na'kaox,* the morning star, and little lines for buffalo grazing on the prairie."

Utica had been quiet. Now he held up one hand. "Symbols only went on one side of the dice. You got that, Father?"

Father John said he got it.

"You'd make your bet," Utica went on. "What're you

gonna bet? Your best pony? Good buffalo robe? You'd toss the dice in a basket and roll it out onto the ground. Sometimes, you used two dice, sometimes four or six, maybe more. If you shook out dice that fell the same, all the symbols on top, or all the blank sides on top—either way, you won the bet."

"Ah"—Will tapped his mug on the table again—"the grandfathers had themselves a good time playing dice. The grandmothers, too. We didn't discriminate none, when it come to gambling."

There were other games. All three elders were talking at once now. Games with sticks and hoops. Games with balls and cups. All played for ponies or blankets or buffalo robes.

"*Chi'chita'ne* was a good game," Utica said. "One of the boys'd get his bow and arrow ready to shoot. He'd have some grass that was bound up with sinew in one hand. He'd bet that he could drop the grass and shoot it with the arrow before it touched the ground. *A'ba'ni'hi', a'ba'ni'hi', aticha'bi'nasana, aticha'bi'nasana, chi'chita'ne, chi'chita'ne.*"

"Got that?" Will bent his thin shoulders over the table, eyes blurry with amusement.

"I got the name of the game," Father John said.

"My friend. My friend. Let us go out gambling. Let us go out gambling. At *chi'chita'ne.* At *chi'chita'ne.*" Will settled back in his chair. "Now we got craps, blackjack, roulette, bingo, poker, and slot machines. Same games, just different ways. Biggest thing people learned from gambling was that life's a chance, you know. Nothing's for certain. Can't take nothing for granted."

For a moment, the elders fell quiet. Then Utica flopped both forearms on the table and dropped his head, like a bull about to charge. "You hear what happened at Fort Washakie last night?"

Father John waited, his muscles tensing. More trouble, he could see it in the way the elder's eyes had turned to stone.

Utica went on. "Truckload of whites from over Riverton showed up and pulled a couple Indians outta their pickup. Beat 'em up pretty good. Said they was paying back Indians for the white man got shot over at Double Dives."

"Who were they?" Father John could still see Rodney Pearson's wife sitting in his office. "You find that Indian that killed Rodney," she'd said, "or Rodney's friends are gonna find him."

"They took off." Utica tightened his fingers around his mug until his knuckles showed white. "They was probably halfway to Riverton before the cops showed up."

The nearby tables had gone quiet, and Father John had a sense that the other elders were listening. He remained quiet a moment, an old idea working its way into his mind. Suppose Monroe had sent Tommy Willard to kill Dennis Light Stone and Tommy had shot Pearson instead. Gianelli had scoffed at the idea. *Mistake a white man for an Indian?* And Lela Running Bull had seemed relieved that the murdered man was white, as if that proved Tommy couldn't have been involved.

But what if Gianelli and Lela were both wrong? What if Pearson had happened along, blundered into a murder about to take place, and gotten shot instead of the intended victim?

Father John pushed his chair back and got to his feet. He thanked the elders for their time and their stories and said he'd better get back to work. They nodded in unison, not taking their eyes from him, and told him to come around soon. He could still feel their eyes on his back as he crossed the room and flung open the door.

18

FATHER JOHN SLID into the pickup, found the cell phone in the glove compartment, and punched in Gianelli's number. The answering machine picked up, and he heard his own voice speaking into the void. I have to talk to you. Call me.

He tossed the phonc next to the tape player, flipped on *Tosca* again, and jammed the stick shift into reverse. He backed around the truck on the right and, forward now, spun out across the graveled drive and headed east on Seventeen-Mile Road.

He didn't see the late-model, tan-colored truck until it had pulled around him, the noise of the engine roaring into his thoughts, tires thumping the asphalt. The truck cut in so short he had to step hard on the brake. There were two men inside, Indians by the black heads above the seat. Coming up in the rearview mirror was a dark-colored truck that looked almost purple in the sunshine. An Indian hunched over the steering wheel, another in the passenger seat.

They were crowding him now. He kept flicking his gaze between the tan truck ahead and the purple truck hugging his bumper in the rearview mirror. The driver was reaching out the window and setting something on the roof.

The siren wailed over the sounds of "*E lucevan la stelle*"; a blue light flashed on the roof. Ahead, the driver had turned on the right signal and raised his hand, motioning him toward the barrow ditch.

Father John kept going straight, waiting for the chance to swerve around the tan truck and gun the engine. The road stretched ahead as far as he could see. Empty. There were no houses, no one out in the fields. Nothing but the vast openness of the plains.

The Indians were not BIA police in unmarked vehicles, he was certain of it. Not state patrolmen or sheriff's deputies or any other law-enforcement organization. He was being waylaid. Carjacking? Robbery? He stifled a laugh. He had twenty-some dollars and a few coins on him, and what would these Indians in their shiny trucks want with his old pickup?

There was a growing impatience in the whirl of the siren and the blue light behind him. Then he felt the shove against the rear bumper. The pickup lurched ahead, the music skipped a half measure. The Indian in the tan truck was gesturing with his fist toward the ditch.

Father John put on the right blinker. The instant the tan truck veered right, he jammed down on the accelerator and shot out into the oncoming lane, but the truck had swerved back. A blur of motion outside the passenger window. He stomped on the brake pedal, but it was too late. The jolt came in a cacophony of metal crumpling against metal and glass shattering. The steering wheel crashed into his ribs.

It was a moment before he understood that the pickup was standing still, the front end pushed up against the bed of the tan truck. The siren had stopped, and so had *Tosca.* The tape player lay upside down on the floor. Except for the hush of the wind coming over the plains, it was quiet.

"Now look what you done, Father."

Father John winced with the pain that burned through his chest with every breath and looked up at the large Indian with short-cropped gray hair outside his window. The man was wearing army camouflage pants and a shirt with a silver bar on the breast pocket. Father John had to squint to read the black letters: Fasthorse. Another Indian, also in camouflage and burr haircut, had come up behind. Father John felt a twinge of surprise at how old they looked—at least his age, forty-eight. Maybe even older.

Ahead, the two men were crawling out of the tan truck. They were younger, probably in their twenties, dressed in camouflage that looked worn, battle-fatigued, the sleeves cut out, as if the men had just emerged from a firefight in a jungle. The driver was short and big-bellied with bowed legs. He walked with the stiff gait of a man who'd just gotten off a horse. The other Indian was close to six feet, gaunt looking, with long black hair slicked back from a narrow face and hooded eyes, and a blue-black tattoo of a bird that rippled on his skinny arm.

"You went and wrecked your nice pickup here," Fasthorse was saying. "You should've pulled over."

Father John pushed the door open, got out past the two older Indians, and walked to the front. The right bumper was smashed, the headlight broken, but with any luck, the engine would still run.

"Jack Monroe send you?" He looked back at Fasthorse, aware of the others moving in, like a lasso tightening around him.

"Captain wants to see you." Fasthorse had planted his black boots a couple of feet apart and was standing with hands braced on his hips, thick, brown arms crooked out of the short sleeves of his shirt.

"Who the hell are you?"

"Sergeant Joe Fasthorse." The Indian clicked his boots and straightened his arms. For a moment, Father John thought he was about to salute.

"Tell the Captain I'm unavailable." He shouldered past and was about to get back into the pickup when he felt the hard grip on his arm.

"It's an order, Father."

Father John yanked his arm free and turned to face Fasthorse. "This isn't the army, and I'm not one of Jack Monroe's rangers."

Out of the corner of his eye, he saw the two younger Indians rear back, as if he'd tossed gravel in their eyes. Then the squat, bow-legged man took a step forward. Fasthorse shot him a look, and the man backed off.

"Captain says it's urgent," Fasthorse said, his voice strained, barely controlled. "Either you come with us on your own, or I have instructions . . ." He hesitated.

"Instructions for what?" Father John heard the sharpness in his own tone.

The Indian threw a glance over one shoulder at the gaunt young man with the tattoo, hovering near the tan truck. For the first time, Father John saw that the kid was holding a coiled rope next to his pants.

"Tommy here'll escort you."

"Tommy Willard." Father John squared himself toward the young man with the sneer on his face and the hollow, drug-dead eyes. "I've heard about you," he said.

The kid held his gaze and gave him what passed for a smile. He didn't say anything.

Turning back to Fasthorse, Father John said, "Where's Monroe?"

"Field headquarters. Tommy'll drive you."

"I'll drive myself." Father John nodded toward the lanky kid. "He can ride along."

An argument played out behind Fasthorse's eyes a couple seconds before he tossed his head toward Tommy and stepped back. The kid started toward the passenger side of the pickup, snapping the coiled rope against his thigh as he went. Father John threw open his door and got inside.

"We'll escort you, Father, so I suggest you follow Dan's truck . . ." Fasthorse nodded toward the bow-legged Indian about to drop into the tan truck. "Don't try anything, or we'll have to force you into the ditch. Wouldn't want to wreck your pickup permanent-like and put you in the hospital for a good long time, now would we?"

"I have a meeting at the mission . . ." Father John glanced at his wristwatch. "One hour from now. If I'm not there, my assistant will notify the police." The door slammed on the passenger side, and he was aware of Tommy sinking into the seat. "You understand? Every cop on the rez will be looking for this pickup."

Fasthorse held his gaze a moment, then shrugged and followed the other gray-haired Indian back to the purple truck.

FATHER JOHN TURNED the key in the ignition and held his breath. The engine sputtered, then died. He jiggled the key again, coaxing the old pickup into life. Finally, the engine turned over, still sputtering, skipping beats, but running, thank God.

"Where's Lela?" Father John pulled out behind the tan truck and glanced over at the kid beside him. The wind was blowing his hair around his face, and he lifted a skinny arm and pushed it back. The bird tattoo wiggled on his biceps.

"Lela who?" The kid's voice came from down in his throat, behind clenched teeth.

"I know all about you, Tommy." Father John kept his eyes on the truck no more than ten feet ahead, rolling down the road at about thirty-five miles an hour. The purple truck was on his tail. They were like a funeral cortege turning onto Rendezvous Road.

"You were with Lela out at Double Dives," Father John went on. "You saw the body, just like she did."

"Yeah, well that bitch pokes her nose into lotta things that ain't none of her business."

"That right? Is that why you hit her?"

The Indian didn't say anything, but Father John could hear him taking in a breath, as if he were sucking air through a straw. "You like hitting girls, Tommy? Makes you feel like a big man?"

"So I hit her. So what? Nothing like what the Captain did to her."

"What did he do?" Father John felt the constriction in his throat.

"Said he had to teach her to keep her mouth shut, that's all. Knocked her around a little."

"Jesus, Tommy. Is she okay?"

The kid started laughing. It was a sharp, metallic sound. "Learned her lesson, that's for sure."

"You've got to take her home, Tommy."

"Home? All her old man cares about is booze. He don't give a shit about Lela. I'm the only one looks after her."

Father John threw another glance at the kid. He had one elbow propped on the door, holding his hair back, staring straight ahead. There was a trace of pimples along his hairline. What the kid said was true, Father John realized, and it gave him an immense sense of sadness.

"That's how you look after her? Let Monroe beat her up?"

"Hey, what was I gonna do? Captain'd beat the shit outta me, too."

"If you care about Lela, you've got to get her away from Monroe. You could be in a lot of trouble," he pushed on. "Doing the man's dirty work. Lela could be in trouble, too, if you keep her with you. It'll look like she's in on whatever you're doing."

"What're you talking about?"

"Dennis Light Stone. What did you do to him?"

"Nothing!" The kid shot forward on the seat and braced himself against the dashboard. "I didn't do nothing to him."

"You harassed the man, tried to intimidate him into giving up the job at the casino." The tan truck turned west onto a gravel road, and Father John followed. Stripes of shadows lay over the rooftops of the little community of Arapaho. "When that didn't work, what did Monroe order you to do? Beat him up? Shoot him? What?"

"Man, Father!"

Father John looked over. The kid was shaking his head so hard that his whole body was shaking. "I ain't into killing people for nobody, not even the Captain. I mean, he tells us we gotta make it tough on the collaborators and contain the enemy and all that, but he ain't telling us to go kill the enemy. I mean, he don't say that!"

"What happened to Dennis?"

"I don't know, I'm telling you. I ain't seen that Indian in a while. We got other collaborators we been assigned to."

"Such as Vicky Holden?"

The kid was quiet. Out of the corner of his eye, Father

John saw him sink back against the seat, settle his elbow against the door, and start mopping at his hair. "I gotta follow orders."

"How'd you get mixed up with Monroe anyway?"

Tommy sucked in his breath again, then he said, "Captain comes here, makes jobs that pay real money. I don't see nobody else hiring me around here. Sure as hell, the casino didn't wanna see my skinny butt in their fancy place. So I work for Monroe. It's a job, that's all."

"Intimidating people. Throwing rocks through windows. That's your work?" Father John glanced over again. In the resigned look flowing across the narrow face, he knew he'd hit on the truth. "Where's Monroe get his money to bankroll the rangers?"

"Ain't my business. All I care about is he's putting some of it in my pocket."

"You're looking at an assault charge, Tommy. You could be on your way to some jail time."

"No way." The kid shouted into the wind blowing through the window. "I'm just following orders, doing my job. We got a war going on, Father."

"War?" They were in Arapaho now, winding along a gravel road past the block-like houses that erupted out of the flat, brown earth. The tan truck turned into a bare-dirt yard in front of a small, rectangular-shaped house with white paint peeling from the front and a concrete stoop that sloped sideways.

"What are you talking about?"

"War between good and evil, between the good spirits and the devil. Devil got that casino started here, and our mission is to get it outta here."

Father John bumped across the yard after the truck and stopped. The purple truck nudged against his rear bumper. He turned off the engine and looked at the kid. "Do something decent, Tommy. Lela's a noncombatant. Get her away. Bring her to the mission. She can stay at the guest house. She'll be safe there."

"Captain says she'll blab to the fed if I don't watch her."

"Lela's scared. She's not going to blab to anybody. She wouldn't have said anything about the body at Double Dives if her aunt hadn't called the police."

The kid clenched his jaw; the muscles in his cheek started twitching. He kept his eyes straight ahead as he pulled down on the door handle and got out.

"Let's go, Father." Fasthorse was outside his window again. "Captain doesn't like to be kept waiting."

19

FATHER JOHN FOLLOWED Fasthorse across the yard, up the concrete steps, and into the living room. The door banged shut behind them. The house could have been any house on the reservation: kitchen in the back, bedrooms off the hallway. A middle-aged man, Indian, dressed in camouflage, sat at a card table in the middle of the living room, studying the papers spread in front of him. Strips of duct tape were wrapped around the edges of the table.

Fasthorse stood at attention a few feet away. Finally the man shifted the papers into a stack, which he laid on top of another stack, and lifted his eyes. "At ease, Sergeant."

"Sir, we have the padre for Captain Monroe."

"Go on back. Captain's waiting."

Fasthorse made an about-face. "This way, padre," he said, motioning toward the hallway behind them.

They walked past two opened doors to rooms with small beds pushed under the windows and papers and books piled on card tables and chairs.

The Indian stopped at a closed door and gave three sharp knocks.

"Enter." The order was an impatient bark.

Fasthorse pushed open the door and stepped inside. "Father O'Malley, sir," he said, then he backed into the hallway.

Father John shouldered past and went into the room. Hunched over a desk, writing something on a form-like sheet of paper, was a large man with a fleshy, beet-red face, and balloon shoulders and chest that pushed against the fabric of his camouflage shirt. Two silver bars were pinned on his shoulders. Beneath the thin strips of the man's gray hair, Father John could see the pink scalp and the top of the furrowed forehead.

"Be with you in a minute," Captain Monroe said without looking up. He dipped a pen into the ink bottle at his hand and went back to writing. The pen made a scratching noise on the paper, like the noise of a bird pecking at seeds.

"You brought me here, Monroe," Father John said. "What do you want?"

The man took his time arranging the pen in a perpendicular line to the paper before he raised his eyes. He was in his fifties, Father John guessed, light-skinned with a square-set jaw and narrow, gray eyes filled with a mixture of contempt and amusement.

"Obviously, my intelligence reports are correct," he said. "They say you're a maverick, Father O'Malley. Take a seat." He waved one hand across the desk toward a folding chair against the wall. "There are a few matters I want to clear up."

Father John pulled over the chair and sat down. "You're right, Monroe."

"Captain, Father."

"There are matters we have to clear up. Where are you holding the girl?"

"The girl?" A note of surprise rang in the man's voice. "I assume you're referring to Lela Running Bull. I'm not holding her or anyone else. The people working for me are free to ask for a discharge at any time."

"You're saying that Lela works for you?"

"Her boyfriend has enlisted in the rangers. I assume you've met First Lieutenant Willard. As long as she chooses to stay with him, she will be treated as a military dependent. Loyalty will be required of her."

Monroe squared his massive shoulders and regarded him a long moment. "The first matter I wish to clear up is that Lela Running Bull has given you"—he picked up the pen and began waving it like a baton—"erroneous information. Loose lips"—now the pen was tracing large circles in the air—"sink ships, I believe the old motto was. Loose lips can destroy my mission. I won't allow that to happen."

"You brought me here to tell me that?"

"My rangers had nothing to do with the body found at Double Dives. Nothing whatsoever." Monroe set the pen down again and rolled it against the side of the paper. "The girl, I'm afraid, made you believe otherwise. Let me assure you, I had no reason to want the white man—what did the newspaper say his name was? Rodney Pearson from Two-Valley Road—dead." He shook his head, and a strand of gray hair fell over his forehead. He smoothed it back into place. "We will do nothing that is counterproductive to our mission, Father."

"So you send out your employees . . ."

"Rangers, Father."

". . . to lob rocks through windows, assault people in the parking lot."

"Assault? You mean the unfortunate incident in the casino parking lot two days ago?" The man picked up the pen again and stabbed it in the air. "That brings me to the second matter I wish to clear up. The incident was an accident. As for the broken window, let me assure you that Tommy has been disciplined and confined to quarters, except for limited exposure, such as today's mission to bring you in."

The man drew in a long breath that inflated his chest. "Unfortunately, we received a visit this morning from Chief Art Banner and two other BIA police officers. They had a warrant from the tribal court for the arrest of Tommy Willard. Naturally, I explained that Lieutenant Willard was deployed elsewhere in the field and, until he checked in, I had no idea of his exact whereabouts. The police insisted upon interrogating the other three men who witnessed the incident. They searched the premises. To no avail, I may add. I had to restrain my men from taking offensive action. We must keep our eye on the primary mission."

"You can't hide Tommy forever. Sooner or later, he'll be arrested."

"In that unfortunate case, the other rangers who witnessed the incident will testify on Tommy's behalf that it was nothing but an accident." The man gripped the edge. "This morning, we had another visitor. Special Agent Ted Gianelli who interrogated me about the demonstrators at the casino. All of this pressure, Father O'Malley, is due to the girl's loose lips and the lies she told you. I order you to stop spreading the lies immediately."

"I'm not one of your rangers, Monroe."

"Captain Monroe." The man gave Father John a hard look, then lifted his head and squared his shoulders.

"What happened to Dennis Light Stone?" Father John pushed on. "What did you do to him?"

The man didn't blink. A hint of a smile played at his

mouth, and then he said, “My intelligence tells me that Light Stone hasn’t been at his post for several days. He’s the first to desert the casino. Other Arapahos who have sold their souls to the devil will follow his lead. I can only conclude that our preliminary tactics are succeeding.”

Father John shifted forward, braced his arms on his thighs, and drove a fist into his palm. “You really believe you can scare people enough that they’ll stop showing up for their jobs?”

“Our tactics are appropriate to the circumstance, Father O’Malley. Appropriate to enemy resources. Tell me, were you in Vietnam?”

“The army didn’t want high school students.”

“Didn’t want college students either, as I recall.” Monroe’s lips parted in a slow smile, as if he were smiling to himself. “Let me guess, after high school, you went directly to college. Draft-deferred college student. Am I right?” He pushed on, “I met guys like you after my tour of duty. College students still sucking on their mother’s teats, and conscientious objectors scurrying around the hospitals like rats. Yeah, I knew guys like you, and I decided back then, you can’t ever trust them because they don’t know. They just don’t know. You gotta fight evil without them. You got to search out the collaborators to destroy the enemy.”

The man lowered his jaw into the folds of his neck and stared up at him. “You ever heard of Pleiku? Nah, you wouldn’t know about that. We culled out the collaborators and turned them into God-fearing, freedom-loving Vietnamese. That’s what we thought. In the daytime, they were God-fearing, freedom-loving Vietnamese, and at night they’d come out firing at our camps. You know what I learned? We have to stay with the collaborators, keep them in sight at all times. Don’t ever turn our backs on them. You can never trust collaborators.”

"This isn't Vietnam."

"Like I said, Father, we gotta fight evil where we find it. Indian people got sucked into this gambling filth. It's draining their souls. I've got rangers all over the country helping to stop this scourge. But the politicians are selling us out, like in Nam. This time, we're gonna win the war without them, because we got the people behind us. You should've seen the crowd that came to my rally in Florida couple years ago. Good Christian people that believe in our mission and want to save the Indian people. Show how much they believe with the checks they write. We got a vast army fighting against gambling, and we're gonna win."

"The casino's operating, Monroe. You can't shut it down by intimidating Arapahos who work there."

"Collaborators!" He spit out the word. "They're the ones we have to turn and keep watching. Soon's they see the light, they're gonna come forward, tell people what's really going on. We won't have to shut down that den of thieves. The Indian Gaming Commission's gonna do it for us."

"What do you think is going on, Monroe?"

"Ask Dennis Light Stone."

"I will as soon as I find him. Now I'm asking you."

"The usual evils, Father O'Malley. Must I list the evils? Thievery, fraud, debauchery." He shrugged. "They're found in every casino."

"Every casino, Monroe? What proof do you have of any wrongdoing at Great Plains Casino?"

The man made a clicking noise with his teeth and sat back, lacing his fingers over his chest. After a minute, he said, "It's always the same. First, the evildoers co-opt the guy that's supposed to be watching them. I believe you've heard of Matt Kingdom, Gaming Commission chairman? Usually, they co-opt guys like him with fancy cars and vacations to the Bahamas, but Kingdom . . ." He shook his head. "All that Arapaho wanted were some jobs for his nearest and dearest and other jobs to hand out. Done!" The man snapped his fingers.

"So you've targeted people you think were hired because of Kingdom?"

"They got the best jobs. More than likely, they're gonna know what's going on. All we gotta do is convince them to come over to the God-fearing side, Father, and when that happens, they will speak the truth. They will confirm our intelligence."

Father John was quiet a moment. "You're wrong about Vicky Holden. She's not one of Kingdom's people."

"No? Then why did she suddenly take the job?" Monroe slapped his palm on the sheet of paper and rose to his feet. He was shorter than Father John had expected, not more than five and a half feet tall, with hips as thick as his waist. "You should consider joining our mission, Father."

"You mean, help you intimidate people?" Father John got to his feet. He towered over the man.

Monroe laughed. "A man like yourself, people respect you. You start telling the truth about the evils of gambling, they're gonna listen. They're gonna stop going to that cesspool."

"Not interested, Monroe."

"Surely you don't condone gambling?"

"I don't condone your tactics."

"That's because you don't know, Father. You weren't there in Vietnam. You don't understand what works. Light Stone's ready to come over now. I know the signs. He's gone off somewhere to think about it, and he's gonna come back and speak out about what's going on. You'll see. Our tactics are working. My men will escort you back to your headquarters."

"I know the way." Father John started for the door, then stopped and looked back. "Stay away from Vicky, Monroe."

"Oh?" The man's face cracked into a smile. "You got an interest in the lady?"

"Just stay away." He held the man's gaze a moment, then headed down the hallway, through the living room, and out into the blast of mid-afternoon heat. Tommy and the others were leaning against the purple truck, hands cupped over cigarettes. They jumped to attention as he walked past. He got into the pickup and, cutting around the truck, drove out onto the road, rear tires spitting back kernels of rock. He kept the speed down past the cluster of small houses, wondering how many people living in the area were part of Monroe's army, then turned left onto Rendezvous Road.

The pickup was straining over a rise, the engine knocking, when he saw something move in the tall grasses in the barrow ditch. An antelope, he thought, easing up on the accelerator. You never knew when a frightened animal would dart onto the road.

And then he realized it was a person—a girl with long black hair billowing around her thin shoulders. He slowed almost to a crawl, keeping his eyes on the girl darting through the ditch. Suddenly she turned and lifted her head, squinting into the sun. Then she bounded up onto the road waving both hands over her head. A purple bruise spread over one side of her face.

Lela Running Bull. He was struck by how small she looked, like a child dressed in blue jeans hanging low on her thin hips and a white T-shirt clinging to her small breasts.

He stopped the pickup on the side of the road, close to the girl, leaned over and pushed the door open. She clambered inside, breathing hard, little dots of perspiration glistening on her forehead. Blue-black bruises, like tattoos, ran down her arms. The purple bruise ran into the blackness around her eye. The whites of both eyes were bloodshot.

"I seen you go into headquarters," she said, pulling the door shut. She was still gulping in air. "Tommy and me been staying in the house across the road. I ran out the back door, so he didn't see me."

"Are you okay?" He glanced over at the girl. A stalk of grass clung to the side of her jeans, and there was an odd odor about her—a mixture of sweat and sex and dried earth. "Do you need a doctor?"

"Just get me away from here," she said, shaking her head.

Father John stepped hard on the accelerator, keeping one eye on the rearview mirror, expecting the tan truck to appear over the rise. The road was empty, a line of asphalt shining in the sun.

"Do you want to go home?"

"You said you got a guest house." She was wringing her hands, then combing her fingers through her hair. Wringing. Combing.

They were heading east on Seventeen-Mile Road now. The sign for St. Francis Mission loomed ahead.

Dear Lord, he'd told Tommy about the guest house. He was going to have to keep a close watch on the girl.

20

VICKY SPOTTED THE commission chairman the instant she turned into the gravel parking lot that wrapped around the tribal office building. Matt Kingdom, dressed in blue jeans and a short-sleeved white shirt, was leaning against the red-brick façade, one boot crossed over the other. The rim of his black cowboy hat threw a half-moon shadow over his face. He took another draw from the cigarette cupped in his hand.

Vicky parked at the cement curb that marked off the lot from the sidewalk in front of the building. She could feel the man's gaze on her, like a light beam flashed in her direction. A gust of hot air slapped at her skirt as she got out of the Cherokee.

"Hey, Vicky, how ya doing?" Kingdom blew the cigarette smoke out of the side of his mouth. Gray smoke curled up over the rim of his hat.

"Can I see you for a minute, Matt?"

"You're seein' me." The man laughed at his own joke. "You mean in the office?" A mock look of comprehension clouded his dark eyes. "I guess I can work that out." He uncrossed his boots, pushed away from the brick wall, and tossed the cigarette onto the gravel where it blinked for a moment like a firefly.

Kingdom led the way inside the building and across the tiled entry. "Hold my calls," he called to the dark-haired woman in front of a computer monitor. They kept walking. Down the corridor. Past the doors with wood plaques and black letters identifying the offices of various tribal officials. He stopped at a door on the left and pushed it open.

Vicky stepped into the office behind him, the way it had always been, she was thinking. Arapaho men always went ahead of women to make certain there was no danger, that the path was clear so the women would be safe.

"Make yourself comfortable." Kingdom nodded toward a side chair, then tossed his hat onto the coat tree and walked around the oak desk that sprawled into the middle of the room.

"Gotta tell you, Vicky"—he dropped into the swivel chair—"hearing you started work at the casino sure brought back memories."

Vicky took the chair he'd indicated. The polite preliminaries would last a minute or two.

"Got me thinking about Ben," the man went on.

"Ben!" Vicky heard the note of surprise in her voice. Ben had been dead more than three months. Why was she still surprised by the fact?

"Ben and me were buddies, you know." A blank look had come into Kingdom's eyes, as if he were watching a scene taking place far away from the cramped, stuffy office. "Got me through school, Ben did. Used to do my English homework and pass me the answers in the tests." He lifted his head and laughed. "Went rodeoing together, Ben and me, soon's we got outta high school. Colorado, Texas, Arizona, Nevada. We was in Utah one day, and Ben says, 'Let's you and me join up.' 'Join up? What're you talking about?' I said. 'We already joined up with the rodeo.' 'Army,' Ben says. 'Join up and see the world.' "

Kingdom grinned and shook his head. "So we drove his old truck back to Lander and enlisted. That sonabitch Ben gets himself sent to Germany, and you know where they sent me? Right back to Utah! Except I wasn't rodeoing anymore. I was in the fucking—excuse me, Vicky—army."

"Listen, Matt." Vicky could feel the impatience rising like gorge in her throat. She wasn't here to reminisce about Ben Holden.

"Soon's Ben and me got discharged," Matt went on, as if she hadn't spoken, "we went right back to rodeoing. Then he met you and, man, it was like a bronc threw that cowboy on his head. He wasn't never the same. Settled down, started ranching, got himself a couple kids off you, and become a good family man."

That wasn't the way it was, Vicky wanted to say. It only looked that way to the outside world where no one saw the drinking and the beatings. And when she'd tried to tell people, even her own family, no one had believed her. Ben Holden? How could it be? That was when she first realized she was alone. She raised the palm of her hand, fingers outstretched, in the traditional sign of peace. She understood. Matt Kingdom had brought up her former husband to set the ground rules for their meeting: He and Ben had been buddies; he was Ben's friend. He was not her friend.

"We have to talk about the casino," she said.

"I been expecting you to come around." His eyes had become as hard as obsidian. "Hell, I was outside waiting for you this morning. Smoked a goddamn pack of cigarettes. What took you so long?" He gave a mirthless laugh.

Vicky studied the man on the other side of the desk. Obviously Stan Lexson had called the chairman and told him she'd tried to see the personnel records yesterday. A wave of futility passed over her. She'd hoped to catch Kingdom off guard. Off guard he might let something spill out.

She said, "Jack Monroe says you have a lock on the best jobs at the casino."

"Captain Jack Monroe!" He blew out a long breath, as if he were exhaling cigarette smoke. "Still fighting his own goddamn war. All dressed up in an army suit like those Japanese soldiers that came stumbling out of the jungle forty years after World War II was over. Goes around the country trying to stop Indian gaming. Says it's another way for white people to rip off Indians. What a load of shit! We been making bets since before white people heard about this land. You gonna believe what Monroe says?" He threw up both hands.

"I've checked on some employees," Vicky said. "At least two of your relatives have very good jobs."

"So what? They got the jobs 'cause they're qualified."

"What qualified your sister to be the director of human resources?"

The man chewed on his lower lip a moment. "The Lexson Company has a real good training program. They're walking Annette through the steps. Besides"—he hunched over the desk and lifted his eyes in supplication—"she needs that job. She's been outta work three years now."

"That's the point, Matt. A lot of people have been out of work, and some might be more qualified. But your sister got the job."

"You're looking to cause trouble." His voice was tight with anger.

"I'm trying to avoid trouble," Vicky said. "If there's any evidence that you've misused your position, Lodestar Enterprises could face a class action lawsuit from people better qualified for jobs that went to your relatives. The tribe could also be sued."

Matt Kingdom tucked his chin into his throat and let out a guffaw that sounded like a groan. "You got it all wrong, Vicky. Nobody's gonna be suing anybody. The casino's a cash cow around here. People are working and making money. Maybe some folks didn't get a job right off the bat, that don't mean they won't get a job tomorrow, and that keeps 'em going. In the meantime, a lot of 'em are winning at the tables. So everybody's happy, except you. Just like Ben used to say, no matter what he did, the man couldn't make you happy. He give you the world, but you was always looking for something else."

Vicky felt the heat spreading in her face. "Is it true, Matt," she struggled to keep her voice steady, "that people looking for a job have to see you? That would be a major conflict of interest."

The man didn't say anything for a long moment. His Adam's apple bobbed up and down in his thick throat; a blue vein pulsed in the center of his forehead. When he spoke, it was in a monotone. His eyes were almost closed. "Maybe you forgot I'm the chairman. Business Council appointed me to oversee the casino operations for the tribe. So what if people come here first? I'm not about to let some stumbling drunk take on a big job and make a mess of things. We gotta have good, reliable people in important jobs. You know why you got the job in the legal department? 'Cause I told Lexson to hire you."

"You!" Vicky swallowed hard. Not Adam, not Stan Lexson. The man who had wanted to hire her was Matt Kingdom.

"So don't tell me about conflicts of interest and all that legal crap. If you didn't have a connection to me through Ben, you wouldn't be sitting here looking holier than thou."

Kingdom pushed himself to his feet, a signal that the meeting was over. "I sure hope I didn't make a mistake."

Vicky stood up, her eyes locked on his. "How many people came here looking for a job, Matt? How many were hired?" She drew in a long breath. "How much did they pay you?"

"Go back to your contracts." He hissed the words. "You can't prove anything."

It was true. She felt as if he'd lifted his hand and slapped her. She waited a couple of beats before taking her eyes away. Then she let herself out the door and headed down the corridor. In the lobby, she glanced back over her shoulder.

Matt Kingdom was standing outside his door watching her.

THE CASINO LOOKED different, Vicky thought as she made her way past the floor to the hotel lobby. Same rows of slots with Indians and tourists slumped on the stools, same kaleidoscope of figures jumping on the screens, same jangle of coins and beehive of voices, and red-neon signs—Raven's Nest—shining overhead.

All the same, but different, unreal, like props dragged onto a stage to create an imaginary world.

She stopped at the elevator, inserted the security card Adam had given her, then rode upward against the smallest pull of gravity. The bronze doors pulled open. Everything seemed different, even the sign on the door that said, "Legal Department." Nothing at Great Plains Casino, she knew now, was as it appeared.

Inside, the secretary was flipping through a folder and

murmuring into the phone tucked between her chin and shoulder. Through the opened door, she saw Adam at his desk, staring at the computer monitor.

She shut the door in her office, sank into the chair behind the desk, and turned to the computer. In a couple seconds the contract that she'd been reviewing floated onto the screen. Another routine contract. They would never let her get close to what was really going on. She was going to have to play her own hand very close, be patient, wait for the opportunity . . .

It would take time. She forced herself to concentrate on the lines of black type scrawling down the screen. Edgeware Equipment. Contract to supply Great Plains Casino with linens, china, stemware, flatware, cooking pans, and utensils.

She moved to the second page. Nothing unusual. Specifications as to frequency and type of service, quality of merchandise, methods and dates of payment.

There was a low rap on the door before it swung open. Adam stood in the doorway, his broad shoulders nearly filling out the frame.

"Hello," he said. "Just wanted to see how you're doing."

Vicky had to look away. She felt a sense of betrayal as acute and lasting as a puncture from a dull instrument. What if Kingdom had been telling the truth? After all, Lexson had also said that *he* was the one who had wanted an Arapaho lawyer on board. Yet Adam had insisted that he had suggested her to Lexson. What if they were both wrong, and it was Kingdom who had wanted her here all along? God, what was she thinking? How could she have ever thought there could be anything between her and Adam? A man who would lie to her. A man that women followed with hungry eyes. She could never trust Adam Lone Eagle.

It was a moment before she could face the man. "I'm fine," she said, making her voice light, as if they were just a couple of employees passing the time.

"I was going to ask you to lunch," Adam went on, "but Stan's called an emergency meeting of the department heads, so I guess I'll be having lunch in the executive dining room."

"I plan to skip lunch today," she said because she couldn't think of anything else except that she wanted him to leave.

"You free for dinner tonight? New restaurant opened up south of Lander. I hear it's pretty good."

"I don't think so, Adam."

He nodded, almost as if he'd expected the rejection. Then he moved forward and shut the door. "I'm almost sorry I told you the truth about my marriage. Now you don't think you can trust me. I hope I can convince you that it was a long time ago, and I'm a different man. I'd like to get to know you better, Vicky." When she didn't reply, he said, "I'm not giving up. Unless you tell me to go away and leave you alone and that you hate my guts. If you tell me that, I won't bother you anymore, but, you know what? That isn't what I see in your eyes."

"I really need to get back to this contract, Adam," Vicky said.

"Right." He reached behind for the knob, yanked the door open, and stepped backward into the reception room, not taking his eyes off her. Then he was gone.

Vicky spent another thirty minutes scrolling through the lines of type, correcting a couple of discrepancies, rewriting several sentences to clarify the meanings. At one point she heard Adam tell the secretary he'd be back in a couple hours. The door to the reception room slammed shut.

She finished the Edgeware contract and was accessing

the next contract when she realized the secretary was in the doorway. "Adam said I should see if you want me to bring you anything to eat," she said. "Some of the secretaries are going to the restaurant."

"No, thanks." Vicky gave the woman a smile, then went back to the monitor. Edgeware again, but this contract was for paper products. She'd read through the first page when she heard the outer door shut. A stillness dropped over the office.

Vicky sat back and gazed at the oil painting of the Wind River mountains on the wall, trying to grasp an idea playing like a faint melody in her mind. Stan Lexson had called a meeting of the department heads, which meant that Annette Addley was also in the executive dining room. And it was possible that the human resources secretary had gone to the restaurant. There was a chance the office was unlocked. The floor was secure; no need to lock the offices in midday.

Vicky got up and went out to the corridor. There was no one around, no ringing phones or clacking computer keys. Nothing but the thick, enveloping silence. She rode the elevator to the third floor and walked down the corridor to the human resources office. The doorknob turned in her hand. There was no one at the desk.

She slipped inside and closed the door behind her. She had about thirty minutes, she figured.

21

THE OFFICE WAS deserted, as if the fire alarm had sounded and everyone had left. Brochures and forms sat in neat stacks at the edge of the secretary's desk, next to the computer with a picture of the casino blazing on the monitor. Vicky hesitated a moment, her gaze on the computer. She had no idea of the password the secretary might use, but she knew Annette and there was a chance . . .

She rapped on the door to Annette's office, waited a half-second, then turned the knob and looked inside. The office was vacant: the square-shaped oak desk with the clear top gleaming under the ceiling light, the leather chair pushed against the side wall, a depression in the cushion, as if someone had just gotten up. The computer stood on the side table that formed an L with the desk. On the screen saver, Appaloosas were running against the blue sky.

Vicky closed the door, walked over and sat down at the computer. Her heart was thumping as she moved the cursor and clicked. Human Resource Information System came onto the screen. An empty box appeared with the word *Password* below it. She typed in *ho'heisi.* "Denied" flashed in the box.

Vicky flexed her fingers over the keys, then typed in "Madwoman." A menu came up. She clicked on Employees, then Department Heads. Two columns of black text appeared. On the left, a list of names. On the right, the positions. She scrolled down, glancing through the names. Several Arapahos. She returned to the top and clicked on résumés.

A new document opened—thirty-two pages of résumés for department heads. She couldn't read them all—it would take at least an hour.

She glanced at her watch. Twenty minutes had passed.

She pulled open the desk drawers searching for a diskette, then glanced at the shelves behind the desk. Nothing resembling a diskette box. Turning back to the computer, she tapped the print keys and clicked on "Print all pages." The printer next to the computer stirred into life, green lights flashing on the front. A sheet of paper flitted into a tray, then another.

Vicky started lifting off the first sheets as they spit out. She glanced through the names and sorted the résumés of Arapahos on top. A tremor, as slight as a whisper, started through the floor. She sat very still, listening. She could hear the whoosh of the elevator rising through the building.

She took off more sheets. Twenty-two, so far. Still ten to print. She held her breath, waiting for the clang of the elevator. It didn't come, which meant the elevator was heading upward into the hotel. The floor was still trembling beneath her feet.

The printer disgorged another sheet, which Vicky added

to the stack in front of her. The building seemed to be coming alive, and she realized the elevator was dropping through the floors. Another sheet floated into the tray, then another. Still five sheets to print.

Now the elevator was coming back up. She pulled off another sheet. Come on. Come on.

From the corridor came the muffled clang of the elevator stopping on the third floor. In the quiet that followed, Vicky could imagine the swish of the doors parting, the cushioned sound of footsteps on the carpet. The voices, when they came, were real, crashing around her like drumbeats.

Vicky exited the program, then leaned over the printer and caught the last page before it dropped into the tray, listening for the sound of the door opening in the outer office. There was a peal of laughter, the secretary's voice shouting good-bye.

Gripping the stack of papers, Vicky darted across the office, closed the door, and slid into one of the visitor's chairs against the wall. She grabbed a magazine from the side table, and stuffed the printed sheets inside, her gaze fixed on the door across from her.

The door burst open. "Oh!" The secretary flinched, as if she'd been struck by an unseen force. Her dark eyes flitted about the office, lighting for a half-second on the computer next to her desk, then on the closed door to the inner office. "Ms. Holden," she said, a note of relief in her tone. "I didn't realize you had an appointment."

"I didn't." Vicky kept her own voice nonchalant. She turned to a page in the magazine, as if she'd been perusing an article. Her fingers were trembling. "I was hoping to catch Annette when she got back from lunch."

The other woman swung her shoulder bag, walked over to the desk and sat down, dropping the bag on top. "Sorry," she said. "Annette's in a meeting with Lexson that will probably last all afternoon. I wouldn't wait, if I were you."

Vicky closed the magazine and got to her feet, conscious of the smile frozen on her face. "In that case, I'll stop by tomorrow." She tucked the magazine under her arm.

"You want me to pencil you in?"

Vicky was across the office now, still smiling. "It won't be necessary," she said, stepping into the corridor. She headed for the elevator and pressed the down button. A shiver ran through the floor as the elevator doors opened.

"Oh, Ms. Holden."

Vicky swung around. The woman was crossing the corridor, hand outstretched. "I believe you have our magazine."

"Oh, I just started an interesting article. You don't mind if I borrow it, do you? I promise to return it," Vicky said, stepping into the elevator.

"No, no. Of course not." The secretary withdrew her hand and began moving backward. "I'll tell Annette you want to see her," she said, her voice muffled by the closing doors.

In the legal offices, the secretary was leaning over the desk, stuffing her bag into the lower drawer. "You must've gone for lunch after all," she said, looking up.

Vicky nodded, hurried into her own office and closed the door. Then she lifted her briefcase onto the desk, slipped the magazine and papers into a pocket, and zippered it closed. She found her black bag in another drawer and, gripping the soft leather in one hand and her briefcase in the other, walked back into the reception room.

"If anyone wants to reach me," she said to the woman behind the desk, "I'll be at my office in Lander."

■ ■ ■

THE SUN RODE overhead in a sky whitened by the heat. A dust-dry wind swirled through the Cherokee. Vicky drove with one hand on the steering wheel, the other holding her hair back from her face. She was in a line of campers and SUVS with out-of-state licenses heading south on 287. Tourists, and most had no doubt gone to the casino, stayed in the hotel, eaten in the restaurants, fed coins into the slot machines, and lost at the tables. All of which was good for the rez, good for her people. Except that . . .

Even the brief glance through the names on the computer screen had confirmed her suspicions. She'd spotted the names of several people she doubted were qualified for management positions. And several others, she knew, were connected to Kingdom.

She was connected to Kingdom! She laughed into the wind. What did Captain Jack Monroe's accusations matter? Vicky Holden, Arapaho attorney, was at the casino, which meant there couldn't be anything illegal in hiring the chairman's friends and relatives. What else would she be able to say, if she were asked, when she owed her own job to Kingdom? Unless one of the managers turned against the man, she would never be able to prove he'd done anything wrong.

Clever, she thought. The used-up rodeo rider was still as sharp as barbed wire. He'd made a deal with Lexson, she was sure of it, and the management jobs were his to hand out. But in exchange for what? What was the casino watchdog expected to overlook?

Vicky passed a camper, then settled back into the flow of traffic and tried to shake the unsteady feeling, as if she were walking a tightrope that bucked and swayed in the wind. She could have gotten it all wrong. It wouldn't have been the first time that she'd struck out with some theory that had gotten hold of her and refused to let go. Even if Kingdom had conducted the investigation into Lodestar

Enterprises, the lawyers in Cheyenne hadn't found anything improper. And the Business Council had approved the company. Even the state of Wyoming had approved.

Vicky slowed into Lander and took the side streets to her office. Esther glanced up from the half-sandwich and potato chips spread over the brown paper bag on her desk. "Didn't expect you in today," she said.

"Hold my calls." Vicky waved the briefcase. "I'll be working here this afternoon."

She closed the doors to her own office, settled at the desk, and plucked a card from the Rolodex. Then she dialed the Secretary of State's Office in Cheyenne and asked for Myrna Hancock. She was put on hold, a mechanical voice describing the advantages of Wyoming.

She could still see Myrna Hancock, the tall, angular woman with black hair, long and parted in the middle, who'd walked into contracts class the third semester in law school. Another Indian. Vicky had felt almost faint with relief. They'd become friends right away, she and Myrna, an Arapaho and a Lakota making their way in the outside world, like two fish swimming upriver.

"Myrna Hancock here." There was a business-as-usual tone in the woman's voice. Vicky smiled at the flash of memory: she and Myrna giggling in the law library, too exhausted and scared to stop.

"It's me, Vicky," she said.

"How *are* you?" The old Myrna was on the line now. "Everything okay?"

"Fine, I hope." Vicky stopped herself from plunging into the reason for the call. The pleasantries had to be observed. After a couple of minutes, she said, "I'm doing some contract work for Great Plains Casino. Can you get me some information on the management company, Lodestar Enterprises?"

A long whistle came over the line. "We must have a hundred documents. State wasn't happy about the Arapahos getting a casino, you know. What exactly do you need?"

"Corporate history," Vicky said. She was fishing. "Anything you have on Stan Lexson and the other principals."

"Hold on." The line went blank again. After a moment, Myrna was back. "It's going to take a while to pull the files. What's going on, Vicky?"

"I'm not sure." Vicky drew in a long breath. Whatever Kingdom had learned about Lodestar Enterprises, he'd used to get control of jobs that he could hand out, like some chief in the Old Time, decreeing who could pitch their tipis near the stream, who could graze their ponies in the best grass. Kingdom had made himself an important man.

"I'll have to get back to you, but . . ." The voice on the other end broke off for a half-beat. "If anything's going on the state ought to know about, you'll keep us informed, right?"

Vicky closed her eyes. Her stomach muscles clinched. If there was any illegality, the state would ask the federal court to close the casino. The jobs, the tribal income would all disappear, and she would be responsible.

"Right," she heard herself saying.

22

A COLLECTION OF trucks and rust-patched sedans stood in front of Eagle Hall. Through the opened door, Father John could see the knots of people seated on the folding chairs scattered about the floor. A woman stood in front, the high, tinny sound of her voice drifted out into the evening.

Father John continued down the alley to the guest house sheltered among the cottonwoods and the tall grasses, like the dwelling in a village in the Old Time. The house wasn't much larger than a garage, with white siding, a gray peaked roof, and oblong windows with lacy curtains in front. He stepped onto the cement stoop and rapped on the door.

It was a minute before the door creaked open and Lela Running Bull peered around the edge. She had a vacant stare, a disheveled look, as if she'd been sleeping. Father John hadn't seen her since he'd left her at the guest house this afternoon with some apples, cans of soda, and crackers that he'd found in the kitchen in the residence. Dinner was at six, he'd told her. When the girl didn't appear, Catherine had taken a bowl of stew to the guest house.

"Wanted to make sure you're okay," he said.

"Yeah, I'm okay."

"Did you call your aunt Mary?"

Lela feinted a glance at a watch that hung over the bruise on her wrist. "She don't get home from work for a while."

"Would you like me to call your father?" He knew the answer even before the girl started shaking her head. She'd told him earlier that her father was drunk, so what was the use? Besides, the house would be the first place Tommy would look for her. So she'd just stay at the mission for a while, if that was okay. He'd said she could stay as long as she liked. The police had a warrant for Tommy's arrest. It wouldn't be long before the man was looking at more serious problems than a runaway girlfriend.

He told her to lock the door and get a good night's sleep. Then he headed back to Eagle Hall, the sound of the door shutting behind him punctuating the click of his boots in the gravel.

He slipped through the opened door and took the nearest vacant chair. The air was close, suffused with perspiration, stale cigarettes, and shame. He counted nine people: five women, four men. Except for two men he didn't recognize, they were his parishioners. He knew where they sat at Sunday Mass—second pew, third seat; fifth pew, center; and Abe Lewis, always in the last pew.

Julia Walker, thirty years old, mother of five, was finishing her story at the front. No gambling last week, she said, raising a fist into the air. There was a flurry of applause as she threaded her way around the chairs and sat down.

Another woman lumbered to her feet and faced the group. Lucy Cutter, also in her thirties, small and pretty, despite the deep lines of worry cut into her brow.

"My name is Lucy," she said, holding the floor with her eyes. There was a soft vulnerability in her voice. "I'm a gambling addict."

Several people thrust their heads forward, giving the woman their full attention. There was no need for the pretense of anonymity, he was thinking. Everyone here knew everyone else. They could probably tell one another's stories. Or was it that all the stories sounded alike? He used to think his own story at AA meetings was unique. How the thirst would overtake him, almost knock him to his knees when he least expected it. Then he'd heard the other stories and realized they were the same. The thirst was insidious and powerful and universal.

He tried to catch up with what Lucy Cutter was saying: She'd started going to the bingo hall seven years ago; she'd been lucky, got good cards; always won the blackouts. Then somebody at bingo said, "You want some real action?"

She started going to the gambling house in Arapaho. She was shocked. She'd driven by the house a thousand times and had no idea there were craps, poker, and roulette going on day and night. You could show up any time and get action. She'd seen piles of bills won and lost on the throw of the dice.

"God, it was exciting," she said, her voice still low, and hollowed out, as if all the excitement she'd once felt had been drained away. "I felt like I could do anything. I doubled my bets 'cause I was a winner. Then I started losing, and I had to keep doubling so I could win back what I lost. Truth was, it was the rush that kept me goin'. I wanted the rush."

Heads nodded. People looked around, caught one another's eyes a moment. It wasn't the rush he'd looked for in whiskey, Father John was thinking. It was the plug to stop up the loneliness and the courage to live the life he'd chosen.

"Trouble was," the woman was saying, "I had to borrow money to pay off the debt. I borrowed from my mom and sister, 'til they told me 'no more.' Then I started borrowing from a couple guys at the house."

She stopped. For the first time, she lifted her eyes and gazed out across the hall, as if she were watching an invisible movie starring people she used to know. "One night at the house, they said, 'Where's our money, Lucy?' "

She flinched, her gaze still fastened on the rear wall. "They took me out back. It was real cold, and the snow was coming down, and they started hitting me, and then, you know, they threw me on the ground in the snow and they . . ." Her voice trailed off into not much more than a whisper. "They kept doing it for a long time. Afterward, I was throwing up, I remember, in the snow and mud."

Father John walked to the front and put his arm around the woman's shoulder. The experience seemed to cling to her like static. "You're safe here, Lucy," he said.

She was shuddering. "It was five years ago. I quit cold turkey after that. It was hard."

"I know," he said. He'd quit cold turkey—how many times?—before he'd gone into treatment at Grace House.

"I was doing real good 'til the casino opened up."

"We've all backslid."

"I don't wanna borrow no more money, so I said to myself, Lucy, you just gotta quit. It's been three weeks now."

Someone started clapping, then others joined in. There was a scraping noise as chairs were pushed back on the vinyl floor and people got to their feet, clapping harder. Father John led the woman back to her chair.

It was then that he noticed Leonard Bizzel standing next

to the door. Nodding. Nodding. His eyes following Henry Yellowhair to the front.

Father John took his own chair and made himself keep his eyes on Henry. *I'm a gambler. I love to gamble.* Leonard was a private man, Father John was thinking. He never talked about any problems. He had never mentioned gambling.

And yet, Catherine had said that they could use some extra money.

There was another burst of applause, and Father John realized that Henry had sat down and a woman was making her way to the front. He glanced at the door. Leonard was gone.

Father John got up and went outside. In the yellow glow of the overhead lamps, he spotted the caretaker heading toward the truck on the far side of the alley.

"Leonard!" he called, hurrying after him.

The caretaker swung around, then started backing toward the truck. "How's it going, Father?"

"I saw you at the meeting." Father John caught up to the man. "My office is always open if you ever want to come in and talk."

"Nah, nah." Waves of shadows crossed the caretaker's face. "I just come in to see how many people was there, case we needed extra chairs."

"Is that right?" The man was lying, Father John knew. He'd counseled hundreds of people, heard a thousand confessions. He could almost taste the lie. "Anything you and I talk about, Leonard, is confidential."

"Hey, Father." The man clasped his arm. "Don't you worry none about me. I got things under control, you hear? Next week I'll move some chairs outta the hall over to Father George's office. He's got a good crowd for the convert class."

"Remember what I said."

The caretaker flung open the door and slid inside. "See you tomorrow, Father."

FATHER JOHN FOUND his assistant in the kitchen sipping at a mug of coffee and studying the newspaper flattened on the table.

"How'd the gamblers do tonight?" The other priest didn't look up.

Father John poured himself some coffee and took a sip. "They're going to be okay." He hoped that was true. "How about the converts?"

"Eight tonight." Father George turned the page and smoothed it against the others. "Four women and four men, willing to make a nine-month commitment to study Catholicism. Two thousand years of theology and history rolled into nine months."

Father John smiled. He usually taught the convert classes, but they'd flipped a coin, he and George, and he'd gotten the gamblers. It was where he belonged, he guessed.

"Oh, by the way." The other priest shifted and looked up at him. "Herb Straighter called this afternoon."

"Who?"

"President of the bank. Says he found the discrepancy in our deposits."

This was good news. Father John took a long draft of coffee. George could pay the bills tomorrow.

"Wants to talk to you."

"I'll give him a call in the morning."

The other priest shook his head. "He said you'd better come to the bank."

23

THE BANK LOBBY was suffused in a chilly quiet broken by the tap of footsteps on the marble floor and the sound of a phone ringing behind one of the glass-walled cubicles on the left. Across from the cubicles, four or five people were lined up in front of the tellers. Father John stopped at the counter across from a young woman who gave him a sideways glance, then went back to thumbing through a sheaf of papers. She was pretty—tall and willowy with shoulder-length blond hair and long, red nails at the tips of slim fingers, and he had the sense that she was used to men watching her.

"Help you?" She lifted her eyes.

"Father O'Malley to see Herb Straighter."

"Oh, Father!" A faint blush rose in her pale cheeks, the

red nails tapped at the papers. "Herb's waiting in his office." She tossed her blond head toward the door.

Father John made his way across the lobby, past the tellers' line. Through the glass walls of the last cubicle, he could see the muscular man with a large head, gray hair combed across the pate, and half-moon glasses perched on his nose. He leaned back in his chair, holding the phone to his ear.

"I'll have to get back to you later," the bank president said into the mouthpiece. He waved Father John into the cubicle.

"I understand you've located our missing deposits." Father John sat down in a chrome-framed chair, took off his cowboy hat, and hung it over one knee.

"A simple misunderstanding." Straighter dropped the receiver into the cradle and began rummaging through a drawer. He pulled out a file folder, spread it open on the desk, and pushed the glasses into the small of his nose. Peering down, he said, "I have the printouts here of the deposit records this month. Three separate deposits, twenty-two checks, totaling three thousand, six hundred fifty dollars."

"No cash?" There had been about three hundred dollars in the Sunday donations. Father John felt as if he'd swallowed lead. Leonard sometimes delivered the deposits to the bank, and last night, Leonard had been at the Gamblers Anonymous meeting. Dear Lord, what was going on?

Straighter was reading off the dates and the exact amounts of the deposited checks. "It's all right here," he said, thumping the folder. Then he pulled one of the printout sheets free and peered down at it. "All the deposits went to your new account, as you instructed, Father, along with the transfer . . ."

"Wait a minute." Father John put up one hand. "What are you talking about?"

"You also transferred a thousand dollars from your old account to the new, Father."

"There's some mistake," Father John said. "We have only one account." Father George hadn't said anything about opening another account.

Straighter dipped his large head and stared through the half-moon glasses at the printouts. "The longstanding account opened by St. Francis Mission . . ." His gaze crawled down the top page. "Goodness, how many years ago? Ah, here we go. Nineteen seventy-two. And the account opened . . ." The man shuffled the pages. "Four weeks ago," he said, pushing two sheets of paper across the desk. "You opened the second account yourself, Father."

Father John glanced down the first sheet: New Account Form, Valley Bank. Typed in the top line was: St. Francis Mission. John A. O'Malley, S.J. On the signature line, his name was scrawled in black ink. He studied the writing. Much like his own, a careful copy.

He slipped the sheet behind the other. A similar form for additional signatories on the account. Above the signature line was the name: Catherine Bizzel.

He handed the forms across the desk, struggling to believe what he knew was true. "Our housekeeper must have opened the account," he said.

"It's your signature, Father." The banker peered over the glasses.

"No, it isn't."

"Oh, my. We have a serious problem then. Our records show that forty-five hundred dollars has been withdrawn from this account." Straighter picked up the receiver and tapped a couple numbers. "Linda, I want to see you a moment."

The man had barely replaced the receiver when the willowy blond slipped through the door and positioned herself at the corner of the desk.

"You handled this, right?" Straighter thrust the papers into her hand. "Who requested the account?"

"Oh, yes, I remember," she said, glancing from one page to the other. "Ms. Bizzel said the mission wanted a separate account for auxiliary groups. Ladies aid society, AA, Gamblers Anonymous, religious education. Said the pastor"—she nodded toward Father John—"wanted to keep the finances separate from the general finances."

She handed the papers back to Straighter, a smile of satisfaction remaining in her expression a moment. Then, as if she'd sensed the charge in the atmosphere, she pulled her mouth into a thin line. "Is anything wrong?"

"Father O'Malley did not authorize this account." The president kept his gaze on the pages in his hand.

"I don't understand." The woman turned toward Father John. "Ms. Bizzel said you were too busy to come in, so I told her you could sign the form and send it to the bank. Well, she brought it back that very afternoon. Everything looked fine."

"Everything is not fine, Linda." Straighter swiveled sideways and tossed the pages onto the desk. "You know our policy. Father O'Malley should have signed for the new account in person."

"But Ms. Bizzel said the mission needed the account right away and Father O'Malley was too busy to get into town. I mean, it was the mission, Herb, and the signature was Father O'Malley's. We already had a copy of his signature on record."

Straighter directed a long gaze at the woman hovering at the corner of the desk, hands shaking at her side. Finally, he said, "Leave us, Linda. We'll discuss this later."

The woman backed out of the cubicle and hurried past the glass wall, her heels clacking on the marble floor.

Straighter braced his elbows on the desk and blew into clenched hands, his large head bobbing back and forth. "So what do we have here, Father? Embezzlement by one of your employees?" When Father John didn't reply, he said, "We see this from time to time. Some employee finds a way to open a new account, shuffles funds from the original account and puts in new deposits, then makes withdrawals and clears out the funds. Very smooth, until someone catches on."

"I'll talk to Catherine," Father John said. The leaden feeling was spreading inside him. "She's a good woman. Something must have happened." He knew what it was. He tried to imagine the housekeeper in front of a slot machine, pulling the handle, pushing the buttons, eyes locked on the bright, rolling images of promise. Leonard had come to the meeting last night hoping to help his wife.

"I'm sorry, Father. It appears we were lax about the account. Our insurance will cover the loss." Straighter got to his feet. "Of course I'll have to report the embezzlement to the Riverton police."

Police! Father John stood slowly, a sense of unreality swimming around him. He didn't want to think about the gray-haired woman who liked to make pancakes being pulled into the legal system: arrested, jailed, charged with a felony, shuffled through the courts . . .

"Can't we work this out privately?" Father John asked.

Straighter came around the desk and clamped a thick hand on his shoulder. "I wish that were possible, Father," he said, ushering Father John to the door. "You understand, we have to follow bank regulations." The blond woman kept her eyes averted as they passed the counter in the lobby.

Straighter held the front door opened for him. "We'll keep you informed, Father," he said.

FATHER JOHN SAT in the pickup a couple minutes before he turned the key in the ignition. The engine sputtered into life. He backed through a wall of sunshine, then drove out into the light traffic on Federal, his thoughts filled with Catherine and Leonard and the missing money.

She must have taken the cash out of the deposit bags and filled in new deposit slips for the amount of checks. He'd already endorsed the checks. All she had to do was deposit them in the new account. She'd also transferred a thousand dollars out of the original account.

Catherine Bizzel was desperate.

He drove south, then took the right turn into the reservation, the sun hot on his hands gripping the steering wheel. Another mile and he made a left into the mission. Leonard's truck was nowhere in sight, but Catherine's twenty-year-old Ford was parked in front of the residence. He pulled in next to the Ford.

The aroma of fresh bread rolled over him the minute he opened the front door. He followed the aroma down the hallway to the kitchen where Catherine was standing at the sink, her back to him. Water gushed out of the faucet.

"That you, Father?" She glanced over one shoulder, then turned off the faucet and faced him, drying her hands on the white apron tied at her waist. "Give me a few minutes, and I'll have your lunch."

"I just came from the bank, Catherine." Father John motioned the woman to the chair on the other side of the table. Her expression froze, as if the muscles beneath the skin had seized up. Then she groped for the top of the chair and worked her way down into the seat.

He kicked back the chair across from her and sat down. "Tell me what's going on," he said.

"I guess you know."

He nodded. "I don't know why."

There was a scuffle of footsteps behind him, and Father John looked around. Leonard loomed into the doorway, a circle of perspiration on the front of his denim shirt.

"Come in," Father John said to the man.

"No, Leonard!" Catherine screamed. "You go away. I gotta talk to Father John alone. This ain't got nothing to do with you."

Father John clasped his hands on the table and leaned toward the woman. "He's your husband, Catherine. He has a right to know."

"I already know." Leonard strode into the kitchen, pulled over a chair, and sat down, facing his wife. Perspiration glistened on his cheekbones; his black hair looked wet. "This gambling you're doin' has gotten out of hand. I seen our savings account. It's cleared out, Catherine. All that money we been putting aside."

The woman dropped her head into her hands. Her sobs, when they came, were low and muffled, her shoulders shook against the back of the chair. After a moment, she steepled her hands under her nose. She might have been praying. "I borrowed some money from the mission," she said, her voice as small as a child's.

"You what?" There was a bark of incredulity in her husband's voice.

"They said they was gonna take it outta you, Leonard. I got scared. I didn't know what they'd do."

"Hold on." Leonard took his wife's hands and cushioned them in both of his. "You're not making sense. What're you talking about?"

"The night I lost at craps. I was winning, Leonard," she

said, warming to the topic. "I was winning big. We was gonna retire, go live in Denver by the kids. Then, all of a sudden, my chips was swept away. This white man—he looked real nice—comes up to me and says, 'You were on a roll.' Boy, was he right. 'You can get lucky again.' I thought, that's also right. Sometimes my luck went away, but it always came back. So he says, 'We can stake you.' He handed me a couple hundred."

"Oh, God, Catherine. You took money from a loan shark?" Leonard let go of his wife's hands, straightened himself against the chair, and stared up at the ceiling.

"I didn't know he was one of them loan sharks. I never seen him before."

"Well, what did you think?" Leonard was shouting now. "Some nice guy trying to help you out?"

"Let her finish, Leonard." Father John kept his own voice calm.

Even before the woman had cleared her throat and begun talking, he knew how it would go: She'd lost the money, then borrowed more. She'd lost that. The loan sharks had demanded payment with so much interest she could never pay it back. She'd cleared out the savings account, taken money from the mission.

"They kept coming around," she said. "I got scared."

"God, Catherine! Why didn't you tell me? Some white men threatening you, and you didn't tell me? I would've taken care of 'em."

The woman was crying softly, blowing her nose into the tissue she'd pulled out of her apron pocket, wiping at her eyes. "It was my problem, Leonard. I figured I'd borrow from the mission and pay it back, just as soon as . . ."

"You kept on gambling!" Leonard said.

Catherine blew her nose and looked down at the table. "How else was I gonna pay everything off?"

Leonard exchanged a glance with Father John, then looked back at his wife. "It was the deposits wasn't it? You said you'd run the deposits over to the bank so I could finish my work around here. You helped yourself to the cash."

Silence settled over the kitchen. Outside the window, a bird was chirping. When Catherine looked up, there was so much pain in the woman's eyes that Father John had to force himself not to turn away. He said, "You'd better tell him the rest."

Slowly, in a monotone voice, as if she were talking about someone she didn't know, Catherine explained about opening the account and making the withdrawals.

Leonard went as quiet as stone, the circle of perspiration widening on the front of his shirt.

When Catherine finished, Father John told them the bank was going to report the embezzlement. "You have to talk to a lawyer," he said to Catherine. "Vicky'll help you."

The woman reached over and placed a hand on her husband's. "You don't have to stay by me, Leonard. What I done was wrong. I turned into some old Indian woman I didn't know."

"Well, you're my old Indian woman." Leonard took his wife's arm and helped her to her feet. "We're gonna stick together, Catherine."

Father John got to his feet and followed the couple down the hallway and out onto the stoop. He watched Leonard help his wife into his brown truck with trimmed branches sticking out of the back. Watched the truck slow around Circle Drive and gather speed before turning onto Seventeen-Mile Road and disappearing behind the stand of cottonwoods.

Then he walked over to the administration building, the sun searing his back through his shirt, the wind washing over him. He found Father George in the back office, staring at the computer monitor. He dragged over a chair, straddled it backwards, and set both arms over the top.

"The bank mystery's solved," he said.

That got the priest's attention, and when Father George looked up over the monitor, he told him about Catherine and the loan sharks.

The man shook his head. "Only thing I know about loan sharks, I learned in the movies. Don't think I'd want to cross them. Those guys shoot people in the head and bury them in the desert."

"What?"

"I said . . ."

"I heard you." Father John jumped to his feet. He hadn't understood. It had been right in front of him, and he hadn't understood . . .

Until now.

He swung the chair back under the window and headed for the corridor. "I'll be back in an hour or so," he called over his shoulder.

24

VICKY STARED AT the list of Arapaho names. It read like a Who's Who of casino operations: human resources, hotel, restaurant, buffet, maintenance, security. Only one, Dennis Light Stone, pit boss, worked on the casino floor. A total of thirteen, and every one connected to Matt Kingdom.

She could hear Kingdom's voice in her head: He knew everybody on the rez; he'd recommended the best people for the job, and they were getting training; he'd wanted the casino to succeed.

And the casino was successful. There were jobs, an influx of cash to the tribe, plans to build the first hospital on the rez, an infusion of money for schools. She slipped the roster of names into a Manila envelope and closed the clasp. Her fingers felt like ice. Everything about the casino was working just as the tribe had hoped. Nobody on the

Business Council would want to hear about conflicts of interest and the appearance of impropriety.

The sound of the telephone ringing jarred her out of her thoughts. She waited for Esther to pick up, then remembered that, thirty minutes ago, the secretary had stuck her head between the doors and said she was leaving for the day.

She lifted the receiver. "Vicky Holden," she said.

"I've found the information you want." It was Myrna Hancock at the Secretary of State's Office.

Vicky pulled a yellow legal pad across the desk. "What do you have?"

The woman at the other end of the line started rattling off the legal minutiae of Lodestar Enterprises. Chartered in Delaware, nineteen ninety-six. The usual list of officers: president, vice president, treasurer, secretary. Vicky didn't recognize any of the names.

"What about Stan Lexson?"

"Vice president in charge of casino operations," Myrna said. "He's managed the company's casinos in the Midwest."

"Do you have any idea who owns the company?"

There was a pause, a crackle of papers at the other end. "I can tell you what I've heard," Myrna said finally. "The Hastings Group, an umbrella company that owns fourteen smaller companies, all related to the entertainment industry." She started reading off a list of unfamiliar names: Adolphis, Edgeware, Mariette, Jevron, Omega . . .

"Edgeware!" Vicky felt as if she'd gotten a jolt from a raw electric wire. "Did you say Edgeware?" She balanced the phone under her chin and turned to the computer. Click. Click. The file of casino contracts came onto the monitor. She scrawled down, finally stopping on a page with black letters typed across the top: "Contract between Lodestar Enterprises and Edgeware Supplies."

"You know the company?" A hint of disbelief came into Myrna's voice.

"Give me the names again."

The other woman started over with about as much enthusiasm as if she were reciting the alphabet. Vicky stopped her two more times—at the names of Jevron and Omega. She pulled up two other contracts. Jevron supplied the hotel linens and sundries, soaps, lotions, shampoos. Omega supplied the kitchen equipment.

"Who owns the Hastings Group?"

There was another crackle of papers at the other end. "We've heard rumors that Mickey Vontego is the majority owner. Listen, Vicky, we went up the chain of command to Vontego himself after the Arapaho Business Council informed us they were bringing in Lodestar. We wanted to know what kind of people would be moving into the state. Everybody checked out. No criminal records, no reason for concern. Nothing but years of experience running casinos from Las Vegas to Atlantic City to the Bahamas. Vontego was the only one . . ." She hesitated.

"What, Myrna?"

"Came under suspicion about ten years ago. The Nevada gaming authorities took his license for some minor infraction of the rules, but he disputed the allegation and the license was reinstated."

Vicky was quiet, trying to arrange this new information into some kind of pattern. Suppose the casino were overpaying for equipment and supplies? Cutting into the tribal profits by enriching the Hastings Group? There was no way to know, not without access to casino accounting records.

Accounting. She flipped through the pages of résumés and slipped out the résumé for the accounting manager. Kevin Newman, seven years experience at Indian casinos in Michigan.

Vicky realized she hadn't said anything for several moments when Myrna said: "You promised to keep me informed, Vicky. Well? What have you found?"

"I'm not sure yet," Vicky managed. God, she was still circling the same problem: Matt Kingdom's control of the jobs. How could she bring her concerns to the state if she didn't first go to the Business Council? Her people would never forgive her. She'd have to move back to Denver, because no Arapaho would ever trust her.

"Listen, Myrna, I appreciate the information."

"There's somebody else you might want to talk to," Myrna said hurriedly, as if she sensed the call was about to end. "Alan Peterson works for the Indian Gaming Commission. Trust me, Vicky, the man knows every casino scam anybody ever thought about. If you think Great Plains has a problem, give Alan a call." She gave a telephone number, which Vicky scribbled on the legal pad.

"Don't forget, Vicky," Myrna said. "You promised to keep the state informed."

Vicky said she'd get back as soon as she had anything definite. Then she pressed the end button and dialed the number.

She'd expected to have to work through a maze of secretaries, but a man answered on the second ring. "Alan Peterson here."

Vicky introduced herself and said she was a lawyer with Great Plains Casino.

"Just a moment." The voice was formal, constrained. "Yes, I have the file on Great Plains. Arapaho casino on the Wind River Reservation, correct?"

Vicky said that was correct. "I'm concerned," she began, choosing the words carefully, "about the company operating the casino. Lodestar Enterprises."

"Lodestar." The name hung on the line a moment. "Stan

Lexson at the helm, I believe. What can I tell you, except the company's been around seven, eight years, running profitable casinos in . . ." He paused. "Mississippi, Michigan, Wisconsin."

Vicky told him what Myrna said about the umbrella company, the Hastings Group, and the fact that the majority owner, Mickey Vontego, had lost his gaming license in Nevada ten years ago.

"I'm sure you also know the license was reinstated. Mr. Vontego was accused of associating with unsavory characters." A little laugh, like a cough, burst through the line. "Hard to work in the gaming business in Las Vegas without associating with unsavory characters. In any case, Mr. Vontego proved the accusations were false. Let me say this, Ms. Holden, we've never found reason to believe that Hastings or Lodestar Enterprises were anything but legitimate companies."

"You've investigated them?"

Another laugh erupted at the other end. "We have four auditors, Ms. Holden, and fifteen full-time investigators. Oh, and did I mention that there are more than three hundred Indian gaming operations in twenty-nine states? To answer your question, no, we haven't investigated Hastings or Lodestar. Even if we got a complaint, it would be several years before we could look into it."

Vicky was jotting notes as fast as she could, but she felt as if the pen were moving in slow motion. What the gaming commissioner was saying was that Indian gaming was wide open, except for tribal or state regulations. She said, "Suppose a management company wanted to cheat the tribe?"

"Are you making a complaint?"

"No," she said quickly. Complaint? She had nothing but a hunch, a half-formed theory. "I want to make sure there aren't any infractions of regulations here."

"Cheat the tribe, you say?" Vicky could imagine the man pushing back in a chair and staring out a window across a landscape of concrete and steel. "I see here that Lodestar Enterprises loaned eighteen million to the Arapaho tribe to build the operation. Any company with that kind of money out is going to make certain the tribe gets enough profits to repay the loan. Profits beyond that could be up for grabs."

"What are you saying? The company might skim off money in the cage without the tribe's knowledge?" Vicky held her pen in midair over the tablet. Was this what Kingdom had been paid to overlook?

"Not easily," Peterson said. "There are videos surveying the cage, documenting the counting. Clever managers have more subtle ways of making sure a large percentage of the profits goes to the company. Placing ghost employees on the payroll, for example. Or purchasing supplies at inflated prices from friendly companies that give them a kickback. And you heard of the fill?"

Vicky jotted down the word and drew a sharp line underneath. She'd never heard of the fill until yesterday. "You mean," she said, "chips brought to a table?"

"Let's say," the man hurried on, "that the dealer needs one thousand dollars worth of chips. He signs a slip for ten thousand. Of course, three other people have to sign the slip. Security guard, cashier, pit boss. A thousand dollars is delivered to the table, and nine thousand goes to the company. Multiply that by several tables, it adds up to a nice evening's take."

"But that requires cooperation from a lot of people." Vicky heard the incredulity in her voice.

"Exactly," Peterson said. "The name of the game is having the right people in the right places, people you can trust."

Vicky thanked the man and set the receiver in the cradle. She stared at it for a long time. People you can trust, he'd said, and that's what Matt Kingdom had delivered. The Arapaho managers were working side by side with Lexson's own people, those he'd trusted for years. Dennis Light Stone, the pit boss who signed for the fill, along with the dealers and the cage manager—all Lexson's people.

Adam was right. Stan Lexson ran a cozy, tight operation.

"Where do you stand, Adam?" she said out loud, as if the man were in the office, a sense of sadness and regret and lost possibilities radiating back at her.

It was a long moment before she could bring herself to lift the receiver and dial the local FBI office. The answering machine came on, Gianelli's voice delivering the usual instructions.

After the beep, she gave her name and said she had to talk to him about operations at the casino. She'd be waiting at her office, she said.

25

TWO-VALLEY ROAD angled west out of Riverton, a strip of asphalt laid through the scrub brush and stunted pines. The music of Tosca rose over the wind and the thrum of the tires. Father John guessed he'd come about two miles from town. He'd grown accustomed to judging the distances by the landmarks: the streams and bluffs, the shadows, the blue intensity of the mountains in the distance, the same way the Arapahos had once navigated the vastness of the plains.

The *Gazette* had said that Rodney Pearson lived two miles outside of Riverton. The house, cabin, trailer—whatever it was that Pearson had called home—should be coming up. Father John let up on the accelerator and scanned both sides of the road. No sign of any dwelling.

He'd gone another half-mile, when he spotted the trailer

almost lost in the grove of cottonwoods on the right. He turned into the driveway and stopped behind a pickup truck with cardboard cartons stacked in the bed. The door to the trailer stood open. Inside, it looked as if everything had been cleared out.

By the time he snapped off the tape player and got out, Mo Pearson was standing in the doorway, her light hair held back with a scarf that fluttered in her face.

"What d'ya want?" she called, pushing away the scarf.

"I'd like to talk to you, Mo," he said, crossing the graveled yard.

"You found the Indians that killed Rodney?" She stepped outside and pulled the door shut behind her. There was a sense of futility about the place, as if, at any moment, the trailer might shift off the cement blocks and sink into the earth.

He said, "I think we both know your husband wasn't killed by any Indians."

"I don't know what you're talking about." The woman's hands were trembling. She jammed them into the front pockets of her blue jeans. "Those Indians out on the well were all the time giving Rodney shit . . ."

Father John cut in. "So you told me. You forgot to tell me about Rodney's gambling."

She flinched. The wind whined around the side of the trailer and whipped the scarf across her face.

"How much did he lose?"

Mo Pearson brushed the scarf back and sank down alongside the door, a slow folding together of her legs and arms and shoulders. Father John reached out to steady her as she dropped onto the step. Her breath was coming in quick, hard gasps.

"So Rodney left some cash at the tables," she said after a moment. "So what?"

Father John crouched down beside her. The shadows of the cottonwoods flitted across the woman's face. "Did Rodney lose the trailer? Is that why you're moving?"

"You don't get it, do you?" She glared at him. "You come around here like you got everything all figured out, and you don't know shit."

"Why don't you tell me?"

The woman looked away. He could see the moisture glistening in her eyes. "Yeah, Rodney lost the trailer. And the two acres we scraped and saved to buy so we could build ourselves a real nice house someday and live like decent people with kids and a couple horses, instead of white trash drinking and fighting all the time. We was gonna change all that." She was crying now, the tears running down her cheeks. She made no effort to wipe them away.

"I'm sorry." He gave her a moment, then he said, "Tell me about the loan sharks, Mo."

The woman slid her eyes toward him and started laughing. Laughing and crying at the same time. Finally, she said, "I guess I underestimated you, Father O'Malley."

"How did Rodney get involved with them?"

He could see the argument playing out in her eyes. A couple of seconds passed before she said, "They come up to him in the casino parking lot after he lost his paycheck. Lost two or three paychecks, for all I know. You need some cash? they said. Goddamn fool, Rodney. Always gonna make the big pot. Win so damn much money, we was gonna be floating in it. So he borrowed a couple thousand off 'em, like they was his best friends. Pretty soon, they started calling here. Called all night long. Gotta have payment, Rodney, they said. Don't wanna have to crush your fingers, Rodney."

The woman squeezed her eyes shut. "They said, we can fix it so you won't be good for nobody, Rodney, especially not your wife, you understand? So he sold his truck and give 'em the money. That kept 'em happy for about a week. Then he sold the acres with the trailer, but they said he owed more. All a sudden, he owes 'em nine thousand, and there's no way . . ."

Mo Pearson tipped her head back into the door and sobbed out loud a moment. Finally, she said, "They shot him like a dog out at Double Dives. They give me a week to come up with the nine thousand. I ain't never seen that much money. They said they could make an arrangement, that's what they called it. They said they got places where I can work it off."

"Who are they?"

"How do I know?" She rolled her head against the door. "Voices on the phone. I don't wanna die."

"They threatened to kill you?"

She let out a shout of laughter. "They know that I know they shot Rodney. All I gotta do is tell the fed how Rodney borrowed money off guys in the casino parking lot, and they're gonna do me like they did him."

"So you tried to convince Rodney's killers that you didn't know the truth. You told Agent Gianelli that Arapahos on the drilling site had shot your husband. You told his friends, and you gave me the same story." Father John tried to swallow back his impatience. There was no logic to it, no sense, except . . .

The woman was scared to death. You could never account for what people might do when they were scared.

"I gotta get out of here." Mo Pearson started rising along the door.

"Listen, Mo." Father John got to his feet beside her. "You have to tell the fed about the loan sharks."

She stared at him out of eyes wide with disbelief. "You crazy?"

"He can protect you."

"How's he gonna protect me? Nobody knows who those guys are 'til they come at you out of the dark."

"They'll find you, Mo. The fed's your only chance."

For the first time, she raised her hands and wiped away the moisture on her cheeks. Then she glared at him. "What do you know about it? I'll just bet you come from a fancy home. Nice mamma and daddy that didn't knock you around. Nice fancy school and a big education, but you don't know shit about me and Rodney and where we come from. We come from dirt, Father O'Malley. The fed might come runnin' to protect your kind, but me and Rodney? He don't see us. He don't know we exist, 'cause we're nobody. Well, Rodney's dead, and I'll be damned if I'm gonna end up the same way. I gotta take care of myself. That's the way it is where me and Rodney come from. So back off. It ain't your business."

She kept her eyes on his a moment, then ducked past and walked around the front of the brown pickup. There was fury and determination in the way she opened the door and threw herself inside, as if she dared him to stop her.

He watched the back end of the pickup bounce over the ruts as she drove down the driveway. She turned left, tires squealing, a gray plume of exhaust shooting out of the tailpipe. The exhaust still hung over the road after the pickup had rounded the bend out of sight.

FATHER JOHN PRESSED the cell phone hard against his ear with one hand and guided the pickup back along Two-Valley Road. There was a faint crackle of static. He'd already lost the connection three times. And then the answering machine came on. "You've reached the local offices of the FBI . . ."

He hit the end button. Mo Pearson could be on the highway—heading who knew where?—before he got ahold of Gianelli. Wyoming was a big state with vast, open spaces and networks of dirt roads that dumped into dried streams and cottonwood groves and meandered over mountains. The woman could get lost, if that's what she wanted. Except that—he felt chilled with the certainty—whoever had killed her husband would find her.

Father John guided the pickup through a curve and punched in the number of the BIA police. When the operator answered, he told her about Mo Pearson, a woman in a brown truck, trying to outrun her husband's killers. "Somebody has to stop her. BIA, state patrol, sheriff. Agent Gianelli's going to want to talk to her."

"Take it easy, Father," the woman said. "We'll notify the other departments. Looks like we got another homicide on the rez. Some kids found another body out at Double Dives. Chief Banner and Agent Gianelli are out there now."

26

THE ASSORTMENT OF police vehicles in the cottonwoods at the river looked like refuge tossed about in a flood. Father John drove down the steep dirt road off the bluff and stopped behind Gianelli's white Blazer. About fifty feet away, wedged between a couple of thick trees, was a brown truck. Someone was slumped over the steering wheel.

Father John lifted himself out of the pickup. The lapping sounds of the river mingled with the subdued voices of the officers milling about and the name, Dennis Light Stone, playing like a drumroll in his head. Missing five days, and now this . . .

"Who is it?" Father John asked Gianelli who was coming toward him. He could feel his muscles tense, waiting for the reply.

"Looks like Captain Jack Monroe put a bullet through his right temple."

"What?" Father John walked past the agent toward the truck, trying to absorb the reality. In his mind was the image of Captain Jack Monroe, square-shouldered behind his desk, a commander planning the next battle in the mission to close down the casino.

"You ever meet the man?" Gianelli fell into step alongside him.

"He arranged for me to pay him a visit out at his headquarters yesterday."

"Why the hell didn't you tell me?"

"Check your answering service, Ted."

Gianelli stopped behind the truck. "What else do you have to tell me?"

"Let me say a few prayers first."

The photographer was leaning into the cab, sending white flashes of light over the body. When he stepped back, Father John moved in close. Monroe's chin rested against the far side of the steering wheel, his eyes wide and fixed on something beyond the windshield, mouth opened as if he'd died in the midst of a scream. His right hand flopped a couple inches from the black revolver on the passenger seat.

Father John reached through the opened window and made the sign of the cross over the body, praying silently. May God have mercy on your soul. Forgive you your sins. Take you to everlasting life. The old prayers that usually brought his own soul a moment of comfort, but now he felt only a jarring sense of unreality, as if he'd wandered into a world of chaos where there was no logic, no patterns that made sense.

When he'd finished the prayers, he nodded across the

truck toward the photographer and two police officers, then walked back to the fed. "Monroe wasn't the type to commit suicide," he said. "He had a mission, something he believed in . . ."

"Mission ended this morning," Gianelli cut in. "The tribal judge issued a restraining order that prohibits Monroe and anybody working for him from trespassing on casino property. The man was also looking at a charge of conspiracy to commit assault. He was losing control, John. Maybe he snapped. People can snap, you know, things stop going their way."

Blue-uniformed officers were moving through the trees, pushing aside the brush, checking the ground. The photographer kept the camera pressed to one eye; white lights flashed through the shadows. A couple of plainclothes men from the coroner's office, Father John guessed—were spreading a gray plastic body bag on the ground.

Maybe Gianelli was right, Father John thought. Maybe Monroe had given up.

He didn't believe it. He couldn't reconcile the image of Captain Jack Monroe with the idea of the man holding a gun to his head and pulling the trigger.

Father John looked back at the agent. "There's something else," he said, and he told him about Rodney Pearson and the loan sharks.

"Loan sharks!" Gianelli stood with both hands jammed into the pockets of his tan slacks, the fronts of his blue blazer pulled back. He squinted into the sun. "Mo Pearson told me they sold their property so they could move out of the area. Said Rodney wanted to put as much distance between himself and the Indians as possible."

"She's scared, Ted. She's been covering up the truth, hoping whoever killed her husband would think she didn't know what was going on. She packed up her truck and drove off about an hour ago."

Gianelli turned, walked over to the Blazer and, leaning through the opened window, grabbed a radio. There was a scatter of static, a high-pitched whine. Holding the radio close to his mouth, he told somebody—probably the state patrol—to locate a woman named Mo Pearson, driving a truck . . . He glanced at Father John.

"Chevrolet. Brown."

The agent repeated the information. "She could be sixty miles outside of Riverton in any direction," he said, then set the radio into place below the dashboard. "She ID the loan sharks?" he asked, turning back.

Father John shook his head. "They approached her husband in the casino parking lot."

Neither spoke for a moment, Father John could almost see the propositions clicking together in the other man's mind, rolling toward a logical conclusion. Monroe's men stopped people in the casino parking lot. The loan sharks stopped people in the parking lot. Ergo . . .

"Maybe Captain Jack decided to work both sides of the fence." Gianelli kept his gaze on the riverbank littered with whiskey bottles and beer cans. "Maybe the Captain started loaning people money, making it hurt enough to teach them a lesson, and making himself a nice little profit on the side. Clever." He shook his head, as if the criminal mind never failed to surprise him. "Some guys, if they decided to go straight, could run General Motors."

"Then why shoot himself?"

The agent was working his jaw back and forth, as if he were forming the words to a new and unfamiliar idea. "Maybe the Captain's rangers decided to take over the business."

That was possible, Father John thought. Lela Running Bull believed her boyfriend capable of murder.

He let a moment pass before he said, "Pearson wasn't the only one mixed up with loan sharks."

This got Gianelli's full attention, and Father John told him about Catherine Bizzel and how she'd embezzled money.

The agent walked a few steps away, then swung back. "I knew we'd have nothing but trouble soon as gambling got here. Pearson did business with loan sharks and ended up shot in the head. Now a little old lady like Catherine Bizzel is doing business with loan sharks. What next?"

He took a step closer. White spots of anger flashed in the man's eyes. "Names, John. I need names. Catherine has to talk to me."

"She wants to talk to Vicky first."

"Ah. Vicky." Gianelli jammed his hands back into his pockets. "I see. Catherine Bizzel's committed embezzlement and fraud at a Riverton bank, and Vicky's going to suggest a deal. Catherine will cooperate in a homicide investigation and the district attorney won't press charges."

"You're pretty good, Ted."

"You and Vicky come up with this strategy?"

"I haven't talked to Vicky."

"What's the difference? You two don't need to talk. You communicate telepathically, or some such thing. You think the same."

"Catherine's a good woman, Ted. She deserves another chance."

"Maybe so. Doesn't mean you and Vicky can't be a pain in the neck."

27

IT HAD BEEN more than an hour since Vicky had left the message on Gianelli's answering machine. Most of that time she'd spent at the copying machine in the outer office, making duplicates of the notes she'd scribbled while talking to Myrna Hancock and Alan Peterson, the list she'd compiled of the supply and equipment companies owned by Lodestar's umbrella company and a man named Mickey Vontego, and the résumés of Kingdom's managers. She'd slipped the copies into a file folder, which she set on a stack of papers at the edge of her desk. The originals went into another folder, the one she intended to give to Gianelli. She wrote Casino on a Post-It note and slapped it on top. Fifteen minutes ago, she'd left another message with Gianelli before she started rereading the pages in the folder.

The knock at the front door, intruding as it did into the

quiet, made her jump. She took a couple of breaths, then walked through the office, opened the door, and froze. She'd assumed it would be Gianelli. Instead, she was facing a white man in a light-blue shirt and trousers who looked like a bear, with a massive head above the rounded shoulders and thick chest and a belly that strained against his black belt. It was Felix Slodin, the pit boss that Lexson had brought from Mississippi to back up Dennis Light Stone.

"What is it?" She pulled the door closed beside her.

"Vicky Holden? Mr. Lexson'd like to talk to you."

"Tell him I'll be at the casino tomorrow." Tomorrow, she was thinking, she would call Lexson and resign. Then she would take the information she'd compiled for Gianelli to the Business Council.

"Why not invite Felix in?" From behind, a man's voice, easygoing and polite.

Vicky swung around.

Neil Barrenger, operations officer at the casino, stood in front of her desk, gray head tilted sideways, eyes peering at her through wire-rimmed glasses, as if he were about to deliver a report at a meeting of employees. A hint of irony played at the corners of his thin mouth. He gave her a friendly smile, but the determination, the falseness underneath, sent a cold spasm through her.

"What do you want?" she asked. The edge of the door hit her as the other man stepped inside. He kicked the door shut behind him.

"As Felix said, Vicky, Stan's called a meeting. He's sent us to bring you to the casino."

"I'm waiting for Ted Gianelli," Vicky said. "Maybe you know him? The FBI agent? I thought he was at the door."

There was an almost imperceptible exchange of glances between the two men before Barrenger said, "Stan would appreciate your bringing the diskette of the contracts and the personnel records you stole."

Vicky walked back to her desk, conscious of the men closing in behind. She pushed a computer key, popped out the diskette and handed it to Barrenger.

"Tell Stan Lexson I resign," she said.

The other man, Felix, peered around his boss's shoulder. They studied the diskette a moment, Barrenger turning it over in his hand as if the square of plastic and metal might divulge its contents. "Personnel records?" Barrenger said.

Vicky picked up the file folder she'd intended for Gianelli and, sliding off the Post-It note, handed it across the desk.

The man smiled. "I'm sorry, but your resignation's unacceptable," he said. "The van's in back. Stan doesn't like to be kept waiting."

"I'm not going anywhere."

"We can make this easy, or we can make it hard. Your choice." Felix started around the desk, like a panther stalking her, a glint of anticipation in his eyes. He would prefer the hard way, she thought. And yet, it was the relaxed, gray-haired man a couple of feet away—holding the file folder and diskette, headed tilted to the side—who made her shudder. Behind the careful control, she could sense the cold, implacable will.

"Lead the way," she heard herself saying.

Barrenger nodded her into the kitchen.

As Vicky reached down to open the lower desk drawer, Felix grabbed her arm. "I want my bag," she said.

He stepped back. Vicky lifted out her black bag with one hand and, with the other, slid the Post-It note onto the desk blotter. Edging past the desk, she could see the black letters she'd scribbled earlier: Casino.

She followed Barrenger out the back door, across the

yard, and through the gate to the alley, the other man behind her, so close that when she stopped at the white van, she felt his hand jab the small of her back pushing her forward. She grabbed the door handle to steady herself. He stayed close, his shirt scratchy against her arm, his breath sour over her, as Barrenger slid open the side door. Felix gripped her arm and pushed her into the backseat.

She scrambled into a sitting position and moved into the far corner. Barrenger crawled in beside her, Felix got in behind the steering wheel. He swore at the engine that spurted and died before finally turning over. The van jumped forward, swerved past the link fence, and headed down the alley.

"I can't tell you how sorry we are that things didn't work out," Barrenger said. He stretched his arm over the back of the seat and let the tips of his fingers brush her shoulder. "We had high hopes for a long and mutually beneficial relationship."

"Don't touch me," Vicky said.

He gave a little laugh and lifted his fingers. They came out of the alley and turned onto the street. Rows of bungalows passed outside the windows, firs and spruce fluttering in the breeze. A kid pedaled a bicycle down the sidewalk.

They were heading north on Main Street now, flowing with the sedans and pickups. Nothing unusual, nothing out of the ordinary. Vicky stared out the window, searching for a familiar face—anyone she might wave to—among the people walking past the storefronts. No one she knew. No one who might say later—*later!* When would that be?—"I saw Vicky Holden in the backseat of a white van. The driver, a big-headed guy. The man in back, light, curly hair. Just happened to get the license . . . "

There was the sound of a cry, and Vicky realized it had come from her. She was alone. She might have been a spirit moving through town, invisible.

The van was speeding north on Highway 287 now, the pit boss drumming a pudgy fist against the steering wheel to the jazz music blaring from the radio. A line of RVs snaked ahead, and, from time to time, Felix swung out and passed two or three before darting back into the lane ahead of an oncoming truck or sedan.

Ahead, the neon sign blinked against the blue sky, the giant-sized Indian warrior standing guard over the highway, the dice fluttering at his side. Felix turned beneath the sign and headed toward the casino entrance.

And kept going. Past the curved glass doors, around the north side of the hotel and the service trucks parked in the back. He pulled in a few feet from a door that blended into the stucco walls, the same dusty color, no knobs or hinges. He jumped out and knocked on the door.

Barrenger had already gotten out on his side. "Get out," he barked, allowing the gentle, polite mask to slip and revealing, for the first time, the cold steel underneath.

Vicky gripped her bag and stepped out into the heat radiating off the asphalt and the stucco building. She glanced around. There was no one about, no drivers in the trucks, no maintenance crews heading toward the Dumpsters at the far edge of the lot. But six or seven floors above, a man in a white shirt that billowed in the wind was leaning over the balcony.

"Help! Help!" Vicky shouted. The words scraped at her throat, but she was shouting into the wind. The man looked off into the distance, and Barrenger's slim fingers dug into her arm, pulling her through the door and into a narrow corridor. The door slammed behind them. Streaks of white light from the fluorescent bulbs overhead ran down the beige walls and across the green tiled floor. Except for the scuff of their footsteps, it was silent.

Vicky tried to figure out where they were: The outside

door was almost in the center of the building, on the east side, which meant the corridor ran parallel to the restaurant.

Barrenger was still gripping her arm, his fingers digging into her flesh, hurrying her down the corridor. She jerked herself free. "Video cameras are recording us," she said.

"No cameras in the hallways." Felix let out a loud guffaw from behind. "Just you in this here hall and two big, bad men."

Barrenger stopped at the metal staircase and waved Felix ahead, then Vicky. She started climbing, conscious of Barrenger close behind, the scrape of their heels on the steps echoing around the concrete walls.

At the top was another door similar to the one outside: flush with the wall, painted the same beige color, no molding or hardware. Barrenger's fist reached past and gave the door three short raps. It swung inward.

They came out into the corridor on the second floor: elevator on the left, offices on the right. First, the legal office. She winced as they passed the closed door. At the far end, behind the double wood-paneled doors, was Stan Lexson's office.

And that's where they were heading—marching, Vicky thought, shoulder to shoulder. She, wedged between the two men, their footsteps muffled now in the plush blue and red carpet. It was past quitting time for Adam and the accountants and bookkeepers and secretaries who worked behind the closed doors. The floor was deserted.

Barrenger burst ahead and pushed through the double doors. They crossed the reception area, past the desk on the right, and stopped at the door with tipis and drums carved into the wood panels. He knocked, then opened the door and slid one shoulder past the edge. "We have her," he said.

28

"COME IN." IT was Stan Lexson's voice, bored and disinterested.

Barrenger went first, taking his time crossing the office to the man seated at the desk. The curved wall of glass behind the desk shimmered in the fluorescent lights. The operations chief laid the diskette and file folder down in front of his boss, then leaned over and whispered something in his ear.

A couple seconds passed before Lexson waved the other man aside and got to his feet. He walked around the desk and leaned against the edge, stretching out his long legs, crossing them at the ankles. "Good of you to come," he said.

"What's this all about?" Vicky tried to keep the panic out of her voice.

"They were gentlemen, I assume." Lexson glanced from Felix to Barrenger. "Leave us," he said.

"If you need anything . . ." Barrenger began.

"Just get out."

Lexson waited until the two men had filed past and closed the door, then he motioned Vicky toward one of the upholstered chairs around the glass table in front of the desk. "Make yourself comfortable," he said. "I apologize if my men made you uneasy. I'm afraid they sometimes get carried away with their duties. May I get you something to drink? Coffee, tea, whiskey?"

There was the slightest tinge of a smirk as he spoke, and Vicky realized that she was supposed to have been uneasy. Barrenger and Felix were supposed to have gotten carried away.

"What's this about?" She dropped onto a chair and let her bag slide to the floor.

"Two years ago," Lexson set his hands gripping the edge of the desk and leaned toward her, "Lodestar Enterprises entered into a contract with the Arapaho Business Council. For our part, we were to loan the tribe eighteen million dollars to build the casino property. A lot of money, wouldn't you agree? We would operate the casino and hotel for the tribe because, well, because, we know how to run casinos and hotels and Indian tribes don't. We've been operating casinos for a long time. Bahamas, Las Vegas, Atlantic City. You understand what I'm trying to tell you? It's in our own interest to see that the Arapahos make a lot of money."

He paused and braced himself against the desk. "We thought you'd make a nice addition to our team. You'd want the tribe to pay off the debt. Instead you started asking questions, looking into matters that were none of your business, which could make people think we're not doing our job. Maybe we're cheating on our partner."

"Are you?"

Lexson lifted his chin and laughed. Then he cleared his throat. "What did you hope to find in the human resources records? The secretary knew within five minutes that the computer had been violated."

Vicky got to her feet and walked over to the glass wall. The floor below was crowded with tourists in shorts and T-shirts milling about, clustering around the slots. She moved along the window until she was directly above the tables. Knots of people sat hunched at the blackjack tables. Someone had won at craps, judging by the crowd pressing around.

She turned back to the man who had shifted sideways against the desk. This was an interrogation, she realized, which meant that Lexson didn't know how much she'd put together. All he had were suspicions—hunches—which, he hoped she would confirm. He was looking for information.

Think, Vicky. She could almost hear her grandmother's voice, as if grandmother were standing behind her. *Think, before you speak. Words have power.*

She said, "There's a rumor on the rez that Matt Kingdom has placed his relatives in good jobs. I wanted to see if there was any truth to the rumor. The casino could be open for civil lawsuits. As a legal counsel, I'd have the duty to warn you."

"So? Are you going to warn me?"

"There doesn't seem to be enough evidence."

"I see." The look in Lexson's eyes was as hard as stone. "Why were you checking on our suppliers?"

Vicky tried not to blink; she made her face unreadable.

Lexson smiled. "You have a friend in the Secretary of State's Office, a Myrna Hancock, I believe. We also have friends there. We make it a point to cultivate friends in high offices everywhere we do business."

"As a legal counsel . . ."

"Yes, yes. You were exercising due diligence . . ."

"To make sure the companies the casino does business with are legitimate."

"And what did you find out?"

"They appear to be legitimate."

"So your worries are allayed. You can go back to reviewing contracts without having to worry about all these extraneous matters." He shook his head and pushed himself to his feet. "You're very clever, Vicky. Adam said you were clever, and he was right."

Vicky felt her stomach heave at the mention of Adam. How could he not be suspicious? How could he not question the hiring of unqualified people like Kingdom's sister? Wonder about the companies that supplied everything to the casino? What kind of deal had Adam made with Lexson?

The man leaned over her chair, his face so close she could smell the sourness of his breath. "I don't believe you for a moment," he said. "The question now becomes, what shall we do with you?"

"Let me give you the answer. I'm resigning."

"I'm afraid that isn't possible. The Business Council and elders would become suspicious. They'd think you found something that, shall we say, you couldn't live with. There would be unfortunate rumors. The council might even remove Kingdom and appoint someone else to oversee our operations. I'm sorry, Vicky. You're going to have to stay on as the Arapaho lawyer for a little longer. You'll be our guest."

"I'm leaving." Vicky got up and started for the door.

"Barrenger and Felix are waiting for my signal. I don't believe you'd want them to stop you."

She turned back. "You can't hold me against my will. There are laws . . ."

"Yes. Yes." He nodded. "No one will ever know."

"I'm supposed to be meeting with Agent Gianelli now. He's waiting at my office."

"So I've been told. We must take care of that little matter." He went back to the desk, picked up the phone, then walked over and held it out to her. "Call him. Tell him something came up and you have to cancel the meeting."

"Go to hell, Lexson."

"Call him!" He took her hand and jammed the phone against her palm. "Do as I say or I'll have to call my men and tell them you're being difficult."

Vicky tapped out the number. The answering machine picked up, and she said, "I'm at . . ."

Lexson yanked the phone out of her hand. The opened palm of his other hand cracked across her face, sending her stumbling sideways. She grabbed onto the back of the chair. Her face went hot and tight, as if she'd been singed by a fireball.

"That was stupid." Lexson moved toward her and she braced herself for another blow. Then he walked back to the desk, dropped the phone, and pushed a button on a small brown box.

"She's all yours," he said, leaning toward the box.

Vicky lunged for the door, flung it open, and kept going across the reception room, out into the corridor. An eerie silence followed her, punctuated by the sound of her own footsteps pounding the carpet. She glanced back. The corridor was empty.

She stopped at the elevator and jammed in the down button. Her breath came in burning gasps; her heart was knocking. The floor seemed to vibrate beneath her, or was it her own legs shaking? Numbers flashed above the elevator: seven, six, five. *Come on.* She kept one eye on the opened doors at the far end of the corridor. Still no sign of Lexson.

And then Barrenger and Felix burst out of another door and started running toward her.

Three flashed overhead.

Vicky darted for the opposite wall, her eyes searching for the cracks that marked the edges of the concealed door. She had them: two vertical cracks almost three feet apart.

"Hold it!" It was Barrenger's voice. Out of the corner of her eye she saw him thrust out one hand. He was holding something thick and white, like a folded towel.

She knocked hard on the wall between the cracks. Something gave way, as if the joists had shifted. She rammed her shoulder against the plaster. The door swung open, and she stumbled onto the metal landing at the top of the stairs. Kicking the door shut, she started running down the stairs into the dim hallway below.

She was almost down when she heard the muffled knocking sound on the wall above. She flung herself down the last steps and raced toward the rim of light around the outside door. The sound of boots thudding on the stairs came at her like bursts of thunder.

"Where the hell are you?" Barrenger shouted over thuds.

"Right here." A man's voice sputtered through a radio.

Vicky sprinted for the door only a body-length ahead, the boots ringing behind her. The door swung inward. She stopped. The sound of her own gasps filled the air. In the opening was a large man with dark hair and bulky shoulders and thick torso. Legs spread apart, one hand resting on the doorjamb. For a half instant she thought it was Adam, a black shadow looming out of the harsh light.

The man stepped into the hall and closed the door. The ceiling light flickering over his face made him look like an untrue person, a ghost materializing out of the painted walls. She realized he was Arapaho.

"I hear you been looking for me," Dennis Light Stone said.

An arm lashed out from behind and caught her around the shoulders and chest. She felt herself floating off her feet, the arm crushing her neck, forcing back her head. She opened her mouth to scream, but no sound came. In the glare of the ceiling light, she saw the white towel coming toward her. The towel pressed over her nose, jammed into her mouth. The chemical smell made her retch. She was aware of trying to kick backward against the man holding her, aware of the hall swirling around, like some carnival ride.

And then there was only blackness.

29

FATHER JOHN DROVE out of Double Dives and headed toward the mission, only partly aware of the two-lane road shimmering ahead in the late afternoon sun and the oncoming trucks and cars whizzing past. His thoughts were on the two white men shot in the head and left in a desolate, out-of-the-way place. Except for the way they'd died, where were the connections? Loan sharks, as Gianelli suggested? Shadowy figures stopping gamblers in the parking lot after a big loss and offering to help?

Maybe the fed was right. Monroe was a commander, determined to win the war he'd declared, willing to use any tactics available, as long as they worked, even loan sharking. And maybe the tactic had worked better than he'd planned. Suddenly he was making a lot of money. Frightened people were paying back the debt, embezzling money, selling property. When Rodney Pearson couldn't pay his debt, Monroe decided to make an example of the man, teach others a lesson.

A good business, Gianelli had said, until one of the captain's men decided to take it over.

Father John thumped his fist on the steering wheel. He was trying to talk himself into Gianelli's theory, he realized. He still didn't believe it.

He turned into the mission grounds and drove for the residence, surprised to see Catherine's blue sedan parked in front. He hadn't expected the woman to return to the mission today.

He was in the hallway, patting Walks-On, when the door to the living room slid open. Father George peered around the jamb. "You'd better come in here," he said.

Father John followed his assistant into the room. Catherine sat in the middle of the sofa, the cushions on either side rising like pillows around her. She kept her face in her hands. Her sobs sounded as if she were blowing up a balloon.

"What's going on?" He glanced at the other priest.

"She won't tell me. She said she had to talk to you."

Father John walked over and sat down next to the woman. "What is it, Catherine?" He could sense the sadness in the woman. It was often the third presence in the confessional.

She turned her face toward him. Strands of gray hair clung to her cheek. "Everything's ruined," she said. "Leonard's gonna shoot them."

"What? Who?"

"The guys I borrowed money from. I seen the white van driving by the house after me and Leonard got home. Letting me know they know where I live so they can come get me anytime they want."

"Wait a minute, Catherine. Are you sure they were the same men?"

She was nodding, and her hand was shaking inside his. "I'd know 'em anywhere. Leonard seen 'em, too. He said he was gonna find 'em and put an end to it. He got in his truck and took off."

Father John exchanged a glance with the other priest. Leonard Bizzel was a warrior, and the men—whoever they were—had come by his home. They'd threatened his wife. He would protect what belonged to him.

"Where do you think he was going?"

Catherine raised her head and blinked at the moisture in her eyes. "He might go to the casino. They'll kill him, Father."

Father John got to his feet, walked over to the side table, and picked up the phone. The operator answered on the second ring, and Father John told her that Leonard Bizzel was looking for a couple of white men in a white van and—selecting the words, aware of Catherine watching him—that the police should pick him up before he did anything he might regret.

From outside, came the roar of an engine. Tires squealed around Circle Drive. Father John looked over at the other priest who was already heading into the hallway.

"Leonard could be heading for the casino," he told the operator. The front door slammed shut, sending a little jolt through the floorboards.

"We've got a couple cars in the vicinity," the operator said. "We'll pick him up."

Father John had just dropped the receiver into the cradle when the other priest stuck his head through the doorway. "A tan pickup just turned into the alley."

God. He'd told Tommy Willard about the guest house, and now the Indian had come for Lela.

Father John told Catherine to wait, then he hurried outside after the other priest who was already down the sidewalk and starting across Circle Drive. Father John sprinted ahead. He cut a diagonal line through the grasses, crossed the other side of the drive, and turned down the alley. The pickup was parked in front of the guest house. He could hear the shouts, muffled and angry, followed by a scream that sounded like the cry of a wounded animal.

He dodged around the pickup and burst through the door. Lela was huddled in the corner of the sofa, small and drawn into herself. She was crying. The red imprint of a hand rose into the bruise on her cheek. Tommy hovered over her, black hair hanging over the back of his army camouflage shirt, ropy arms dangling out of the cut-off sleeves.

"You hear me?" He raised his fist like a club.

Father John lunged for the man and grabbed the upraised arm. He swung him around and started pushing him across the room. The man stumbled against a side table, sending the lamp crashing onto the floor, and Father John kept pushing. Past the table, through the doorway, into the tiny kitchen. He drove him against the edge of the counter and gripped the skinny shoulders hard, aware only of the lights bursting behind his own eyes.

"You like beating up women, do you?" he said. "Why don't you try me?"

"Hey, hey." The Indian tried lifting both hands, curling them into fists in front of his face. Father John shoved him again until he was leaning backward over the counter, head tilted up, his Adam's apple bobbing up and down in his skinny neck.

"Take it easy, John." Father George's voice made a clean cut through his anger. He could feel the pressure of the man's grip on his arm. He held on to Tommy another moment, then let him go.

Tommy slumped alongside the counter, then swung around, gripping the edge for support. He was gasping and coughing.

"You don't get it," the Indian said, running his forearm under his nose. A long string of mucus glistened on his brown skin. "I ain't hurt her none." He was talking to the counter. "She won't listen to sense. We gotta get outta here, man."

"What are you talking about?"

"Them guys that come to headquarters and took Captain Jack this morning. They're gonna kill us. We ain't got no time."

"Good heavens," Father George said.

Father John ignored the other priest, who was standing at his side. "You saw somebody take Monroe?"

"I was across the road working on my pickup." He kept his eyes on the counter. "I seen this white van pull into headquarters. I didn't pay no attention. Captain gets visitors sometimes. Next thing I know, three guys are pushing the Captain across the yard. They got a gun on him. One of 'em gets in the Captain's truck with him and they take off, the van right behind."

"Did you recognize them?"

"The guy with the gun. I seen him plain as day. It was Light Stone."

Father John took a step back and studied the Indian a moment. "You're sure it was Light Stone? The man you've been harassing at the casino?"

Tommy looked up out of the corners of his eyes. "Me harassing Light Stone? Man, you got it all wrong. It was the other way around. Me and the rangers was trying to talk to Indians working at the casino, make 'em see how bad gambling is, get 'em to stop going there. There was three of us in the parking lot last week, and Light Stone and a couple security guards come out and started slapping us around, and Light Stone, he started choking me. I was seeing stars, man. I was dyin'. He says, tell the Captain to call off his dogs—like we're a bunch of dogs—or we're all gonna be dead."

"Was Lela there?"

The Indian nodded. "She was in the pickup."

Father John stepped back and stared at the cottonwoods swaying outside the window. He'd gotten it wrong. Oh, he had part of it right: Lela had expected the body at Double Dives to be Light Stone's. What he'd gotten wrong was the reason. It wasn't because Tommy had threatened Light Stone. It was because the girl had seen Light Stone threaten Tommy, and she'd concluded that Tommy had killed the man to protect himself.

"What did you do when Light Stone took the Captain?" he said.

"I didn't know what to do." Tommy bit his lower lip, and for an instant, Father John thought the man might burst into tears. "Nobody was around. I went over to headquarters and started calling the rangers. We decided to drive around the rez 'til we found the van. First I went looking for the Captain's gun, thinking I was gonna need a gun. But it wasn't where the Captain always kept it. Finally I got in my truck and headed over to the casino. There was a lot of white vans in the parking lot, 'cause that's what them security guards drive, but I didn't see the Captain. So I headed over to Ethete and Fort Washakie and back to Arapaho. Captain wasn't nowhere. Then I hear that Captain Jack's out at Double Dives, and he's dead, and the radio says he shot himself."

Tommy pushed himself upright and faced Father John. "What a load of shit. The Captain was shot by that bastard, Light Stone."

Father John backed away. For a long moment, he studied the Indian still sloped against the counter. The man had seen the murderers. He could identify the men who'd killed Pearson and Monroe and threatened Catherine. No telling how many others they'd threatened—people too frightened to come forward.

And there was more—the realization made him feel as if he were heading into the wind. Light Stone and the others—the men who drove white vans—were only errand boys, enforcers. Stan Lexson, the man who ran the casino, gave the orders. And Lexson was making a sweep of everybody who'd gotten in his way—Captain Jack Monroe, sending rangers to harass casino employees, raising questions about the gaming chairman, and Rodney Pearson, unable to pay his debt and frightened. Maybe frightened enough to blow the whistle on the casino's loan sharks.

Dear God. Vicky was in Lexson's way.

Father John reached around the Indian and pulled the phone across the counter. "You've got to talk to Agent Gianelli," he said.

"I ain't talking to no fed." Tommy spit out the words. "Light Stone and them other security guards'll come after me and blow my head off. You say anything about what I told you, and I'm gonna deny it. I didn't see nothing. I don't know nobody named Dennis Light Stone. You must've been smokin' weed."

Tommy pushed himself away from the counter and, head lowered with determination, started forward.

Father John jabbed the receiver against the man's chest and pushed him back. Then he started dialing. Out of the corner of his eye, he saw the other priest's bulky figure blocking the doorway. "You got a choice, Tommy. Either you talk to the fed about Light Stone, or you talk to him about how you assaulted Lela."

"What! Lela's my girlfriend."

Father George let out a guffaw. "Didn't your mother ever tell you not to hit girls?"

"You've got two witnesses right here. Make that three." The ringing phone at Gianelli's office sounded far away. "Lela'll be more than willing to tell the fed about how you've treated her. You're looking at serious prison time, Tommy."

The Indian rolled his eyes from Father John to the other priest blocking the doorway. "You're nothing but a couple of bastards. You priests are supposed to help people. Instead you're gonna get me killed."

The fed picked up in mid-ring. "Special Agent Gianelli."

"Tommy Willard's at the mission," Father John said. "He saw Dennis Light Stone and two guards from the casino take Monroe at gunpoint this afternoon." Keeping his gaze hard on the Indian, he added, "Tommy wants to tell you everything."

"I'm on the way." There was a click. The line went silent, and Father John dropped the receiver into the cradle.

Fear blazed like diamonds in the Indian's eyes. "I'm a dead man."

"This will be over soon." Father John tried to inject more confidence in his voice than he felt. "Light Stone and the others will be arrested. You'll be okay."

Except for Lexson, he was thinking. A man like Lexson didn't depend on only a few people. He'd have others to call on. In the flat look of resignation that came into Tommy's eyes, Father John understood that the man had reached a similar conclusion.

"John!" Father George's voice came like a shot through the kitchen.

Father John turned to the door.

The other priest was standing in the middle of the living room. Beyond his white shirtsleeves, Father John could see the vacant sofa with the small impression of Lela's body in the cushions.

"She's gone, John," Father George said.

30

"STAY WITH HIM."

Father John shouldered past the other priest and went outside. A gust of hot wind took the door from his hand and banged it against the wall. He searched the alley with his eyes. Nothing but a vacant stretch of brown gravel road running between the church and the cottonwoods and sagebrush in front of Eagle Hall. He searched the road in the other direction where it meandered into the path that cut through the trees to the river.

And from there, Lela could follow the river to the cluster of trailers in the low, mushy ground next to the highway. She was on the way to her aunt Mary's trailer.

Father John took off through the cottonwoods, ducking around the branches, his boots knocking against the fallen logs. Ahead, dodging through the trees, he spotted the flash of white. He cut to the left, crashing through the underbrush, his eyes on the girl's white T-shirt. She was running along the riverbank, and he sprinted toward her.

Suddenly she looked around. All eyes, startled and despairing at the same time. "Go away!" she screamed.

"Lela, wait!" But she was running full-out now, head down, arms pumping. Running with an awkwardness, feet flipping sideways. He could see the white soles of her sneakers. He dodged around a clump of willows and came out in front of her. She stopped, then threw out both hands to hold him off. She was tossing her head between the river and the trees, like a wild animal groping for the way out of the trap.

"Don't be afraid," he said. "I'm not going to hurt you. I want to help you."

"He's gonna make me go with him. He gave me a lot of b.s. about Monroe getting shot, so I'd get scared and come back to him, but I don't wanna be with him anymore." She gave him a look filled with misery, then hunched her shoulders and started to dart past.

"Tommy's not leaving the rez. The FBI agent's on the way here now to talk to him, and the police have a warrant for his arrest." The man was lucky, he was thinking. He'd be safer in custody.

The girl blinked up at him, trying to decide if he was telling the truth. "Tommy's not gonna talk to the fed," she said finally.

"You saw what happened at the casino parking lot, didn't you? You heard Dennis Light Stone threaten Tommy and the rangers."

The girl shook her head and looked away.

"Captain Jack was shot this afternoon at Double Dives. He's dead, Lela. Light Stone has to be stopped before he kills anybody else, and you and Tommy have to tell the fed everything you know."

She was crying now, holding on to her arms and rocking back and forth. Tears flooded out of her eyes and ran down her cheeks. "I gotta get away from Tommy." Her voice sounded like a little girl's.

"Where will you go?"

"Aunt Mary's got a girlfriend in Casper that Tommy don't know about. Maybe I can stay there awhile, 'til Tommy forgets me and gets himself a new girlfriend."

That was good, Father John was thinking. Even better, Dennis Light Stone wouldn't know about Casper. "Will you call Gianelli's office and let him know where you're staying? You're going to have to talk to him, you know."

She didn't move. Finally she gave a little nod and started forward, her palms over her cheeks, wiping away the wetness. "You won't tell Tommy where I'm going?"

"I won't tell Tommy," he said, stepping aside. "Go on."

The girl hesitated, then plunged forward and broke into a run—the same, awkward, feet-splayed run. She seemed so small and helpless and young, he thought. Dear God, what was she? Fifteen?

As he retraced his route through the trees, Father John spotted Gianelli lifting himself out of the white Blazer parked next to Tommy's pickup. The other priest stood in the doorway, one hand propped against the jamb, a human bulwark to discourage any idea Tommy might have about bolting.

The agent slammed the door, walked to the rear and waited, the fronts of his blue sport coat blowing back in the wind.

"Girlfriend here, too?" he said when Father John was within earshot.

"She ran off." Well, that was the truth, Father John thought. Not all of the truth, but the most important part. "She'll get in touch with you, Ted."

"Sure she will." The agent lifted his eyes to the sky. "You let her leave here, and now I'm going to have to spend valuable time finding her."

"You've got Tommy." Father John nodded toward the black head at the kitchen window. "He's the one who saw Dennis Light Stone and another man take Monroe this morning. The men work for Stan Lexson. They killed Pearson, Ted."

The agent seemed to be filing this among the other facts floating in his head. Then, lowering his voice, he said, "A couple other agents are coming over from Casper. This is just the beginning." He jerked a fist toward the guest house. "One witness, and not the most credible witness in the world, against Light Stone. Doesn't matter what Willard says, you can bet Light Stone's going to have a very persuasive alibi for today, backed up by Stan Lexson himself. Even if we get an indictment against Light Stone, it's going to be difficult to connect Pearson's and Monroe's deaths to Lexson, not without hard evidence. Guys like that know how to cushion themselves. It's the guys that work for them who take the fall."

"Talk to Vicky," Father John said. "She's been trying to find evidence that Matt Kingdom has control of jobs at the casino. If the man's been paid off, then he probably knows what's going on."

"That must be why she called." Gianelli looked away a moment. "Left a message couple hours ago that she'd be in her office and wanted to talk to me. But when I got there, her Cherokee was out in front, but she was gone."

"Gone?" It wasn't like Vicky to make an appointment and leave.

"Front door was locked, like she left for the day. Got the answering machine when I called her apartment." The agent hesitated. "She called back . . ."

"When? When did she call back?"

"Thirty minutes ago. Just before you called. We were cut off."

Father John started to ask where the call had come from, but before he could say anything, the agent said, "It was an unlisted number. I figure she'd gotten called away on something else and she'd get back to me."

"Something's happened to her." Father John blurted out the words. He was barely aware of the other priest stepping off the stoop and coming toward the Blazer, head cocked toward them.

"Take it easy," the agent said, but Father John could see in the set of the man's jaw that *he* wasn't taking it easy. There'd been one death today—most likely a homicide—and another homicide five days ago, both connected to the casino, and Vicky could have the evidence to put the casino manager out of business. Maybe into prison.

"I'll have the Lander PD do a safety check at her office and apartment," Gianelli went on. "What about relatives? Friends? Anybody likely to have come and picked her up, headed out for dinner? You know who to call, don't you?"

Vicky's Aunt Rose, Father John was thinking. Will and Josephine Standing Bear. A daughter in Los Angeles, a son in Denver. An ex-husband, dead. She was so alone. Except that now, there was Adam Lone Eagle. Vicky could have gone out with Adam Lone Eagle.

He wanted to believe it was true. Why couldn't he believe?

"She's okay, John," Gianelli said, as if he read his mind. "Somebody probably called needing a lawyer, and she had to leave the office. Could be at the Fremont County Jail right now, talking to somebody arrested on a disturbance charge or DUI. Try not to worry about her."

He knows, Father John was thinking. The fed had

worked with him and Vicky on dozens of cases; how could the man not know how he felt about Vicky? And now Father George knew.

He didn't care. It didn't matter. The only thing that mattered was that she was safe.

"Call me when you hear from her." The agent stepped past the other priest and went into the house.

"I'm sure she's fine," Father George said as they walked down the alley. Gravel skittered about their boots. Somewhere out on the plains around the mission, a dog was barking.

Father John didn't say anything. He didn't want to discuss Vicky with his assistant. He had no intention of defending the way he felt about her; it was as it was. He'd come to accept his feelings, the reality of them. At times, they seemed the most real thing in the world. He'd even come to think of them as a gift and a blessing. So unlike the longing and the emptiness that still came over him at unexpected moments, but something plentiful and generous. How could loving someone else not be a blessing? He'd kept his vows—that had been the hard part—and she had made the only decision she could make. But the feelings remained; they were real.

"Looks like Leonard's back," Father George said as they came around the corner of the church. The brown truck was nosed into the curb in front of the residence, a rifle locked across the back window. Next to the truck was a police cruiser, an officer pulling himself out of the front seat.

"Found Leonard Bizzel," the officer said, walking toward them. "Man's sober, all right."

"Leonard doesn't drink," Father John said.

"Says some guys at the casino are trying to kill his wife."

"The same men who killed Captain Jack Monroe this afternoon." Father John gestured with his head in the direction of the guest house. "Gianelli's talking to a witness now. Tommy Willard."

"Willard's here? We been looking for him. Got a warrant for his arrest for assaulting Vicky Holden in the casino parking lot. Over in the guest house, you say?" The officer's eyes narrowed into slits, as if the situation had suddenly veered onto a familiar path that he was anxious to take. "Bizzel's got himself calmed down. All right if he stays here for a while?"

Father John nodded. He waited until the police car had turned around Circle Drive and nosed into the alley before he started up the sidewalk to the house, barely aware of Father George lumbering behind him and the in-and-out noise of the man's breathing, his own thoughts on Vicky. She'd driven out of the mission yesterday morning, determined to learn whether Matt Kingdom was handing out casino jobs. And this afternoon, she'd called Gianelli. Which meant she'd found something.

Father John could almost feel the danger, like the darkness of a storm moving toward her.

He turned around and started back down the sidewalk, ignoring the startled look in the other priest's eyes. "I'm going out for a while," he said over his shoulder.

31

HOW STRANGE, HE thought, that the evening could be so beautiful, filled with red and violet light that lingered over the deep blue mountains at the edge of Lander and the sounds of children riding bikes down the sidewalks, running and shouting in the yards. Everything normal and safe, and people capable of taking men to Double Dives and shooting them in the head, people capable of hurting Vicky—people like that were a million miles away.

Except that Stan Lexson and Dennis Light Stone and the other killers were close by.

Father John drove through the residential neighborhood west of Main Street. From a half block away, he spotted Vicky's Cherokee parked in front of the bungalow that was her office. He was struck by the irony: On a normal day, the Cherokee would be a sign that she was there. But this evening, he knew it could be a sign that she hadn't yet returned.

He walked up the sidewalk, past the sign with Vicky Holden, Attorney at Law, shimmering in the light, and tried the front door. Locked. He knocked hard, but there was no sound except for that of kids playing down the street and a car backfiring somewhere. He peered through the sliver of glass next to the cardboard in the window frame. There was no one in the reception room or in the office beyond the opened French doors. She wasn't at her desk.

He knocked again, waited a moment, then he stepped off the porch and made his way around the side of the house and pounded on the back door. Still no answer. He tried the knob. To his surprise, it turned in his hand, and he stepped inside, standing on a landing below six stairs leading up to the kitchen. A sense of wrongness gripped him like an icy hand that he couldn't shake off. Vicky wouldn't have walked away and left the back door unlocked.

He took the stairs two at a time, calling out her name. The kitchen was deserted. Her office, the reception room, the two bedrooms turned into storage rooms and the bathroom on the side of the house—all deserted. He walked back into her office and sat down at her desk. The top was nearly clear, except for the phone, the caller ID machine, and a stack of papers at the edge with a file folder on top, as if she'd finished her work and left for the day.

He opened the folder and glanced through the copies of her handwritten notes; lists of casino managers connected to Matt Kingdom; lists of companies from which the casino bought supplies and equipment. Sister companies, Vicky had written at the top of the sheet, owned by the same company that owned Lodestar Enterprises.

There was more: three sheets of notes on conversations with Alan Peterson in the Indian Gaming Commission that detailed the ways in which a casino management company might cheat an Indian tribe, and pages of personnel records.

This was the information Vicky intended to give to Gianelli, the reason she'd called the fed. Father John knew now with a certainty as real as the wood desk he was leaning into that she wouldn't have left before the agent arrived. Unless, someone had forced her.

He reached over and started pushing the button on the caller ID. Names flashed behind the narrow glass: Unidentified, three times, Federal Bureau of Investigation, twice. No other calls this afternoon.

He picked up the receiver, dialed her apartment and listened to the sound of a phone ringing into the void, the receiver cold and inert. When her recorded voice answered, he hit the disconnect button. He was about to call Gianelli when the phone rang in his hand. He pushed the on button and waited.

"Vicky?" It was a man's voice, a note of panic sounding below the surface.

"Who is this?"

"Adam Lone Eagle. Let me talk to Vicky."

"She isn't in."

"Where is she, and who are you?"

"Father O'Malley."

The unidentified calls were from Adam Lone Eagle, Father John realized. The Lakota who'd brought Vicky into the casino. Why? To allay suspicions, discredit Captain Jack Monroe, and camouflage the truth? Which side was the man on?

There was a half beat before Lone Eagle said, "What's going on? I've been trying to reach her all afternoon."

Father John closed the folder and pushed it aside.

And then he saw it, stuck to the edge of the desk blotter, a yellow Post-It with one word scrawled on top: *Casino.*

"Vicky's at the casino," he said, his voice hard with certainty.

"She hasn't been here all day."

"Ask your boss where she is."

"What the hell's going on?"

"Ask your boss."

Father John pushed the disconnect button and dialed Gianelli's office. Another answering machine, and after the beep, he told the fed what he'd found at Vicky's office: the unlocked back door, the Cherokee, the file folder with the evidence, a Post-It note that said casino. "She left us a message," he said. "They've taken her to the casino."

He could imagine the fed's response: Whoa, John. You saying the guys that killed Monroe came for Vicky? Why would they take her to the casino?

He heard himself hurrying on, the logical sequence spilling out. "Lexson wants to know how much she knows and whether she's told anybody. When he gets the information, he'll have his goons kill her. I'm going after her."

32

THROUGH THE DARKNESS came a throb of pain. Swimming upward toward consciousness, Vicky struggled to open her eyes. The room swirled around—window, draperies, dresser, chair; her head was pounding. She could still see the white towel pressing down on her face. The sticky, anesthetic smell clung to her nose and mouth, or was it a memory of the smell? How long had she been unconscious?

She tried lying very still, waiting for each new stab of pain until, finally, the pain was no more than a dull throb. Scarcely moving, she surveyed her surroundings. She was lying on top of a satiny bedspread in the middle of a large bed in a large room that had the plastic, superficial look of a hotel room. The red-tinged light of early evening floated past the filmy curtains at the window. Heavy draperies were folded at either side. Across the room, a small desk and a two-door armoire that probably concealed a television. On the table to the left was a remote control next to a clock with lighted red numbers: 8:08. On the other table, a phone.

Vicky managed to prop herself upright against the headboard, a slow, deliberate motion, not wanting to set the pain loose again in her head. She picked up the receiver. There was no dial tone. Her fingers danced at random over the buttons. Nothing.

She tossed the receiver across the bed and swallowed back the hysterical laughter erupting in her throat. How could she have imagined that Lexson would put her in a hotel room with a working phone? Which meant—she stared across the room at the door—she was locked in. She edged toward the bed and swung her legs over the sides. Her shoes thudded against the carpet. She still had her shoes; that was good, but her bag? Where was her bag? She had a cell phone in her bag, a fingernail file, a tiny flashlight—any number of things that might help.

Then she remembered: She'd dropped it onto the floor in Lexson's office and run out without it.

She lifted herself off the bed and, trailing one hand along the edge, almost afraid to step out on her own, moved toward the foot. So far, so good. The dizziness had gone, and the aching was tolerable. Cool air washed over her. She pushed off and walked to the door. The knob stayed frozen in her hand, glued in place. Pressing her face against the smooth wood, she peered through the peephole. The corridor stretched away to either side, empty and silent, a row of doors on the opposite wall. To the right, almost out of sight, were the bronze doors of the elevator.

She sank against the wall. Lexson had her locked in one of the hotel rooms when he could have had her taken someplace and shot. Why hadn't he? Because he still wasn't certain how much she'd learned and—most important—he didn't know who she'd told. It was only a matter of time before he came to the hotel room, and he would bring Light Stone and Barrenger and Felix with him.

She had to get out of there.

She darted to the right and flung open the first door. The bathroom was on the other side—all white marble gleaming in the light from the round bulbs above the mirror. Everything was solid—the ceiling and walls and floor. No panels to kick open and try to crawl through.

She backed away and opened the second door. A narrow closet with wooden hangers dangling from a metal rod. She tried to push the rod out of its brackets with some crazy notion of using it as a tool to break down the door, but she couldn't budge the rod. The tears started coming, hot and salty on her cheeks, and she tried to blink them away. The last thing she needed was to break down and cry.

She closed the door and walked around the bed to the window. It was more than a window; it consisted of two glass doors that extended from the floor almost to the ceiling. She pushed aside the curtain, then slid open one door. The curtain flew around her face as she stepped out onto the balcony. It was small, three feet deep and four feet wide, she guessed, with a solid concrete half-wall around the perimeter. From below, she'd thought the balconies around the windows had looked like blocks erupting from the stucco walls.

She walked over and looked down. She was in a corner room on the top floor—eight stories high, on the north side. On the left, the edge of the building floated into space. On the right, rows of balconies protruded from the floors. Directly below, she knew, was the door through which the Barrenger and Felix had pushed her. The service trucks were gone. There were no vehicles in the area, nothing but the pavement running into the flat, brown earth.

But the wind was blowing, the hot, sacred wind, and the white curtains billowed out onto the balcony and brushed against her arms. *Give me your strength,* she said to the spirit of the wind. *Let me get away from here.*

She went back inside, yanked open the desk drawer, and pulled out a small tablet and pen. She dropped onto the chair and wrote out the same message on every page: Help. Corner room, 8th floor. Then she ripped the phone cord out of the wall, wrapped it around the phone and stuck one of the pages into the cord. Back on the balcony, she hurled the phone at an angle toward a balcony below. It clanged against the concrete and skidded over the floor. She waited. The glass doors remained closed.

She went back into the room, grabbed the clock and pulled the cord free. Then she jammed another message into the slot where the numbers used to show, wrapped the cord around the frame, and went back outside. Leaning over the edge, she aimed the clock for another one of the lower balconies. Bull's-eye. She listened for the sound of the doors sliding open, but again there was nothing. It was as if the hotel was deserted. People in the casino. They could be there for hours. And people behind closed glass doors in soundproofed, air-conditioned rooms.

She gripped the edge of the balcony. She could shout into the wind, but she had no idea where Barrenger and Light Stone might be, and the sound of her voice would alert them that she was conscious. It would bring them on the run.

She got the rest of the pages, ripped them off, and sent them downward, floating one by one out beyond the building toward the highway, out across the open spaces. Watching the last page flutter away, she felt as if she was going to be sick. A few words scribbled on a piece of paper—they were all she had.

The thwack of a door shutting sent a mixture of fear and hope through her. There was a low rumble of voices. She moved toward the sound coming from the adjoining room. Hotel guests, tourists from Billings or Cheyenne or Denver?

It was then she heard the low, confident sound of Barrenger's voice. The glass door started to slide open. She darted back inside, pulling the billowing curtains after her. Flattened against the wall, she could see Barrenger at the far side of the balcony. Light Stone moved beside him and shook out a cigarette, which Barrenger took, bending his gray head into the lighter the Arapaho held for him. The operations chief held the cigarette between his slim fingers and took a couple of pulls before blowing the smoke out of the side of his mouth.

"How much longer we gotta wait?" Light Stone asked.

"Until Stan gets here."

"Let me talk to her. I know how to talk to her. I'll find out how much she knows. Boss is giving her too much time to come up with some story. He moves too slow, you ask me."

"Nobody asked you."

"I'm just sayin', give me five minutes alone with the bitch . . ."

"Shut up, Dennis." A phone started ringing. Barrenger pulled a black object out of the back pocket of his slacks and cocked his head downward. "Yeah? Okay. Okay." He slid the phone back into his pocket. A smile of anticipation spread through his face. "Stan is on the way," he said, turning toward the glass door.

Vicky hugged the wall, paralyzed. Her head was throbbing again, her saliva had turned to acid. She heard the whoosh of the door opening in the adjacent room. It slammed shut. The reverberation ran through the wall and into her fingers. Footsteps sounded in the corridor.

She pulled hard on the plastic wand dangling from the curtain rod and ran the draperies across the windows. Then she slipped outside past the heavy fabric onto the balcony. She could hear the lock clicking loose on the hall door as she slid the glass door shut. She looked around. She felt like an animal in a concrete trap.

A mountain lion. "The lion is stealthy," grandfather used to say when he told his stories. "The lion sees everything before she moves."

Vicky saw the metal vent protruding from the wall about a foot off the floor on the side next to the adjacent balcony. She stepped onto the vent and crawled onto the flat, six-inch-wide top of the balcony. The sound of voices—surprise, anger—floated through the window. Steadying herself by the wall, she managed to stand up. The adjacent balcony was about four feet away, but it was hard to calculate—all that space, all that emptiness in between. Rows of balconies swam below her. And far below, the pavement shimmered gray in the fading light.

"She has to be here somewhere." Barrenger's voice came from the other side of the window.

Vicky took a gulp of air, bent her knees, and jumped.

33

HER FEET CAME down on the top of the adjacent balcony. She swayed forward, backward, clawing at the wall to get her balance and keep from falling backward and down, down, down.

The glass door slid open behind her, and she pitched forward onto the concrete floor. She drew herself into a tight ball against the stucco wall.

"She's not out here," Barrenger said. Boots stomped and kicked against the balcony floor.

"Well, she was here." Light Stone's voice wavered from low to high. "She was laying right here on the bed where we left her."

"Look under the bed." Barrenger's voice fading among the draperies.

"She ain't there. She ain't anywhere. She must've

picked the lock. She had something on her. I told you to let me strip her."

"Where the hell's the clock and the phone?"

"Dunno."

A couple of seconds passed, then Barrenger spoke. "Stan, we're in the room. We got a little problem. She's not here."

Vicky held her breath and clasped her hands over her arms, trying to stop the shaking. "I can't figure how she did it," the operations chief said, frustration crackling in his voice, "but she must have gotten out the door. We'll check the elevator videos. She couldn't have gotten far. Give us a few minutes. We'll have her."

Now the voice came from far away. "Let's go," she heard Barrenger say before the door slammed.

Vicky inched her way across the floor to the sliding-glass doors. Closed, but not locked. Not locked, thank God. They'd forgotten to snap the lock. She pushed the door open wide enough to crawl through, then stood up, her legs shaky and weak beneath her. For a moment, she thought she was going to pass out: The room started moving, blackness closing in. She leaned against the window and made herself breathe slowly, keeping her gaze on the bed, the dresser, the armoire—solid and real, unlike the blue-gray abyss she had leapt across.

After a moment, she felt steadier. She realized the room had been recently occupied: The satin bedspread was pulled to one side, the white pillow propped against the headboard. A man's shaving kit lay opened on the dresser, a little pile of cigarette butts had been stabbed into the glass ashtray on the bedside table. She made her way across the room and opened the closet. Men's shirts and slacks were draped over the hangers.

And then it hit her. Dennis Light Stone had been missing for five days, but he hadn't gone anywhere. He'd been right here, hiding in the hotel, ordering room service and watching TV. The blackjack pit boss, signing off on inflated fills for the tables, cheating his own people: He knew too much, and he was Arapaho. Lexson must have gotten worried that Light Stone might start listening to Monroe's rangers in the parking lot and start believing what they said, so he'd gotten the Arapaho out of the way for a while.

Vicky walked over and checked the door. The knob turned in her hand. She hesitated. Barrenger and Light Stone could be on the way to the surveillance room to check the elevator videos for the last hour. Lexson was probably already there. She couldn't use the elevator. There were real-time screens. They'd see her immediately.

She pressed her eye against the peephole. The panel above the elevator was dark. An eerie calm gripped the corridor, as if she were staring into an unreal world, a void floating in space. The bronze elevator doors across the hall could have been painted in place. A flat, dull light lay over the opposite wall, the row of doors to the other rooms, the wide strip of blue carpeting along the wood floor. She could see almost the entire length of the corridor from the elevator to the neon-red Exit sign at the far end. But there was no door on the other side, which meant the exit door was on her side.

The mountain lion is watchful. Be watchful, like the lion.

Her hand gripped the doorknob, her eye still glued to the spy hole. She was about to open the door when the knob turned to ice in her hand. The numbers above the elevator were blinking, like yellow creatures gnawing at the glass panel: 6, 7, 8. The bell pinged and the bronze doors parted. Stan Lexson stepped out first, determination in the forward thrust of his head. He seemed confident and contained, Vicky thought, as contained as a stick of dynamite. He must have called the surveillance room, learned she wasn't on the elevator videos, and intercepted Barrenger and Light Stone.

They were behind him, coming down the corridor toward her. Her breath turned into a hot lump in her throat.

The three men wheeled in unison toward the door to the adjacent room. Vicky heard the clinking keys, the angry murmurs, a shout of derision from Lexson: "Don't give me that shit. She has to be in here someplace."

The door to the other room burst open. "Check under the bed," Lexson shouted.

"We looked there." This from Barrenger.

"Look again! Check the armoire." The door made a whooshing noise, then crashed shut, and Vicky realized the doors closed automatically.

She opened her own and stepped into the corridor. The exit was farther than she'd thought, the distance distorted by the peephole. She had four or five seconds, no more, she figured, to reach the exit before her own door whooshed and slammed shut and alerted the men in the next room.

She pushed her door back against the wall to give herself another half second, then started running down the corridor. She was almost to the exit when the door behind her thudded shut. She threw herself toward the exit, then stopped. Next to the door frame was a glass-fronted fire alarm. A door cracked open behind her, and Barrenger shouted, "There she is!"

Vicky lunged for the alarm and pulled down the red handle. The wailing siren burst around her, drawing in the air, like fire itself as she wheeled back to the exit and through the door onto a grated metal landing.

Grabbing hold of the railing, she started down the metal steps, swinging around the next landing, the siren bouncing off the concrete walls and muffling the clack of her heels.

Overhead, a door slammed; boots thumped behind her. She reached the sixth floor, flung open the door and yelled "Fire!" Doors were opening up and down the corridor. At the far end, a rotund man in shorts and T-shirt, with a bowling ball head, leaned into the corridor, disbelief plastered on his face.

"Fire!" she yelled again, before slamming the door and starting down the next flight. She ran faster, taking in gulps of air as she crossed a landing, sensing Lexson and the others behind her, not daring to look up. She was on the fourth floor now and hotel guests were pushing one another through the exit door: a woman with her hair tight in curlers, a white robe tied around her bulky figure, terror on her face; several men in shorts, one barefoot.

"What's going on?" a man shouted.

"Out of the way!" Lexson's voice came from above. The steps rattled and shook beneath her as she dodged around the guests and plunged down the next flight. She could feel the man's presence somewhere in the crowd pressing behind her, as pervasive as the screaming siren.

More people were pouring into the stairway. Third floor, second floor—a crush of people running from a disaster, nervous and distracted, rushing and stumbling down the steps. Vicky had to weave her way through the bodies damp with fear and perspiration. She reached the first floor and followed the crowd into a hotel corridor with offices on each side that looked as if the occupants had run out, leaving papers toppling across the desks. A tiny camera perched on a black metal frame under the ceiling, watching everything, looking for an Indian woman in a blue linen dress.

Vicky ducked her head and stayed close behind a heavy-set man. They passed an office with a navy-blue blazer hanging over the back of a chair. She slipped inside, pulled on the blazer, and rejoined the crowd running down the corridor. The siren wailed over the thud of footsteps, the huffing sounds of fear. Behind her somewhere, a woman was crying. The crowd spilled into the hotel lobby along with the guests coming out of the opposite corridor, everybody heading toward the entrance to the casino.

Vicky kept her head low, the blazer collar pulled up around her hair, and worked her way through the crowd—excuse me, excuse me—slipping past the sweaty, muscled arms and the breasts bulging beneath the T-shirts. A low buzz hung in the air, as if people were breathing through their teeth. Through the buzz came the sound of Lexson's voice behind her: "Let me through. Let me through."

The crowd was flowing around a woman who stood still, shock and confusion in her expression, as if having gotten this far, she didn't know where else to go. "Come on," Vicky said, taking her by the arm and pulling her into the crowd swarming across the lobby toward the entrance.

The siren stopped, leaving a silence more unsettling than the bleating noise. The crowd seemed to pull itself to a stop, everyone glancing around, faces frozen in uncertainty. The woman had started whimpering, a sound that darted through the quiet like the cry of a bird.

"Attention!" A man's voice boomed through the loudspeakers. Heads swiveled about. "We've had a false alarm. False alarm," the voice repeated. "There is no fire on the premises. We apologize for your inconvenience. Please resume your activities."

"No fire?" The woman pulled herself free and started back into the casino.

Vicky glanced around. The crowd was parting to let the woman through, and in the opening, Vicky saw Lexson hurrying forward.

She squeezed her way past the crush of bodies at the entrance and started running along the side of the building toward the parking lot.

"Stop her! Stop that woman!" Lexson's voice came like a trumpet blast behind her.

Ahead, one of the casino guards snapped to attention and darted through a group of people. Vicky dodged past his groping hands and kept running. Footsteps pounded behind her, someone gasped for breath. She felt a hand grip her shoulder. She tried to wrench herself free, but fingers dug into her other shoulder, and she was spinning around, her feet sliding across the gravel. She stared up at Adam Long Eagle.

"Vicky! I've been looking everywhere for you."

Behind him, Lexson, Barrenger, and Light Stone were bearing down on the sidewalk through the knots of people. Lexson flicked his head toward a white casino van parked at the curb, and the van started inching through the crowd.

"Let me go!" Vicky pushed against Adam's chest and twisted in his arms, but his hands stayed welded to her shoulders. People were hurrying by, heads down, eyes averted. A lovers' quarrel. No need to get involved.

"We've got to talk," Adam said.

"You're one of them!"

"You don't know what you're saying."

The van pulled alongside and, out of the corner of her eye, Vicky saw Felix dart around the front and slide open the side door. The crowd made a wide circle around them, as Lexson moved in behind Adam.

"Let's take a ride."

"You heard the boss." It was Barrenger's voice behind her. A fist punched into the small of her back.

"Wait a minute . . ." Suddenly Adam let go, and Vicky had to scrabble for balance. And then—the fist in her back again, a hand gripping her arm, and she was stumbling sideways toward the van. The edge of the door cracked her knee as she fell onto the seat.

"Get in!" Lexson shouted. Adam filled up the doorway, then dropped onto the seat. Barrenger got in behind him and, leaning forward, reached around and yanked the door shut. Vicky pulled herself into a tight ball against the far window.

"What the hell's going on?" Adam asked, his voice hoarse with anger. Vicky felt his hand over her knee, as if to reassure her. She tried to jerk away, make herself smaller, but there was no room. Lexson was already in the front passenger seat, and Light Stone had replaced Felix behind the wheel. The man was now standing in the middle of the drive, stopping the other traffic as the van started moving forward, horn pounding in intermittent bleeps that sent people scurrying forward or jumping back. Then the van broke free and sped through the parking lot toward the highway.

"I demand some answers!" Adam shouted at the back of Lexson's head. "Where we going?"

Barrenger snorted beside him and stared into the darkness outside his window.

It was a moment before Lexson twisted around and glanced from Adam to Vicky. "You two make me laugh," he said. "You're the last problem we have to clear up today."

34

DRIVING AS FAST as he dared, taking the shortcuts, keeping one eye on the rearview mirror for flashing lights behind him—*Now Father O'Malley, can't keep giving you warnings. Gonna have to ticket you this time*—it still took forty minutes before he'd crossed the reservation and was heading north on Highway 287. Great Plains Casino, gleamed a neon violet against the evening sky. Tumbling, tumbling down the side were giant white and black dice.

Father John slowed for the turn into the casino. Cars and trucks, headlights blazing, were waiting to turn onto the highway. Other vehicles streamed out of the parking lot, jockeying for places at the end of the line. Groups of people spilled out of the casino entrance and headed toward the lot. He gripped the steering wheel hard. Something was wrong. People were usually heading toward the casino, not trying to get away.

He swung into the drive and pulled up alongside a pickup about to leap into the highway. An Indian couple sat in front, heads bobbing sideways—man looking left, woman looking right.

"What's going on?" he yelled out the window.

The man swiveled around. "That you, Father John?"

He recognized the couple—Henry and Stella Whiteman, fourth pew from the back, ten o'clock Mass. "Fire alarm went off!" the woman yelled past her husband. A cacophony of horns had started up. "False alarm, but me and Henry decided to get outta there. Lotta other folks thinkin' the same." She threw her head back toward the string of vehicles.

He gave the couple a wave and drove toward the casino. The tires whined against the asphalt. On the right, the parking lot was bathed in the white light shining down from poles scattered about. He glanced at groups of people walking toward the cars and RVs, hoping to catch sight of Vicky. She was nowhere.

And then he spotted her—on the sidewalk in front of the casino standing with Adam Lone Eagle.

The Lakota was holding her by the shoulders, leaning toward her. Vicky twisted about, in and out of the shadows. People flowed past. There was no one to help her—why didn't someone help her? In the instant before a white van pulled alongside the curb and blocked his view, Father John saw the three men hurrying through the crowd toward them. He recognized the operations chief. What was his name? Barrenger. One of the others must be Lexson himself.

An RV lumbered into the lane ahead and stopped. Father John jammed on the brake pedal and pulled up close to the front bumper. The headlights washed over him. The RV's left signal started flashing, and the driver craned his head toward the line of vehicles moving toward the highway. Father John laid on the horn. The driver looked around and nodded before inching the RV sideways. Now it blocked the entire lane.

Beyond the RV, Father John could see the white van pull away from the curb, horn bleating into the crowd. Several people jumped out of the way. Vicky was gone! Lone Eagle and the other three men—all gone.

The van made a U-turn, careened into the parking lot, swerving around a couple of cars, then sped toward the highway. In the rearview mirror, he watched the van turn north, and in that instant he knew where they were taking her.

Father John put the gear into reverse and jammed down the accelerator. The pickup lunged backward. A horn squawked, someone shouted, "Hey!" He hit the brake pedal. In the rearview mirror, he saw the driver shaking his fist into the windshield of a green sedan.

He was blocked in. The RV in front, five or six vehicles stacked up behind. He felt sick with rage and helplessness. In the side mirror, he could see the van swing into the drive behind him and turn onto the highway. He shifted into forward and gave the steering wheel a hard right pull toward the curb that abutted the parking lot. He managed to move sideways a couple of feet, then had to back up to keep from sideswiping the RV. Forward. Back. Finally he bumped against the curb, then backed up one last time and stomped down on the accelerator. The pickup shot over the curb and bounced onto the asphalt.

He drove across the lot, dodging around the parked vehicles, blasting the horn at the little groups of people. He managed to pull the cell phone out of the glove compartment and fumble with the buttons as he swung back into the drive. A dark sedan was coming off the highway toward him, and he tossed the cell phone onto the seat and gripped the steering wheel, turning out of the way. Headlights exploded in his eyes. There was the sound of brakes squealing, tires spitting out gravel. The sedan stopped sideways against the oncoming traffic, the driver hunched over the ignition, trying to bring the engine back to life. A cloud of black smoke puffed from the tailpipes.

Father John took off again, around the sedan, back into the parking lot. He thumped across the barrow ditch, shot out onto the highway into the northbound lane, and pulled into the space between two trucks. He made a right onto Highway 26, the diagonal road across the reservation, the fastest route to Double Dives.

The pickup shook around him, going all out at seventy, he guessed, although the speedometer registered the usual five miles per hour. The van had at least ten minutes on him; it could be ten or twelve miles ahead. He closed both fists over the steering wheel and peered at the asphalt flowing into the wash of headlights.

"YOU'LL NEVER GET away with this," Vicky said. The shadows of the reservation flew past outside her window. She was jammed against the side, the armrest poking into her ribs and Adam's thigh pressing against her own. "The fed knows I was taken to the casino against my will. I left a message."

"Don't say anything else." Adam's voice was low and firm, but underneath—what was that?—the faintest crack in the man's confidence?

"She's lying, Stan." Barrenger leaned forward, dipping his head toward the front seat, blinking rapidly behind the wire-rimmed glasses. "There wasn't any message when we took her."

"Took her!" This from Adam. "Damn it, Stan. What's going on?"

"You must've screwed up, Barrenger." Vicky glanced past Adam at the man still bent toward the front seat, nervousness and worry stamped on his face. They were speeding south on Highway 26, moonlight flickering through the darkness outside the windows. "I slipped a message onto the desk blotter before we left."

Lexson twisted around and glared at the operations chief. "You let her leave a message that could be found?"

"I'm telling you, Stan, she's a lying bitch trying to get herself out of this." A note of terror rang like a bell in the man's voice. "I didn't take my eyes off her the whole time . . ."

Adam interrupted. "You have no right to be taking us anywhere."

Us? Vicky tried to shift around. The armrest bit into her ribs. She stared at the profile of the man beside her. Us? She'd been so sure—why had she been so sure?—that Adam was in on the scheme to defraud her people. She'd convinced herself he must have known what was going on. If she had figured it out, why hadn't Adam? And if he had, why did he stay on? Why did he bring her in?

Adam glanced at her, as if he'd felt her eyes boring into him, and gave her a look mixed with caution and reassurance. She could sense the strain of it, the effort it cost. Still, she felt a sense of comfort. She might never know the answers, she realized, and it didn't matter. Whatever happened, she was not alone. There was an "us."

FATHER JOHN SPOTTED the van taking a curve ahead, taillights glowing red like the butts of cigarettes tossed onto the highway. By the time he reached the curve, the vehicle had disappeared. He took the curve on two wheels, accelerator jammed against the floor, headlights flashing over the asphalt, moonlight dropping over the plains. The pickup was still shivering, and something had started knocking. No sign of the van now. For a moment, he feared it had turned off and cut its lights. It could be waiting on one of the dirt roads, Lexson and his thugs laughing as the pickup sped by.

And then he spotted the tiny red taillights again. The van was slowing into the outskirts of Riverton. He kept his own speed up. The knocking sounded as if a rock had gotten inside the engine. Another mile, and he was in the traffic heading into town, and he let up on the accelerator.

Gripping the wheel with one hand, he groped for the cell phone on the seat beside him. Finally he had it. Glancing between the road and the phone, he hammered at the keys, then pressed the phone against his ear.

"Office of the Federal Bureau of Investigation. Leave your name and message."

"They've got Vicky!" He was shouting. "Lexson, Lone Eagle, and two others in a white van. They're taking her to Double Dives. Get out there right away."

He cut off, then going through the ritual again—road, phone, road, phone—dialed the BIA Police. "Father O'Malley," he said when the operator came on. "Get me Chief Banner. It's an emergency."

"What's going on, John?" Banner's voice was like an island of reason bobbing into the turbulence of his own anxiety and fear. He told the chief about Vicky and the van, only part of his mind on the traffic ahead. "They're going to execute her, just like they did Monroe and Pearson."

"Take it easy, John."

"I'm five miles from Double Dives," he shouted over the chief's voice. "They're ahead of me. Get some officers out there, Banner."

"We've got patrol cars on the way. Let the officers handle this, John. Don't get involved . . ."

Father John pushed his thumb on the off button and tossed the phone across the seat. He tailgated an SUV and pounded on the horn.

"ALL YOU HAD to do was handle the contracts. Law school 101." Lexson threw a glance over his shoulder, then looked ahead again. They were on the outskirts of Riverton, flat-roofed buildings and small houses and vacant lots passing outside. "That too boring for a couple of hotshot Indian lawyers like you? You had to start looking into matters that were none of your business."

"Did you really expect us to sign off on your bogus contracts, Stan?" Vicky said.

"Let me handle this." Adam gave her a sideways glance. "Listen, Stan, anything we may have learned at the casino is privileged information, you know that. We couldn't testify against you. What's all this macho crap about? As your lawyer, I'm telling you the smartest thing right now is to pull over and let us out."

"Pull over and let you out?" Lexson gave a shout of laughter. "Let you run to the FBI and the Business Council with your accusations? That wouldn't be very smart, would it? What a pity you couldn't have just left things alone. We have a great business. Everybody was making money. The tribe was making more money than they'd ever dreamed of. You two lawyers were pulling in good money for shuffling papers around. And we were making money. Win-win situation, I'd call it. Everybody rolling around in dough and happy. But you're a couple of do-gooders, the kind that blow whistles. Who's going to thank you? Who's going to want to know what you found out?" He looked back for a moment, then shook his head and laughed. "Nobody. Not the council, not the Indians at the slots waiting for the big jackpot, knowing a lot of profits are going right back to the tribe. You'd probably get run off the reservation. We're doing you a big favor by removing you from the scene before you can ruin everything. Nobody likes troublemakers."

They were stopped at a red light, the right signal clicking.

"Where are you taking us?" Adam's voice sounded frozen, as if the shadow of death, like a raven, had flapped overhead, and Vicky realized that he knew the answer.

And so did she. They were turning south onto Highway 789. They were going to a place where bodies routinely turned up, the casualties of drug deals gone bad or just bad blood between gangs. They were going to Double Dives.

Light Stone glanced over at the boss. Click. Click. "You sure about this, Mr. Lexson? Police might start wondering if a couple more bodies show up there so soon after Monroe."

"Shut up and drive." Lexson motioned toward the light that had changed to green a half second earlier.

Vicky tried to fight back the rising panic as the van turned onto the highway. They drove south across the bridge with the moonlight shining in the Wind River on either side, then turned left onto the two-lane road. The cottonwoods and brush rushed by like specters from the other world.

"So you're going to kill us," Vicky said. "Is that it?"

She felt the pressure of Adam's hand on her thigh. "Don't say anything," he said.

But she understood now, and she pushed on. "Just like you killed Captain Monroe. He was also a troublemaker, wasn't he?" Adam was squeezing her leg hard. "Monroe was onto the fact you'd made a deal with Matt Kingdom.

Was he close to getting the evidence, Lexson? Is that why your errand boys killed him?"

"Evidence?" Lexson shook his head. "You don't know what you're talking about. You think Captain Jack Monroe's a do-gooder, concerned about Indian welfare? The man's a mercenary. He's on the corporate payrolls in Vegas. Who else do you think is going to pay to stop Indian gaming? Bunch of Christians?"

"Be quiet, Vicky," Adam said, but his voice sounded far away, beyond the jumble of her own thoughts. No matter who Monroe was, there was still more. Another white man had died at Double Dives. Had Lexson killed him, too? What was it the Indian gaming commissioner had said? Managers had subtle ways of skimming profits. Putting ghosts on the payrolls, inflating costs of supplies, inflating the fill.

Except that . . . Pearson didn't work at the casino. There had to be something else.

And then she had it. "Pearson!" she spit out the word. "You loaned Pearson money, right? And he couldn't pay you back. What did he do? Threaten to go to the police?"

"You should listen to your lawyer." Lexson was half-turned in the front seat and staring at her. It was as if a mask had slipped from the man's face, and beneath the handsome, polished features were muscles, bones and skin set in a cold, unrelenting hatred. "The more you talk," he said, "the more obvious it is what must be done with both of you."

"Gianelli's looking for me now," Vicky managed. God, where was Gianelli? They turned into the two-track that ran across the barren bluff, the headlights flashing over a wilderness of sagebrush and utility poles. There were no headlights shining behind them. She'd been clinging to a thread as thin as a spiderweb. A word scribbled on a Post-It. No one knew where she was. Not Gianelli. Not anyone.

■ ■ ■

FATHER JOHN DROVE south on Highway 789 and turned left onto Gas Hills Road, the accelerator rammed into the floor. The engine was knocking, as if the metal parts were flying around under the hood, and clouds of steam blurred the headlights funneling ahead. He took the left turn onto the bluff on two wheels. He could make out the fresh tire tracks in the dirt. He was close, but the van was still ahead.

THE VAN HIT something hard, and Vicky put out one hand to brace herself against the front seat. They were thumping down the steep two-track into the trees. Adam took both her hands, and the warmth of his palms against hers was like the sun flowing over her. They had survived in the sun, her people and his. Sun gave life, time to think. She had to think. She had to draw upon the gift of the sun.

The van jerked to a stop, and the interior light flicked on.

Light Stone crawled out from behind the wheel and walked around the hood. Barrenger was still leaning forward, his blue shirt and gray hair reflecting against the black window. "I told you, Stan," he said, "no one's followed us. No one knows where she is. This is a rough place. A lot of people have been killed here. Bodies probably buried all over the place. Even if the police find 'em, they'll never trace anything to us."

"You think I don't know that?" Lexson pushed open his door and ducked outside just as the side door slid open.

"Let's go," Barrenger said, shifting himself out of the van.

Vicky felt as if she couldn't move. She wanted to run—she had to get out and run away—but her legs wouldn't work. She couldn't breathe. She was barely aware of Adam's hand still holding hers, and then he let go.

She watched him crawl across the seat and out the door.

Now, it was her turn, and she was crawling after him, her arms and legs moving on their own with no direction from her, no connection to any wish of hers. She felt Adam's hand closing on hers, helping her out. The light outside was dim, a mixture of moonlight and headlights splaying through the cottonwoods and brush. The beer cans scattered about looked like silver ingots on the ground. Through the trees, she could hear the sound of the river.

For a moment, Lexson and the two other men formed a half circle of shadows around her and Adam. Then Barrenger started toward the back of the van, his footsteps scuffing the dirt. The rear door snapped open.

"Not unreasonable"—Lexson's voice broke into the quiet—"for two Indian lawyers thrown together at the office to develop a powerful attraction for each other." He glanced from Vicky to Adam, and in the dim light, Vicky saw that the mask had reattached itself to his face. He was the man who knew how to run casinos. Handsome. Genial. Deadly.

Barrenger planted himself next to his boss. He was gripping the handle of a shovel.

"I believe I might have hit upon the truth," Lexson said, still glancing between them. "That's wonderful. No one will be in the least surprised that they simply decided to run off together. Decamp in the night, one might say. No one will look for them."

"Think about what you're doing," Adam said. "Whatever's happened is over. You can go forward from here. We walk away and decamp in the night, just like you said, and no one will be the wiser."

Lexson shook his head and laughed. Enjoyment shone like diamonds in his eyes. "I'm not a gambler, Adam. Never was. Never liked risks. I always make sure somebody else takes the risks. The house has to have the edge." He turned to Light Stone. "Take them over there," he said, gesturing with his head toward the clump of cottonwoods near the river. "The soil should be nice and soft."

Light Stone didn't move. A couple of seconds passed before he said, "We'd better go."

It was then that Vicky saw the gun glinting in the man's hand.

"You're the one who's going to pull the trigger, Dennis?" Vicky said. "You're going to kill your own people?"

The Indian was quiet. The gun bobbed in his hand.

"He's an apple," Adam said. "Red on the outside, and whiter than white on the inside. Enjoys doing the white man's dirty work." He made a sucking noise and spit a wad of phlegm onto the ground. "He's like the Indians that led the soldiers to the villages."

"Yeah?" Dennis took a step forward. The barrel looked like an abyss rising toward them. "I'm alive. You're dead."

"I believe that's enough." Lexson waved at Light Stone and Barrenger. "Take them over into the trees."

"You know what happened to the Indians that betrayed their own people?" Vicky said. "The white men killed them, Dennis. They used them and killed them because they couldn't really trust them. Lexson doesn't trust you, either, Dennis."

"I've heard enough," Lexson said. "Pull the trigger."

Vicky saw the hesitation, like the flare of a light behind the Indian's eyes. "That's why Lexson had you hide in the hotel for five days," she hurried on. "He was afraid you'd start thinking about what Captain Monroe said, how the casino is a den of thieves ripping off our people. Sooner or later Lexson's going to start thinking about how much you know. And he doesn't like to take risks, Dennis."

"Pull the trigger now, Dennis!"

"Listen to Vicky," Adam said. "Lexson's going to kill you. Don't you have a wife? He's going to kill her, too, and anybody else he thinks you talked to."

Vicky moved toward the Indian. "The ancestors will turn from you. They won't claim you. You'll walk the earth through eternity . . ."

"*Now,* Dennis!" Lexson shouted.

The gun jerked upward as Dennis swung toward the man next to him. There was a moment, one awful moment, when Lexson's mouth opened in a wide, unbelieving circle and his eyes turned white with fear before the gunshot shattered the air and his cheek exploded into little pieces of flesh and skin and a fountain of blood.

"Bastard!" Barrenger lifted the shovel and smashed it into Dennis's head. The Indian staggered sideways, surprise and pain shooting through his expression, then stumbled onto his hands and knees. The gun slid over the ground. Barrenger lifted the shovel again, but Adam was already diving for him. He caught him around the waist and rammed him backward. The shovel clattered against the van. The air was punctuated with grunts and the sharp sound of fists smashing into flesh. And then Barrenger lay sprawled on his back, arms and legs splayed, chest heaving. His glasses lay smashed next to his head. Adam stood over him, gulping in air.

The gun, Vicky thought. Where was the gun? Stepping around Light Stone's still form, she spotted the silver sheen in the dirt near the van. Adam had spotted it, too, she realized, and had dropped to his knees reaching for it.

Out of the corner of her eye, Vicky saw Barrenger push himself to his feet and lunge for the shovel.

"Adam, look out!" she yelled, but the man had already lifted the shovel overhead. She heard herself scream as Adam turned toward the shovel that smashed into his face.

He crumpled sideways, groaning, and drew his knees up to his chest. Black blood pooled across his face, like oil seeping from the ground.

Vicky started for him, then stopped. Barrenger had moved between them, lifted the shovel again, face contorted in rage, eyes narrowed almost shut.

"Get down on the ground," he said. "First I'm going to have a piece of you."

35

FATHER JOHN SAW the lights glowing in the trees below the bluff. He held down the accelerator and went airborne over the ruts. The tires skidded back over the hard ground, the banging noise in the engine as insistent as the beating of his own heart. It was a moment before he realized the engine had stopped and the pickup was moving forward on momentum.

He jiggled the key in the ignition and pumped the gas pedal, but the pickup was starting to grind to a stop. He flung open the door, jumped out, and started running, surrounded by silence, like the void at the end of the world.

The gunshot came out of nowhere, crashing around him like a strike of lightning.

"No!" he shouted, running as hard as he could for the edge of the bluff, plunging past the pickup's headlights and into the darkness. He was at the dropoff when he saw the van below, lit up like a cabin in the trees, the interior lights shining in the windows, the headlights running through the moonlight and shadows.

Next to the van was Vicky, a figure looming over her, their shadows merging with the shadows of the trees.

Father John started down the steep pitch of the two-track, his boots sliding in the dirt. At the bottom, he headed into the trees, his eyes still on the glow of lights. The branches scraped at his hands and tore at his shirt. He was still about thirty feet away when he heard Vicky scream into the night.

He sprinted across a clearing for the van, his consciousness concentrated into a pinprick of reality that he grasped in pieces: A man was looming over Vicky, lifting a shovel over his shoulder like an ax.

Father John threw himself against the man and grabbed hold of his neck. His other hand went for the shovel. The man was gasping, coughing as Father John gripped the splintery wood handle and yanked it forward and backward until it floated free. Then he pulled the man's head back until he feared he'd snap his neck. He let up a little and, with his other hand, took hold of the man's right arm, and, yanking it up along his spine as hard as he could, pushed him down over the hood of the van. The man let out a long gasp, like air escaping from a tire.

"I've got the gun," Vicky shouted behind him.

He didn't take his eyes away. His fingers were glued to the man's wrist, pressing his arm into his spine. With his other hand, Father John gripped the man's shoulder and rammed it hard against the hood. It was then that he realized the man was Barrenger.

"Take it easy." Barrenger was gulping in air, and Father John could feel his lungs inflating beneath the sweat-soaked shirt. His own lungs were burning; his heart hammering.

"It's okay, John," Vicky said, quieter this time. He was aware of her beside him, arms outstretched, a gun gripped in both hands. "I'll shoot him if he moves."

Father John took in a couple of breaths. "I'll tell you what you're going to do," he said, giving the arm a jerk upward that made Barrenger cry out again.

"You're going to get down on your stomach. Got it? You heard what Vicky said. One wrong move, and she'll shoot you."

The man was nodding. Gasping. Nodding.

Father John eased up on the arm, then let it go. It dangled over Barrenger's buttocks a moment, like a bobbing fish. Gradually he moved the arm sideways and pulled himself up from the hood, rubbing at his shoulder.

"Get down." Father John tightened his grip on Barrenger's other shoulder. He thought he heard sirens in the distance, but he couldn't be sure he wasn't imagining the sound, he wanted so much for the sirens to be there.

Barrenger dropped to his knees, then to his hands before flattening himself against the ground.

"Take the gun, John." Vicky thrust the black metal object at him. "I've got to see about Adam."

Father John gripped the handle still warm from her hand and backed up, taking in the scene for the first time. Barrenger on his stomach near the front of the van, still gasping and coughing; another man lying unconscious behind the van. Indian, it looked like, his black hair matted with blood. Not more than five feet away was the body of a third man, still and lifeless, half of his face gone. Father John realized that it was Stan Lexson.

And Vicky, kneeling beside Adam Lone Eagle, who was curled to one side, arms wrapped around his knees, rocking and groaning. She had torn off a strip from the man's shirt and was pressing the wadded cloth against his cheek.

Dear Lord, what went on here? Who had the gun? Lexson? Maybe, Father John thought, then discarded the idea. A man like Lexson didn't do his own dirty work. He gave it to someone who worked for him. Who? Barrenger was wielding the shovel, not the gun. That left the Indian with the smashed head. Or Adam.

Father John looked back at Vicky. She was sobbing quietly. "It's all right, Adam," she kept saying, soothing him. "Everything will be all right."

Father John understood now. It was the other Indian who'd had the gun. The other Indian who was supposed to kill both Adam and Vicky, but, for some reason, had turned the gun on the man who was his boss.

He looked away. Through the trees, he could see the red and blue lights flashing on the bluff. The sirens were louder now; they were real.

36

ACROSS THE BROWN stretch of land, the white house shimmered in the sun. All around was nothing but empty earth melting into the blue sky. Vicky drove with the windows down, the summer smells of unplowed dirt and wild grasses blowing through the Cherokee.

Lately she'd been noticing everything about the reservation, imprinting the sights and smells and the quiet in her mind so that she would remember, if she had to leave. With each passing day, the possibility seemed more real. She didn't want to leave; the reservation was home. But she couldn't stay if she couldn't make a living practicing law. And she couldn't practice law if she didn't have any clients.

The phone had stopped ringing. Last week, she'd had to let Esther go, and this morning, when the phone rang, she'd been so surprised, she'd stared at the inert object a moment, wondering if the sound was real, before she'd finally answered.

"That you, Vicky?" the voice of Will Standing Bear had boomed over the line. "Sure is a pretty day," he'd begun. And then had followed several moments of pleasantries before he said, "Sure would like to visit with you, if you got time one of these days."

Oh, she had the time all right. A procession of empty days stretched ahead. "I can come by this afternoon," she'd told the elder.

Lexson had been right about one thing, she thought, watching the road flow toward her, like a stream coursing through an arroyo. Nobody liked a whistle blower. The day after Lexson was killed, the Business Council had closed the casino, and a couple hundred jobs had melted away, including her own. Her people blamed her. Not Lodestar Enterprises or Stan Lexson, even though the FBI had launched an investigation into the casino operations. A dozen employees, including Matt Kingdom, had already been charged with conspiracy to commit fraud, loan sharking, tax evasion.

Some of those charged were people Kingdom had placed in jobs—people he could trust to look the other way when the casino skimmed profits, took cash out of the register in the restaurant, altered the books in the hotel to show fewer rooms rented. Of course Kingdom had trusted them. He'd gotten them good jobs, and even if he took a cut of the paychecks, they still owed him. Her people had even spoken up for Kingdom at last week's Business Council meeting. *He'd* gotten them jobs, they'd said.

She could imagine the rumors flying over the moccasin telegraph during the days she spent giving statements to Gianelli and the Wind River police.

A traitor to the people. She'd explained how the casino had been siphoning off money. *Don't belong here.* She'd gone over the details about the night Barrenger and the pit boss—Felix Slodin from Mississippi—had taken her to the casino. She'd even gone back to the hotel room with Gianelli and three other agents and explained how she'd jumped from the balcony. She remembered looking down at the asphalt lot eight floors below and swallowing back the acid in her throat to keep from being sick.

Now she was left with a couple of old cases to wind up, a client or two in need of help, including Catherine Bizzel. It had taken some talking to get the district attorney to agree to a plea bargain. It was the woman's first offense. Fifty-two years of a worthy life; a moment of desperation. Instead of going to prison, Catherine would make restitution. That would take a couple years, Vicky knew, but John O'Malley was willing to let the woman work off her debt at the mission no matter how long it took.

Vicky turned into the dirt yard and tried to set her tires in the ruts leading to the house. The tailgate of a brown truck jutted out from the corner, which meant Will and Josephine were home, most likely in the brushshade. Vicky took the brown bag of gifts and started around the house, making her way down a column of shade between the truck and the paint-chipped siding. She found the old couple seated inside the brushshade, the elder over a newspaper, the grandmother drawing a needle and thread through a piece of fabric. Drops of sunshine fell through the branch walls and spattered the dirt floor.

"Have yourself a chair," Will said, looking up and beckoning her forward.

Vicky stepped inside, dropped the brown bag on a folding chair, and sat down at the table, aware that the elders were reading her manner like a book. They'd heard the gossip on the moccasin telegraph, gossip that hadn't reached her. It was the reason Will had called, and for half an instant, she regretted having come. It was the elder who would admonish her, tell her she'd overstepped, done more than he'd expected. She'd brought about the closing of the casino.

"Get yourself some fry bread and coffee," Josephine said, nodding toward the plastic covered bowl, thermos, and stack of mugs in the center of the table.

Vicky thanked the old woman and explained that she'd eaten not long ago—breakfast, hours ago; she had no appetite—hoping she didn't sound ungrateful. It was impolite to refuse a gift, especially a gift as precious as food.

They talked about the weather, the upcoming powwow—awkward snatches of conversation thrown like a blanket over the real subject. The people had been cheated, that was true, but they'd had something. Now they had nothing.

Finally, Will went quiet, drawing into some deep place within himself. Then, in a low voice, he said, "You did right by the people, Vicky. Maybe they don't know it now they got themselves all worked up about the casino, but they're gonna know it soon."

Vicky felt a wave of relief. No matter what the spectators in the courtroom might think, the judge who mattered the most had found her not guilty. "Thank you, grandfather," she managed.

"Casino ain't gonna stay closed forever," the elder went on. "What we gotta get are some honest people that know how to run the place. Business Council's already interviewing companies that want to work for us."

Vicky glanced away. The wind whistled through the branches. In her mind, she could see the companies, an ever-widening black circle of ravens over the casino. What would prevent them from stealing from her people?

"Before the council makes any decision"—Vicky turned her attention back to the elder—"they're gonna appoint a commission with five people on it. Not just three where a strong chairman can run things." He shook his head and stared off into the distance a moment. "Matt Kingdom was a smart man."

"Maybe too smart," Josephine put in.

"Darn right, he was too smart," Will said. "He seen how Lexson was gonna rob the people. All that money flowing away, so he decided to get himself some. Money ain't gonna do that Indian any good in prison."

The old man sighed, then went on. "New commission's gonna have five smart people investigate the companies that wanna run the casino. Then the commissioners are gonna oversee all the operations. The elders asked Billie Lean Bear to come home and help the people," he said, and Vicky understood that Will was the elder who had called Lean Bear. "Remember Billie? Been an accountant in San Francisco last fifteen years. And we got us a couple guys with good business experience." He named two other Arapahos who had left the reservation for an education and never returned.

So the tribe was calling back the best, Vicky thought. She could imagine Will's pitch on the telephone: The people need you; you gotta help.

"About all we need now is a good lawyer or two." A hint of amusement flashed in the old man's eyes. "You know any?"

"I could think of a couple," Vicky said.

"You think they'd be willing to help the people?"

"If the people wanted them."

"We want 'em, that's for sure. Lawyers you're thinkin' of, could they be that Arapaho lawyer in Lander and that Lakota lawyer?"

"Could be."

"You tell 'em the commissioners are gonna get paid real good. Business Council figures the casino's gonna have a lot more profits, once people ain't stealing. You think them two lawyers are gonna be interested?"

Vicky smiled at the irony. She'd been working at the casino—for a bunch of crooks—caught between her duty toward her clients and her duty toward her people. Now she'd be working at the casino, but her clients would be her people.

She said, "I suspect it's the best offer either one of those lawyers has had in a while."

"Soon's the casino gets up and running again, the people are gonna see all the profits that should've been coming in. Business Council thinks it's gonna be a couple million more this year. That's when people are gonna thank you, Vicky." Will kept his eyes on hers. "Josephine and me, we're thanking you now, daughter, just to hold on 'til the people get around to it."

THERE WAS A lightness to the evening, Vicky thought, as she drove back across the reservation. The sun was still riding over the mountains, and a mixture of shadows and light played across the land and the houses springing up here and there. She passed the casino, the blue neon sign dark, the parking lots empty, a diminished look to the walls of stucco, the rows of empty balconies, the expanse of glass across the entrance, as if everything the casino had promised, those large and grand promises, had been deflated, reduced to a more manageable size, a better size.

She was still a half-block from her apartment when she spotted Adam's green truck parked at the curb. She pulled in close behind. He was already walking toward her before she got out. The large red scar across his cheek made her want to cry.

"I've been waiting for you," he said, opening her door.

"How'd you know I'd be here?"

"You weren't at your office." Adam closed the door behind her and didn't move, staying very close. "I left a message on your cell phone."

She'd turned off the phone, she remembered. She hadn't expected any messages.

"I figured you'd show up here sooner or later. Hope you haven't eaten."

"What are you proposing?"

"Dinner in the pine trees."

THEY WENT IN his truck, winding through the neighborhood streets on the west side of town, then up into the foothills to the small restaurant where they'd eaten before, listening to the sound of the wind in the trees outside, a candle flickering in the little glass vase between them. They sat at the same table.

"Our table," Adam had exclaimed when the waiter seated them. She winced at the idea, so unfamiliar and unexpected, so out of the blue. It had been so long that she'd felt part of a shared experience—a song, a movie, a table—that she wasn't sure how to react.

She sipped on the ice water the waiter had poured and watched the man across from her: handsome and dark—oh, yes, the old clichés applied to Adam, right down to the flashing black eyes and the black hair with the touch of gray at the temples that gave him the distinguished look of an experienced warrior with the scar to prove it, one of the leading men—those who guided the young warriors and advised the elders. Not yet an elder himself, not for a couple decades, but the patience and wisdom of an elder already growing within him.

He was talking about the investigation. Gianelli had interviewed the two of them separately, then together. Their memories of the van and Lexson, Barrenger, and Light Stone were the same, she'd discovered. Another "our," she thought now. "Our" brush with death at Double Dives. They'd have to testify at Barrenger's and Light Stone's trials, he reminded her. Which meant they'd be seeing a lot of each other. He seemed pleased at the prospect, and yet there was a wrong note in his voice. She realized he was trying to ignore the crack that had erupted between them, that would deepen and spread until, finally, it would shatter any other feelings that might have started.

Vicky said, "I owe you an apology, Adam. I thought you were working with Lexson. I misjudged you, and I'm sorry."

In the smile that he gave her, she could see that the crack was already repaired. "You had a right to wonder about me. I should've looked further into the operations. I had a gut feeling something was wrong, but I had so many contracts to deal with—that's why I brought you on board—I didn't have time to follow my instincts. Besides, I kept telling myself that the Business Council had investigated Lodestar and the principals."

"Kingdom was the investigator."

Adam threw up both hands. "There were lawyers looking over the deal. I let myself believe that if anything was wrong, they would have caught it." He stopped, waiting while the waiter delivered their dinners—two filets, medium rare, two baked potatoes, salads. When the waiter left, Adam started cutting into his filet. "I should've done some investigating on my own, the way you did. It wasn't until . . ." He lifted his fork with a piece of meat on the end.

"Until you pulled away from me that I started taking a closer look at Lodestar Enterprises. I'd been hopeful, then, bam, you went into yourself somewhere, and I didn't know how to reach you."

Adam chewed on the piece of steak, staring past her at some point in the dining room, as if he were trying to recall everything that had happened.

Vicky took a bite of her own filet. After a moment, she said, "I should have confided in you, Adam."

"You didn't trust me."

"I was wrong."

"Well, I finally started listening to my gut feelings," Adam said. "I suspected you'd had the same feelings, looked into matters, found something wrong, and assumed I was part of it. I had to find out what was wrong so I could exonerate myself, counselor. Every place I went, you'd already been there. I talked to your friend at the Secretary of State's Office. I talked to an Indian gaming commissioner. The picture started to come together. Bottom line was, I'd gone to work for professional criminals and brought you in. Almost got you killed. I'm the one who owes you an apology."

Vicky was quiet. She finished part of her dinner, then pushed her plate aside and locked eyes with the man across from her. "The tribe wants us both to serve on the new commission."

He grinned at her. "A couple of lawyers who know all the ins and outs on how to cheat?"

"Who better to keep the managers honest?"

"I've been looking at a job with a firm in Denver," he said after the waiter had poured two cups of coffee. "I was thinking you might be moving back to Denver."

"I'd rather be here."

"The commission, huh? Might be interesting." He sipped at the coffee a moment. "We could pick up where we left off."

"Oh? And where was that, Adam?"

"Hey, we were getting along pretty well, remember? Like I said, I was hopeful before you went all weird on me. Come on, Vicky, admit it. You like me a little."

Vicky put her head back and laughed. It felt good, she thought, to laugh. "Okay, Adam," she said. "I admit I like you." She paused. "A little."

Now it was his turn to laugh. "Don't fill me up with too much hope. I wouldn't know what to do with it." He held her eyes. "Be straight with me, Vicky. Is there somebody else?"

"I'd tell you, if there were," she said, feeling slightly unsteady, as if the earth had shifted beneath them.

"Would you?"

Vicky turned her gaze to the window and the moonlight flickering like fireflies in the branches and the darkness falling all around. The gossip on the moccasin telegraph had reached this Lakota lawyer; it had reached everybody except her and John O'Malley.

Adam said, "Father O'Malley came after you at Double Dives . . ."

"He came after us."

"He came after you. He would've killed Barrenger if he'd had to, to protect you."

"There's been nothing between us."

"He can stop being a priest any time he wants to."

Vicky shook her head. "He would never do that."

"Then I'll keep hoping," Adam said after a moment.

When they had finished dinner, Vicky was aware of the pressure of his hand on her arm, guiding her past the other tables, past the hostess station, out the door. He walked beside her across the parking lot without saying anything. They were almost to the truck when she felt his hand grip her arm again and spin her toward him, then his lips pressing on hers. She tried to relax in his arms. She could feel his heart pounding next to hers. This could be home, she told herself, and she wondered if it might be true, if she kept telling herself.

37

CATHERINE BIZZEL STOOD at the kitchen sink, hands plunged into soap bubbles that were frothing over the dishpan. "What would you like for dinner, Father?" She rinsed off a plate, stacked it in the drainer, all the while looking over her shoulder. "Fried chicken? Some real spicy meatballs and spaghetti?"

Father John finished the last bite of the tuna sandwiches she had made for him and Father George and took a draw of coffee. "How about lobster?" He couldn't resist. He wondered how long he'd have to put up with the woman's tender and grateful mercies. *How do you like your shirts ironed, Father? Can I sweep under your feet, Father?*

"Lobster! Well, I don't know . . ."

"Filet with béarnaise sauce?" Father George set his mug down and got to his feet.

The woman faced them and wrung her hands in her apron. "You think lobster and filet drop out of the sky?" She shook her head. "You two! Had me goin' there a minute."

"Anything's fine." Father John stood up.

"You know, Father, I can never . . ."

"Catherine, Catherine." He waved away another thank-you. At least twice a day, the poor woman thanked him for keeping her on at the mission as long as it took to repay the money. Which was going to be a problem when Elena returned in a couple weeks. He couldn't imagine that the kitchen was big enough for both women. He wondered if the house was big enough.

Dear Lord, he thought. Too many women around wasn't a problem he knew how to deal with.

Outside, Walks-On fell in alongside them, as he and Father George headed back to the administration building. He tossed the Frisbee he'd grabbed off the hall bench and watched the dog lope through the grasses on three legs, pivot on his two hind legs, and grab the Frisbee out of the air. Then the dog loped back, and Father John repeated the routine as they passed the church.

"Been quiet here the last week," his assistant said. "Nothing but meetings and services."

"And the Eagles." The kids had beat Riverton and were now looking good for the regional playoffs.

"I keep thinking about the girl," Father George said as they crossed the alley. "What's going to become of her?"

"You want the most likely scenario?" Father John said.

"Let's pray for better."

"She's with her aunt's friend in Casper. Maybe she'll get a new start." From inside the administration building came the muffled clang of the phone.

Father John was about to start up the steps when he saw

the deep red Cherokee turning off Seventeen-Mile Road. Father George must have seen it, too, because he brushed ahead. "I'll get the phone," he said.

Father John threw the Frisbee again and waited as the vehicle came around Circle Drive and pulled to a stop. He watched Vicky get out and come toward him, feeling as if something had lifted in the atmosphere, leaving the air lighter, more buoyant. It always surprised him, every time he saw her, at how different she looked from the last time. He wondered what might have happened, where her life had taken her, that had suggested something new, something still to discover about her.

"I was in the neighborhood." She smiled up at him. They both knew that wasn't true.

"Come on in." Father John ushered her up the steps and across the corridor to his office. Walks-On trotted along, carrying the Frisbee in his mouth.

"I've been meaning to get over here." Vicky perched on one of the side chairs and Walks-On settled next to her. Leaning over to stroke the dog's head and back, she said, "I want to thank you again for coming after me."

Father John sat on the edge of the desk and folded his arms across his chest. She'd already thanked him during the interviews with Gianelli and Chief Banner.

She went on about how she would have been killed if he hadn't come to her office and found the Post-It.

"Gianelli would have found it, Vicky."

"Not before I was dead. Adam, too."

Ah, yes. Adam. They'd been wrong about the man, he and Vicky. Adam had put his own life on the line to protect her. He would have died with her . . .

And now? Father John had the sense that he was watching her from a far distance and, filling up the space between them, was Adam Lone Eagle.

"I like him, John," Vicky said.

Ah, that was what she had come to tell him. "He seems like a good man."

She nodded. There was a nervousness in the way she stroked the dog's back.

"He's worried about you."

"Vicky . . ."

"Don't worry," she cut in. "I've explained how it's always been with us. We're like two horses taking different roads back to the corral, and once in a while, the roads cross."

Father John didn't say anything. After a moment, Vicky gave the dog a final pat and got to her feet. She fixed the strap of her bag across her shoulder, then walked over and took his hand. He was surprised at the softness and warmth of her hand on his. He half-expected her to say, Come on, let's go, and he wondered where that would be, where they might go, and for a moment, what he might say.

"We're still friends?" she said.

"Of course."

"Sometimes I think," she paused, then started again. "I think that in some other place, some other time, we were more than friends. Do you ever think that?"

"It would be nice to think so," Father John said. He paused, letting his eyes hold hers for a long moment. "We are who we are now in this time, Vicky. In this place."

She smiled up at him, then removed her hand and started toward the door, stooping to give Walks-On a last pat on the way. Gripping the doorjamb, she looked back over her shoulder. "I'll be seeing you, John O'Malley," she said.

And then she was gone, her footsteps clacking in the corridor, the door slamming shut.

He started toward the window, then stopped. From outside came the coughing of an engine, the scrunching of tires on gravel, followed by a silence more complete than any he had ever known. He walked around the desk, sat down, and started riffling through the piles of papers. Three infants to baptize next Sunday, a homily to write, one that would match the solemnity and sacredness of the occasion. It was his turn to hear confessions next Saturday—he and George traded Saturdays—and there was another big Eagles game first thing Saturday morning.

The weeks and months stretched ahead, filled with work. It would be enough for him, he told himself. The people and St. Francis Mission and the life he'd chosen—that he knew in the deepest part of himself had chosen him—that life was enough for him, and it was good.